April
in
Spain

Also by John Banville

Nightspawn

Birchwood

Doctor Copernicus

Kepler

The Newton Letter

Mefisto

The Book of Evidence

Ghosts

Athena

The Untouchable

Eclipse

Shroud

Ancient Light

The Sea

The Infinities

The Blue Guitar

Mrs. Osmond

Snow

April

in

Spain

A NOVEL

JOHN BANVILLE

HANOVER
SQUARE
PRESS

HANOVER
SQUARE
PRESS™

ISBN-13: 978-1-335-47140-6

April in Spain

This edition published by arrangement with Harlequin Books S.A.

Hanover Square Press
22 Adelaide St. West, 40th Floor
Toronto, Ontario M5H 4E3, Canada
HanoverSqPress.com
BookClubbish.com

Printed in U.S.A.

To Andrew Wylie

April

in

Spain

LONDON

1

Terry Tice liked killing people. It was as simple as that. Maybe "liked" wasn't the right word. Nowadays he was paid to do it, and well paid. But money was never the motive, not really. Then what was? He had given a lot of thought to this question, on and off, over the years. He wasn't a looney, and it wasn't a sex thing, or anything sick like that—he was no psycho.

The best answer he could come up with was that it was a matter of making things tidy, of putting things in their right place. The people he was hired to kill had got in the way of something, some project or other, and had to be removed in order for business to proceed smoothly. Either that, or they were superfluous, which was just as good a reason for them to be disposed of.

Needless to say, he had nothing personal against any of his

targets—which is how he thought of them, since "victim" would sound as if he was to blame—except insofar as they were *clutter.* Yes, it gave him a real sense of satisfaction to make things neat and shipshape.

"Shipshape," that was the word. After all, he had been in the British navy, for a while, at the end of the war. He was too young to enlist, but he had lied about his age and was taken on, and "saw action," as the fruity-voiced high-ups liked to say, hunting German submarines in the North Atlantic. Life at sea was boring, however, and boredom was one of the things Terry just couldn't put up with. Besides, he was prone to seasickness. A sailor who was seasick all the time, that would be a fine thing. So as soon as the chance came, he got out and transferred to the army.

He served for a few months in North Africa, propped on his elbows in wadis, fighting off the flies and taking potshots at Rommel's famous Afrika Korps whenever they put up their big square heads, while off on the horizon the tanks buzzed like beetles, spitting fire at each other day and night. After that he did a spell in Burma, where he got the chance to kill a lot of little yellow fellows, and had a fine old time.

In Africa, he had caught a nasty dose of the clap—though was there such a thing as a nice dose of the clap?—and in Burma he contracted an even nastier case of malaria. If it wasn't one thing it was another. Life—a mug's game.

The end of the war was a shock for Private Tice. In peacetime, he didn't know what to do with himself, and drifted from place to place around London, and from job to job. He had no family, that he knew of—he had been brought up, or dragged up, more like, in an Irish orphanage—and didn't keep in touch with his mates from the old days in the desert or on the ocean wave. There weren't that many of them, anyway. None, in fact, if the truth were told.

For a while he had a serious go at the girls, but it wasn't a success. Most of the ones he picked up turned out to be on the

game—he must give off a particular scent or something, since
the brassers fairly flocked to him; it was a thing he noticed. Of
course, it was against his principles to pay for it, and anyway, *it*
wasn't much to write home about, in his opinion.

There was one who latched on to him who wasn't a tart. She
was a hot little redhead, halfway respectable—she had an office
job in the Morris motor car factory up near Oxford, though she
was cockney to the bone. He didn't drive a car, himself, so he only
saw her if he went up on the train, or when she came down to the
Smoke the odd weekend for a bit of fun among the bright lights.

Sapphire, she said her name was. Ooh-la-la. In the Dog and
Bone one night he had a rummage in her handbag, just out of
curiosity, while she was off powdering her nose, and came across
an old ration book and found out her real name was Doris—
Doris Huggett, from over Stepney way. That was the same night
he realized, when he took a close look at it, that her hair was
dyed. He should have known, it was that bright, with that fake
metallic shine, like the shine on the curve of a brand-new Morris Oxford mudguard.

Doris-alias-Sapphire didn't last much longer than any of the
others. In a place in Soho on New Year's Eve she had a couple
of Babychams too many and turned away and spluttered with
laughter at some remark he had made. He couldn't see anything
funny in what he'd said. Drunk though she was, he took her out
the lane behind the club and gave her a few smacks to teach her
manners. Next morning, she rang up screaming, and threatening
to have him done for assault and battery, but nothing came of it.

That was a thing he wouldn't stand for, being disrespected
and made fun of. He had just linked in with an East End outfit,
and was doing some profitable robbing and the like. He had to
get out, though, after knifing one of the younger blokes in the
crew for mimicking his Irish accent—the Irish accent, it should
be said, that he hadn't known he had, until then.

He was handy with a knife, and with shooters—he'd been in

the army, after all—and was pretty nifty with his fists, too, when the need arose, even if he was a bantamweight. One of the Kray twins, Ronnie, it was, took him on for a while as an enforcer, but his low stature was against him. That was why he liked Burma, despite the heat and the fever and all the rest of it—the fellows he'd been sent to kill down there were his own size or smaller.

It wasn't easy making a living on Civvy Street, and he was getting desperate, he didn't mind admitting it, when Percy Antrobus came sashaying into his life.

Percy was—well, it was hard to say what Percy was, exactly. Heavy, pasty-faced, with a woman's hips, and bruise-colored pouches under his eyes and a fat lower lip that sagged and turned a glistening shade of dark purple when he'd had a few. Brandy-and-port was his tipple, though he started the day with what he called a *coupe*, which as Terry discovered was just the French word for a glass of champagne. Percy took his champers ice-cold. He had a swizzle stick that was made of real gold. When Terry asked him what it was for, Percy looked at him in that way he did when he was pretending to be shocked, his eyes big and round as pennies and his mouth pursed into a crimped little circle that looked less like a mouth than a you-know-what, and said, "Dear boy, surely you wouldn't think of drinking champagne before noon *with bubbles in it?*"

That was Percy.

And you had to give it to him, it was he who saw Terry's potential, and introduced him to his true vocation.

Funny, the way it turned out, that his first paid-for target should be, of all people, Percy's old ma. She had a few bob in the bank, quite a few, in fact, and was threatening to cut Percy out of her will, on account of something he'd done or hadn't done. Percy, at his wits' end, had decided the only thing for it was to have her done over before she had time to ring up her solicitor—a "complete stinker," who had it in for Percy, according to the man himself—and order him to bring her the aforementioned document so she could strike from it the name of her only son, the said Percival.

Terry had come across Percy for the first time one foggy November night in the King's Head in Putney. Afterward it occurred to him that it hadn't been a chance encounter at all, and that Percy had picked him out deliberately, as a lad likely to help him in the matter of his inheritance. When, coming up to closing time, Percy started telling him about his problem with "the Mater"—he really did talk like that—and how he intended to go about solving it, Terry thought he was joking.

But it was no joke.

When they were saying good night outside the pub, their breath rising up in big dense puffs through the already dense pea-souper fog, Percy stuck two tenners into Terry's breast pocket and suggested they meet in the same place at the same time the next night. Terry was in two minds whether to go, but go he did. When Percy saw him coming in the door he gave him a big smile, and treated him to a pint of pale and a dish of jellied eels, and whispered in his ear that he'd pay him a hundred pounds sterling to put a bullet in the old girl's noggin.

A hundred quid! Terry had never expected to see that much money all in the one fist.

Two days later he shot Mrs. Antrobus in Kensington High Street, in broad daylight, grabbing her bag to make it look like a common or garden snatch job done by some panicky kid. Percy had supplied the pistol—"Absolutely untraceable, laddie, I assure you"—and arranged for it to be got rid of afterward. This was how Terry discovered just how well connected the fat old poofter was. Untraceable heaters didn't grow on trees.

Next morning the papers ran a big story on the old girl's death, accompanied by "an artist's impression" of "the brutal killer." Terrible likeness.

A few days after the funeral, Terry was treated by his new friend to a slap-up lunch at the Ritz. Terry was uneasy about

them being seen together in such a public place, especially after
the sudden demise of "the Mater," but Percy gave him a slow
wink and said it was all right, that he often came here with
"handsome young chaps such as yourself."

When lunch was over, Terry's head was spinning from the
wine and the stink of the cigars that Percy smoked, which he
did even during the meal. They ambled down St. James's Street
and dropped into the premises of John Lobb, Bootmaker. There
Terry was measured for a pair of brogues—he would have preferred something sharper, but when he took delivery of the shoes
a couple of weeks later and tried them on, he felt like a lord. He
managed to get a look at the bill, and was glad it was on Percy's
account. Percy also bought him a dark-gray titfer at Locks the
Hatters, just a few doors up from Lobb's.

"A young man in your line of work can't afford to look the
part," Percy said, in his plummy, chairman-of-the-board voice,
and sniggered. It took Terry a second or two to get the twist of
it. Wit, that was.

"What line of work would that be, exactly, Mr. Antrobus?"
Terry inquired, putting on the innocent act.

And Percy only smiled, and tried to pinch young Terry's neat
little backside.

Terry still wore the Lobb shoes on occasion, especially when
he was missing Percy, although that wasn't very often. They had
aged nicely, the brogues, and fitted more snugly with each wearing. The gray hat had got badly rained on—at the races at Ascot,
as it happened, to which top-hatted Percy had taken him, for a
special treat—but Terry didn't mind as he had never got the hang
of wearing it. He thought it made him look like a spiv, not the
gentleman Percy had meant to turn him into. Poor old Percy.

He'd had to go, Percy did, in the end, eyes wide with surprise
and his mouth shaped into that little puckered pink hole. Went
down with a bump and a muffled rumble, like a sack of potatoes.

DONOSTIA

2

There was a narrow entrance to the bay, so that the water, once inside, fanned out in the shape of an enormous seashell. In fact, the bay was named La Concha, the Spanish word for shell. Because of that bottleneck channel and the long curve of the beach, the waves didn't run along at a bias, as they did on beaches at home. Instead, there was just one immensely long wave that broke with a single, muffled crash, from the point of the Old Town over to the right, all the way along to the headland far off on the left, where there was a funicular railway that, all day long, inched its laborious way up and down the side of a hill. When Quirke woke at night, with the window open beside the bed, it was as if there were a big, friendly animal asleep and softly breathing out there in the darkness.

All this fascinated him, and he spent a lot of time sitting in front of the window just looking out at the view, his mind a blank. "You look at the sea as other men would look at a woman," his wife said with amusement.

It was she, Evelyn, who had suggested San Sebastián, and before he could think up a convincing objection, she had written off for a brochure to the Hotel de Londres y de Inglaterra. "Honestly," he scoffed, "the names they give to these establishments!" Evelyn ignored him. But when he saw the place he had to admit it was impressive, sitting smack in the middle of the seafront facing the bay, a solid, handsome edifice.

"That's 'the London and England Hotel,' right?" he said, reading the name on the brochure. "Why can't we stay at a Spanish one?"

"It is Spanish, as you very well know," his wife replied. "It's the finest hotel in the city. I stayed there once, when the war was on. It was very good. I'm sure it still is."

"Look at the prices," he grumbled. He knew better than to ask how she had come to be in San Sebastián in wartime. Questions like that were *verboten*. "And this is not even the high season," he added.

It was spring, she said, the best season of all, and they were going to Spain on a holiday, even if she had to handcuff him and push him up the steps and on to the airplane.

"Northern Spain is southern Ireland," she said. "It rains all the time, everywhere is green and everyone is Catholic. You will love it."

"Will they have Irish wine?"

"Ha ha. You are so funny."

She turned away and he smacked her on the bottom, with just enough force to make it wobble in the wonderful way that it did.

Strange, he thought, that the same passion was still there between them, the same erotic thrill. It should have been embarrassing, but it wasn't. They were middle-aged, they had made a late marriage—a second one for both of them—and, so far, they still couldn't get enough of each other. It was absurd, he would say, and "Oh, *ja, ja,* ziss is zertainly zo!" Evelyn would agree, putting on her exaggerated Herr Doktor Freud accent to make him laugh, while at the same time guiding his hands on to her broad, uncorseted, wobbly bum, and kissing him on the lips in that light, peculiarly chaste fashion that never failed to set his blood sizzling.

It was a mystery to him that not only had she married him, but had stuck with him, too, and showed no signs of letting go. Her steadfastness was the very thing that made him nervous, however, and sometimes, in the early morning especially, he would rear up in a panic to check that she was there beside him in bed, that she hadn't given up on the whole project and slipped away in the night. But no, there she was, his large, soft-eyed, mystifying wife, as loving and lightsome as ever, in her always slightly amused, slightly distracted way.

His wife. He, Quirke, had a wife. Yes, the notion of it never failed to surprise him. He had been married before, but never like this; no, never like this.

And now here they were, in Spain, on holiday.

She had been right about the weather—it was raining when they arrived. She didn't care, and neither, really, did he, though he wouldn't say so.

About the greenness of the place she was also right, and about the Catholicism—there was a sense of staid piety that could have been Irish. It certainly wasn't the Spain that old Spanish hands wrote about, with scorching dust, and hot-eyed señoritas stamping the low square heels of their clunky black shoes, and *hidalgos*— was that the word?—in skintight trousers fighting each other with knives, and everybody shouting *Viva España!* and *No pasarán!* and plunging swords between the shoulder blades of lumbering, blood-ied and bewildered bulls.

All the same, however much the place might seem like home, Quirke still resented being on holiday. It was like, he said, being in a drying-out hospital. He had been in more than one such place, in his day, and knew what he was talking about.

"You love to be miserable," Evelyn told him, giving one of her soft, low laughs. "It's your version of being happy."

His wife was a professional psychiatrist, and regarded his many fears and phobias with benign amusement. Most of what he claimed to be the matter with him she diagnosed as playacting, or "performative defense," as she put it—a barrier erected by an overgrown child against a world that, despite his distrust of it, meant him no harm.

"The world treats us all equally," she said.

"Mistreats, you mean," he countered darkly.

She had once compared him to Eeyore, but since he had never heard of Pooh's mournful friend—A. A. Milne was not an author who would have figured in Quirke's blighted childhood—the gibe fell flat.

"You have no problems," she would say gaily. "You have me, instead." Then he would smack her on the backside again, hard, and she would turn and shimmy into his arms and bite him on the earlobe, just as hard.

3

"You know that place name we keep seeing around here, Donostia?" Quirke said. "Well, that's what San Sebastián is called in Basque."

"Or San Sebastián is what Donostia is called in Spanish," his wife responded.

She always managed to have the last word. He could never understand how she did it. Maybe she didn't mean to? Certainly, she didn't do it out of willfulness—she was the least willful person he had ever known—or to get one over on him. She was simply putting the finishing touch to an exchange, he supposed, as she would put down a full stop at the end of a sentence.

It was the morning of the second day of their stay at the Londres. They were in the bedroom of their suite—there was a small reception room as well—and he was sitting on the side of the disordered bed, by the open window, drinking an absurdly tiny cup of coffee and gazing out across the seafront to the beach and the glittering sea beyond. His head felt empty. He supposed this must be what people meant by relaxation. He didn't go in for it much, himself. In the normal run of things he thought of himself as standing on the edge of a precipice and having a hard time not letting go. Or that was how it used to be, until Evelyn came quietly up behind him and put her hands on his shoulders and drew him back from the brink and into her embrace.

What if one day she were to let go her hold? The thought made him shut his eyes tight, like a child in the night choosing inner darkness against the darker dark all around.

The coffee was so bitter that every time he took a sip of it the insides of his cheeks contracted until they almost met.

Outside, the rain had stopped, and the sky was clearing and the sun was making a determined effort to shine. A few tourists, with their towels and swimming caps and paperback books, had ventured onto the still damp beach. The sand was the color of a sucked caramel sweet, and as shinily smooth. He seemed to remember reading somewhere that the Playa de la Concha wasn't a real beach, that the sand was brought here from somewhere else by the lorryload each year before the start of the tourist season. Could it be true? Certainly from up here the stuff did look suspiciously fine and unblemished, with not a stone or seashell to be seen. At night, when the tide was out, people came and wrote elaborate slogans on it, in a strange, cursive lettering that neither he nor Evelyn could decipher. Some antique Basque script, perhaps, Evelyn suggested.

It was easy to tell the visitors by the pallor of their skin and the tentative way they went about choosing a place on the beach on which to settle themselves. Quirke said they reminded him of a dog looking for a spot in which to do its business, and Evelyn frowned and clicked her tongue reprovingly.

For the bathers and the sun worshippers, there was also the tricky matter of how to get into their swimsuits. Officers of the Guardia Civil, in their operetta uniforms, regularly patrolled the promenade, to make sure that no one, especially not a woman, was showing more than the minimum of bare skin. Since there was no official definition of what was and was not permitted in the way of undress, people could never be sure that they wouldn't suddenly be growled at in that particular, guttural tone the Guardia adopted when addressing tourists. Though Quirke noticed that the ones who spoke the most politely were the ones who sounded the most menacing.

Behind him in the room Evelyn gave a small exclamation of shock. She was reading a Spanish newspaper. He turned to her with a questioning eye.

"General Franco has refused an appeal by the Pope to spare the lives of two Basque nationalists," she said. "They will be garrotted tomorrow at dawn. Garrotted! How can such a monster still be in power?"

"Better keep that kind of question to yourself, my dear," he said mildly, "even here in Basqueland, where they loathe the strutting little brute."

It was lunchtime. Quirke had already noted that no matter how the hours dragged, somehow, inexplicably, it always seemed to be just about time for lunch, or for an afternoon glass of wine, for an aperitif, for dinner. He complained about this to his wife—"I feel like a baby in an incubator"—as he complained to her of so many things. She pretended not to hear.

He noticed he was drinking less down here, or less, anyway, than he would have in similar circumstances at home. But could there ever be, at home, circumstances similar to these? Maybe, he thought, the way of life here, the slow mornings, the softness of the slightly damp, lacquered air, the general yieldingness of things—maybe it would bring about a transformation in his character, make a new man of him. He laughed to himself. Fat chance.

Already this morning he had made a fool of himself by mentioning something about the quality of the Mediterranean light.

"But we're on the Atlantic," Evelyn said. "Didn't you know that?"

Of course he knew it. He had studied the map of the Iberian Peninsula in the airline magazine on the flight coming down here, trying to take his mind off the rain clouds through which the frighteningly delicate airplane—an aluminum tube with wings—was making its turbulent way. How could he have forgotten what coast they were on?

He turned his eyes again to the beach and the poor shivering wraiths scattered about the sand. Shaky as he might be in matters of geography, at least he knew better than to bare his blue-gray shanks to the chill spring breeze skimming to shore over the crests of those rolling Atlantic breakers.

There were a few Spaniards among the people on the beach, male, for the most part, easily identifiable by their glistening, mahogany-hued pelts. They were on the prowl after the buttermilk-pale northern girls, new flocks of whom came down on charter flights every week. The would-be Don Juans seemed not to care whether the girls were good-looking or not—paleness was all, the paleness of thick, pulpy flesh that hadn't seen the sun since last year's package trip to the suntanned south.

He drained the last bitter dregs of the coffee and put the cup aside, feeling as if he had dosed himself with an emetic. He would have preferred tea, but in Spain only the English could order tea without self-consciousness.

With an effort he stirred himself out of his torpor, and went into the bathroom, with its unfamiliar appurtenances. Part of his dislike of holidays was that they required him to stay in hotels. He returned to the bedroom, hitching up his pajamas. He told himself he should do something about his paunch, though he knew he wouldn't.

How was it, he wondered, not for the first time, that people seemed oblivious to the brazen confidence trick that was played on them in hotels? Did it never occur to them to think how many greasy holidaymakers, leaky honeymooners, how many oldsters with unpredictable bladders and flaking skin, had slept already in the very bed in which they were themselves just now reclining? Did it never cross their minds that over the years God knows how many poor souls had breathed their last on the same mattress on which they stretched themselves out so luxuriously at the end of another fun-filled day spent prone on the stoneless beach or gamboling in the sea as blue as Reckitt's dye?

The conspiracy begins the moment you arrive, as he pointed out to Evelyn, who was knitting, and wasn't listening. There's the grinning doorman who yanks open the door of your taxi and gabbles a greeting in pidgin English. There's the beaming girl in black behind the reception desk who exclaims, in her bouncy way, that it is a pleasure to welcome you back, even though you've never stayed here before. There is the porter, lean and stooped, with a melancholy eye and a mustache that might have been drawn on with an eyebrow pencil, who festoons himself with your suitcases and staggers away with them, to arrive at the door of your room a mysterious twenty minutes later—was he off in some cubbyhole in the meantime, going through your things?—and, having shown you how the light switches work and how to open and close the curtains, loiters expectantly on the threshold, with his fake, ingratiating smile, waiting for his tip.

"And why," he called out whiningly, Evelyn having taken his place in the bathroom, "why must there be so many staff?"

They were everywhere: porters, receptionists, waiters, barmen, chambermaids, bellboys, cleaners and those unaccountable, bossy-looking, middle-aged women in white blouses and

black skirts who stride along the upstairs corridors bearing in
their chubby hands those mysterious but important-looking
clipboards.

Evelyn came back into the bedroom.

"Why did you bring this woolen jumper?" she asked, holding
up the heavy brown garment by the sleeves. "We are in Spain,
not Scandinavia." She paused, and looked at him vaguely. "What
were you saying, dear, about hotels?"

When they were first married, Quirke would divert himself
by seeing how far he could push her before she lost her temper.
She never did. She responded to everything, all his taunts and
teases, without the least sign of anger or annoyance, but with
what was no more than a kind of clinical interest. It was, he
supposed, another way of having the last word, only more so.

Despite everything, and though he wouldn't dream of admitting it to Evelyn, he had come to quite like the Londres. It
was discreetly self-confident, with an understated style. It didn't
nag, but left him largely to his own devices. The restaurant was
good, the bar well stocked. He was even acquiring a taste for
the briny olives, a fresh dish of which was served with every
drink he ordered.

His keenest, secret enthusiasm was the lift. It ran, or joggled,
rather, up and down through the very heart of the building. It
was ancient and creaky, with a folding iron gate that shuddered
shut with a satisfying clatter. Inside, it was lined with red plush,
and attached to the back wall, below a framed mirror, was a little wooden seat hardly deeper than a bookshelf, covered with
a raggedy piece of carpet held in place by round-headed nails
worn to a shine over the years by the well-upholstered posteri-
ors of countless well-heeled guests.

At the right when you were facing out, there was a brass
wheel, about a foot in diameter, with an invitingly fat brass
knob fitted to the rim. It reminded Quirke of the wheel at the
back of those fire engines you see in films, that firemen spin

with such amazing speed when they're unwinding hosepipes in the glare of a burning building. Every time his eye fell on it, he had a childish urge to grasp the brass knob and give the wheel a turn or two, just to see what would happen. But he lacked the courage. In some ways, Quirke was a timid man.

Yes, he liked the Londres. He was pleased to be here, there was no denying it. This, of course, made him uneasy. What of his long-worked-at reputation as a malcontent and moaner?

4

The Basque language, written down, didn't look like a language at all, to his eye. It seemed made up at random from handfuls of ill-assorted letters. The words were sprinkled thickly with *K*s and *Z*s and *X*s, so that a line of it, in a public announcement or above a shop window, resembled nothing so much as a string of barbed wire. Even Evelyn, who spoke many of the major European languages and some of the minor, didn't attempt it.

The most popular local wine, a very good, slightly fizzy white, was spelled txakoli. That was one word Quirke was quick to learn how to pronounce: *tchacholy*.

"So now, you see," Evelyn said, regarding him with solemn-eyed mockery, "you are learning to speak the language. Today you know how to ask for wine, tomorrow you can find out what is the word for cigarettes. Then all your needs will be taken care of."

"Very droll," he said.

"'Droll'? Tell me, what is that?"

On their first full day at the Londres they had lain down in bed in the middle of the afternoon and made lazy love, to the rhythm of that big friendly sea creature breathing in at the wide-open window.

Rhythm, yes. Life here, for them, on this north-facing southern coast, was simply a matter of matching one's pace to certain regulatory dictates. The sound of the crumpling waves, of church bells tolling the hour, of the lunchtime gong, these were the padded metronome beats that measured out the dreamy melody of their days, of their sea-lapped nights.

Early evening was their favorite time, with twilight coming on and the pace of everything slowing down in anticipation of the rowdy nocturnal excitements that would soon start up. They would step out of the hotel and stroll arm in arm along the front, Quirke in slacks and a light jacket and brown suede shoes—not his usual choice of footwear, though secretly he thought them quite racy—and Evelyn in a flowered cotton frock with a cardigan draped over her shoulders. Darkness, when it fell, fell rapidly in these latitudes, and when it had settled they would stop and lean on the rail above the beach and gaze out over the bay, as black and shining as a vast bowl of oil and scattered with the reflections of lights from houses on the hill on the right, or from the little island of Santa Klara at the mouth of the bay.

At such moments, his wife's happiness was almost palpable to him, a sort of faint, slow vibration running all through her. She was Austrian, and Jewish, and many members of her family had been murdered in the camps. Having ended up by chance in Ireland, she had married, first, a sometime colleague of Quirke's, and been happy for a while, until her husband died. She had lost a child, too, a boy called Hanno, to an illness the doctors had been too late in diagnosing.

She would speak of none of these things.

"That was in the old time, when I should have died with the others," she would say, with a strange, shy little smile. "But I didn't. And now here we are, you and I."

And so the days went on, and Quirke gradually stopped complaining about being on holiday and having to sleep in a bed that wasn't his own and to shave in a mirror that showed him his big fleshy face in a harsher light than it should ever be seen. Evelyn made no comment on this, surely, to her, welcome relief, and for his part he made no comment on her not commenting. His wife was not a woman to let a blessing go uncounted, but she was considerate enough to count in silence.

There was a café on a square in the Old Town that became their favorite haunt of an evening. They took to sitting outside there, under an old stone arcade, as the nights grew increasingly warm. In the space of a few days, late spring had turned to early summer.

One entire side of the square was taken up by a big ugly building with a clock on the top of it, watched over by a pair of stylized cement lions and flanked on either side by rusted, miniature cannons that didn't look as if they would have done much defending even in the days when they were still in a condition to be fired.

The café—or the bar, as Quirke insisted—was a popular spot, not only for tourists, they noted, but for Donostians, too. This was a good sign, Evelyn said, nodding in the slow, pensive way that she did, as if larger thoughts lay behind the commonplace words.

The last light leached from the air, the stars above the square came out, and they sat there, contented husband and happy wife, sipping their glasses of dryly fragrant txakoli and watching the passing promenade.

"Spaniards have no shame when it comes to public display," Quirke observed.

"And why should they?" Evelyn asked, surprised. She reflected for a moment, then said, "But of course, I see. This is a pleasure the Irish have never learned, simply to sit and observe the ordinary things that happen in the world."

Quirke said she was right, or so he supposed. There it was again—relaxation, that problematic concept. He was making himself have a conscious go at it, now, sitting there, but without success. He had a lot of practicing to do.

The people around them were English, Americans, Swedes—he took that singsong accent to be Swedish—and even Germans, who were once again posing as the happy wanderers they used to imagine themselves to be, before the years of madness and their aftermath taught them they were nothing of the kind.

It was only when he heard an Irish voice somewhere behind him that he realized it was the thing he had been listening out for since he had first landed in Spain. You can take the Irishman out of Ireland, he thought despondently, but not the other way around.

It was a woman's voice he had heard. She sounded young, or at least youngish. Her tone was oddly urgent, as if she had more things to say than she could possibly get said. The accent was Dublin, south-side, middle-class. He tried to catch what she was saying with such odd vehemence, but couldn't. He turned his head and scanned the crowd, and there she was.

5

He didn't point her out to Evelyn, that first time. In fact, he didn't pay much attention to her himself, once he had registered the accent and deplored the nostalgic *ping!* it had sounded in his suddenly homesick heart. He took her to be just another well-heeled tourist, doing Spain on Daddy's money, and that the man sitting opposite her, an elegant, lightly bearded, gray-haired gent in a pale linen suit, was Daddy himself. Afterward, he remembered how it had struck him as remarkable that a daughter should address her father with such dark-toned intensity. He decided they must have been having a row. Being on holiday with an elderly parent would try any young person's tolerance, after all.

That was the evening when Quirke and Evelyn themselves had—not a row, exactly, but a sharpish difference of opinion.

They never fought, at least not as other couples did, and as Quirke himself had fought with others of his women in the past. In the old days he was never averse to a bit of argy-bargy, to liven things up and clear the air. But Evelyn, as he had quickly come to realize, didn't know how to fight, or, if she did, chose not to. Their disagreements were hardly disagreements at all, more like slightly overheated debates. Evelyn was unfailingly curious about people and the ways in which they conducted themselves in their dealings with the world. Sitting there at the edge of that busy square, she might have been an anthropologist on a field expedition, sharply alert to the coloring, habits and behavior of the local fauna. Quirke had once told her that she would make a good detective.

"But that's what a psychiatrist is," she said. "Freud was a living version of Sherlock Holmes."

"Yes," Quirke responded, "and his conclusions were about as plausible."

His wife only smiled. Freud, the Nobodaddy of them all, as Quirke, an admiring reader of William Blake, liked to call him, was a subject on which she refused to be drawn.

"Are you hungry?" she asked. "I am."

Quirke wanted to go back to the hotel for dinner, but Evelyn suggested they should stay here and eat. They could make do perfectly well, she said, with the skewered snacks the Basques called *pintxos*. But the *pintxo*, as far as Quirke was concerned, was just a slightly fancier version of the dull old sandwich. He was against the idea of local specialties, which in his experience were all too local, and rarely special.

"But it is so lively here," Evelyn objected.

"Is it?"

"Yes, of course it is. Look at that elderly couple, holding hands."

Quirke wasn't interested in couples, young or old, holding hands or otherwise. He was working himself up, or down, into one of his sulks. It was a thing he did when he was bored and in need of something to occupy himself with. For him, petulance was a pastime.

His wife regarded him in silence for some moments.

She had a broad, heart-shaped face, a fattish nose and a sensuously downturned mouth with a prominent, plump upper lip, due to a slight overbite—that little bleb of glistening pink flesh was one of his favorites among, as he expressed it, her "bits." She never went to a hairdresser but cut her own hair, in a severe pageboy style with a fringe that stopped in a straight line just above her eyebrows. When she looked at him like this, with her chin lowered and her baby-lip protruding, Quirke saw in her the solemn-eyed girl she would once have been. He always resented the expanse of time that had passed before he knew her. It seemed to him astounding that they had both been in the world at the same time, having their lives, being themselves, and each ignorant of the other's existence for so long.

"Do you know what hotel dining rooms remind me of?" she said now.

"No. What do hotel dining rooms remind you of?"

"Places where wakes are held."

He frowned, his forehead wrinkling. "Wakes?"

"Yes. Not the room itself with the dead person in it, you know, but the place next door, where the mourners are gathered, nibbling at their plates of dainty food and speaking to each other in quiet voices, so stilted and polite. All you hear is the murmuring all around you, and the little clinking sound of knives and forks on plates, and now and then the tiny chimes that wineglasses make when a knife or a fork knocks against them."

"I see what you mean," Quirke said, laughing a little. "But it doesn't seem so bad, to me."

After all, he refrained from saying, he was a pathologist; his professional life was carried on among the dead.

"But it is *unnatürlich*, no? Unnatural. People should be with the living. Look around you—here is so much fun."

Quirke shrugged in the way he did, rolling his shoulders inside his jacket. He had in general a low opinion of what people considered "fun." All the same, he found it amusing to think of the gilded dining room at the Londres as an annex to the mortuary. Evelyn gazed at him, perplexed—what was funny?

"You are," he said.

"Am I?"

For Evelyn, no question was rhetorical. Every inquiry required a response.

"The things you say," he said. "The way you look at the world."

"This is funny?"

"Sometimes—often—yes." He paused, and leaned forward. "Someone said of some poet or other that he stood at a slight angle to the world. That's you, my dear."

She thought about this.

"Yes," she said, nodding judiciously, "it is my job to view these things from an angle. Do you think this is wrong?"

"No, I don't think it's wrong at all. It's just—unusual." He glanced about at the crowded tables. "What all this reminds *me* of is a not very engaging bullfight at which the spectators have lost interest and have started to talk among themselves instead. So much chatter."

"What sounds to you like chatter is conversation for the people making it. This is what human beings do, you know." She also looked about at the other people at the other tables. "Don't you think that the restaurant is one of our greatest inventions, as a species?"

He gazed at her, startled, smiling.

"You see?" he said. "I never know what you're going to come out with next."

"Look how people are enjoying themselves, and being nice to each other, talking together—*not* chattering—and making the best of the little bit of time that they will be given here on earth."

He put a hand over hers where it rested beside her wineglass on the table.

"Ah, you confound me in the most charming fashion," he said.

She wrinkled that broad nose of hers. She wasn't beautiful, in any of the generally accepted senses of the word, which was what made her beautiful, for him.

"Confound?" she said. "What is confound?"

Even yet she had occasional difficulties with English, a language that made her cross sometimes by being, as she said, so untidy and illogical. Quirke often pondered the irony of her having settled in Ireland, a more or less English-speaking country, given that English was the language in which she was least proficient. She was the oddest woman he had ever known. If, that was, he could be said to know her.

"To confound," he said, "means that you're always right, and always prove me wrong."

"I don't think you are always wrong. And I am not always right." She frowned again, indignant on his behalf. "Certainly not. You know so many more things than I do. You know all about the body, for instance, the inside of it."

"I only know about the dead ones."

"Well, you know me, and I'm not dead."

He stroked her hand.

"It's time to order another glass of wine," he said. "Don't you think?"

He looked about for the waitress. She was a tall, slim young woman, the type described as sloe-eyed, dark and provocatively sullen. He had already noticed her exquisite wrists. He had a special fondness for the moving parts of women, their wrists, their butterfly-shaped ankles, their shoulder blades like a swan's folded wings. In particular he treasured their knees, especially the backs of them, where the skin was pale, milk-blue, with delicate fissures, little fine cracks, as in the most fragile old pieces of bone china.

The young woman at the table behind him was speaking again, and this time he caught a word: "theater."

He turned halfway around on his chair to get a better look at her, not bothering to disguise his interest—he was sure she wouldn't notice him, anyway. Her figure was slight, and she had a pale, narrow face and skinny shoulders, the bones of which pressed sharply against the thin stuff of her dress. She sat hunched into herself, as though the evening had turned cold just where she was, with her hands folded and her back sloped and her chin lowered to a foot above the table edge.

A strange, striking creature.

Was she an actress? He didn't think so. She was too muted, too self-contained—covert, that was the word that came to his mind. Yet she was demonstrative, too, and used her hands a lot, molding elaborate shapes in air, as if she were illustrating the contours of some complicated thing she had fashioned. A stage designer, maybe? No, not that, either.

Was she angry, to be so animated? Was she airing a grievance? Maybe she was just describing a play she had seen. He couldn't tell.

The man at the other side of the table seemed bored and mildly irritated. It was probably not the first time he had heard her opinions on whatever subject it was that she was expatiating on so animatedly. Quirke sympathized with him. He had a daughter himself. They could be relentless, daughters.

Now the young woman spoke that word again—"theater."

Quirke had once been in love, or something like it, with an actress. Isabel Galloway was her name. She was a thorn lodged in his conscience, too deeply embedded ever to be extracted. She wasn't the only woman he had treated badly, in his time.

They had another glass of txakoli, and, to please Evelyn, Quirke consented to eat some *pintxos* with assorted fillings— ham, anchovies, sliced raw fish, red peppers. The little sandwiches were pierced through the middle with wooden toothpicks, which accumulated on their plates and told the smoldering waitress, she of the sloe-black eyes, how many of them they had eaten and what their bill was to be. Local color, Quirke thought disparagingly, the stuff to tell your mum and dad about when you got home to Birmingham, or Burnley, or Barrow-in-bloody-Furness. There were altogether too many English tourists down here, he considered, however much the musclemen on the beach prized the females among them.

After the wine, Quirke took a risk and ordered a brandy. This turned out to be a mistake.

What was served to him, not in a balloon glass but a chunky tumbler, was a sluggish, brownish stuff, viscous as sherry, with a fragrance reminiscent of cough medicine. He drank it, anyway, though he knew it would give him indigestion. But it might help him to sleep, he thought. On the other hand, it might just as easily keep him awake. Latterly, his nights had become a mixture of stark wakefulness and fitful, ashen dreaming. He had hoped, with faint hope, that down here it might be otherwise. Surely the least that might be expected of a holiday was that it would foster sleepiness.

"Look," Evelyn said, "the girls, they keep their hankies in their sleeves, just like in Ireland."

His wife, now, she slept as if sunk in a coma. It was good that one of them at least was able to rest, though her preternatural stillness puzzled him. How was it the terrors of her past didn't rise up to jolt her awake, like bolts of white lightning striking out of the darkness? On this, as on so many things, he hadn't the nerve to quiz her. From the beginning, she had let it be known that whatever ghosts lingered with her were hers alone, her private hauntings. He used to assume she would confide in him eventually, but she didn't, and by now it seemed she never would. Secretly, in some black cavern of his heart, he was glad. He had quite enough demons of his own to wrestle with.

Yet there was so much he didn't know about this intimate

stranger he was married to, so much he wasn't permitted to know. She wouldn't even tell him her murdered parents' names. Or how many siblings she had lost. Or which camps they had perished in. One day she let slip that her oldest sister—she didn't say how many other, younger ones there were—had perished in a German concentration camp, of tuberculosis. This fact, which immediately he saw her regretting having divulged, he took and stored away, as if it were a formal document, signed and sealed, though what it might be a testament to he wasn't sure.

He told himself the details of her past didn't matter, and they didn't, really, although at the same time they did, precisely because of being withheld.

The facts he did possess were few. An uncle who was a doctor and supplied morphine to someone high up in Hitler's court had got her out of Austria via France and Spain—this, it occurred to him just now, accounted for her knowing San Sebastián and the Hotel Londres. The uncle had gone on to America and made for himself what she, widening her eyes, described as a "big, big career" at the Mayo Clinic.

She had been meant to go onward with him to the States, but at the last minute, entirely on a whim, she had disembarked from the SS *America* at the Cobh harbor and made her way to Dublin. There, through endeavors the nature of which remained vague, she had managed to set herself up in what was to become a successful practice, in spacious rooms in a handsome house on Fitzwilliam Square. It was no small achievement, given that psychiatry was frowned on by the State and anathematized by the Catholic Church—only God had the right to delve into the human soul.

Her success was as much of a surprise to her as it was to others. Quirke told her it was easily explained. The country had been crying out for her, he said, without either she or the country being aware of it. He reminded her that in his will, Jonathan Swift had bequeathed a madhouse to Dublin, since, as the dismal Dean had observed, no place was more in need of one.

She had listened to him gravely, and said he should not use that word.

"Which word?"

"Mad."

Sure enough, a burning sensation had started up behind his breastbone—that damned, so-called brandy.

"Are you telling me there aren't mad people in the world?" he had asked, with mock innocence.

"'Mad' is a meaningless concept. But, of course, yes, there are many people who are sick in their minds."

"And you're here to cure them," he had said, with a scornful smile, and immediately regretted both the words and the smile.

She had ignored his scorn, however, and pondered the question in silence for some moments.

"As I have told you many times, there is no cure. No cure, that is, from what you call madness. There is only—what is the word?—amelioration. Surely you have read of the woman suffering from severe neurosis who went to Freud and asked him if he could cure her. Freud said no, he couldn't do that, but he believed what he could do was restore her to a state of ordinary unhappiness." She had touched his hand and smiled. "That was wise, yes? The old man was always wise."

Quirke could only agree, and look away. He knew a thing or two about ordinary unhappiness.

6

They walked along the sloped streets leading down from the Old Town, and came to the seafront. There were other couples out strolling, aimless and dreamy, like them, perhaps also a little tipsy, as they were. The sea tonight was as smooth and flat as an oval of black glass, traversed by a track of moonlight the color of tarnished gold. Somewhere a palm-court orchestra was playing an old-fashioned, soupy number that Quirke recognized but couldn't put a name to. The music billowed back and forth through the soft night air, waltzing with itself.

"I suppose our being so easy like this makes you anxious, yes?" Evelyn said.

Quirke laughed. "Yes, of course." He looked down at his suede shoes. He wondered if perhaps they hadn't been a bad idea. "But are we happy, or just ordinarily unhappy?"

As usual, she took the question seriously. He watched her considering it from all sides, as if it were something intricately worked, with many gleaming facets, each one requiring the most scrupulous attention.

"Of course, yes, ordinary unhappiness is our condition," she said, "but don't you agree that there are moments—indeed, quite extended periods of time—when everyone, including even persons such as yourself, experiences that famous oceanic feeling of being at one with everything in the world, to its depths and to its heights?"

He began to say something facetious, but stopped himself, beset suddenly by a strange disquiet.

For him, the ocean signified death, always.

Evelyn was waiting for his response, but he wouldn't speak—couldn't, in fact. What was he to say? What right had he to speak of death to her, of all people? She refrained from further prompting. Sometimes silence was more eloquent than words. Her arm was linked through his, and now she drew his elbow tight against her side. "My poor darling," she said. She pronounced it *darlink*, mocking her own accent by exaggerating it, as she often did. Her foreignness—her foreignness to Quirke—was one of the many things she found amusing. How could one be oneself and yet foreign to someone else? It was a puzzle, one of many she had to grapple with in her life as an émigré.

Quirke spoke at last.

"There was an old nun at one of the so-called orphan schools I was sentenced to when I was little," he said. "At least, I suppose she was a nun. She had a black habit, anyway, I remember that."

"A black habit?"

"The outfit that she wore," he explained. "Her uniform."

"Ah. A black habit. I see. It sounds like something sinful."

"She was in charge of the infirmary, and was supposed to look after us when we were sick. Not that we were permitted to be sick, except in extremest cases—there would be a fuss when one

of us had the effrontery to up and die. Anyway, disapproval was
the constant of this woman's life, the iron principle she lived
by. Anything that smacked of tolerance, of tenderness, of solici-
tude, was to be stifled. The saying of hers that I remember best
is 'Laughing will end crying.' It was what she came out with at
the least sign of high spirits, of gaiety, of"—he paused—"of 'happiness.'" He gave a small, bitter laugh. "She didn't have cause to
say it often, since there was precious little to laugh about, in that
place. We learned to keep a straight face, when she was around.
She had a leather strap attached to her belt, and she could use
it, I can tell you."

Evelyn squeezed his arm again, more tightly.

They had come to the steps of the hotel, and here they stopped
short in a mixture of amusement and sudden wonder. Through
a large square window to the right of the main door they were
offered a lighted view, as on a stage, of a crowd of elderly folk,
in pairs, immaculately dressed, dancing. Around and around
they glided, in spritely restraint, their backs straight and silvery
heads held erect, suave, meticulously elegant and expressionless
as marionettes. Here was the source of the waltz music Quirke
had heard earlier.

"*The Merry Widow*," he murmured.

"What?"

"The title of the operetta. I just recognized it."

"I have always thought that a cruel title."

"What is it in German?"

"The same. *Die lustige Witwe.*"

They watched and listened for a minute, and then, without
further comment, they went together on up the steps and entered the hotel.

"Let's sit a while, in the lounge," Evelyn said. "The night is
too lovely to let it end, just yet."

They settled themselves at a table by another of the big windows that gave on to the seafront and, beyond, the bay with the

moonlight on it. Evelyn ordered a tisane, which when it came gave off a delicate fragrance of dried orange blossom.

"It must be like drinking scent," he said.

She made a face at him.

Early on in their stay, Quirke had struck up an acquaintance with one of the barmen, a dusty old boy with large hairy ears and shoe leather that squeaked. This person now, without being summoned, brought to the table a tumbler of Jameson Crested Ten, with a glass of plain water on the side.

"Wine, brandy and now this," Evelyn said, eyeing the whiskey. "Surely tonight you will sleep."

"Surely," Quirke said, taking a sip of his drink.

This was more like it. How he savored the sensation of the whiskey running like slow fire along the complicated tracery of tubes behind his breastbone. His indigestion sent up one last hot flare and was extinguished—good old J J&S, always dependable. He leaned back, and the cane chair crackled under him like a bonfire. Evelyn, sitting opposite, was smiling, in her unfocused fashion, at nothing in particular. Then she lifted her eyes to his. She had a way now and then of looking at him with what seemed like surprise and muted delight, as if she hadn't known him before but had chanced on him just at that moment and was already discovering him to be an object of the profoundest and most pleasing interest.

Yes, he thought, with a faint, inward shiver, nothing is so worrying as happiness, especially when it is of the ordinary variety.

"There was another nun, in that place, I remember," he said. "Much less frosty—warm, in fact. Sister Rose. My first love. She used to give us our weekly bath, on Saturday night, two of us at a time, one at either end of the tub, facing each other. I can see her now, her rolled-up sleeves and pink arms, her wimple tied back with something, a piece of ribbon, I suppose. She would kneel down by the side of the bath and soap us all over, first one of us, then the other, and scrub and scrub. The moment I always waited for, in dread and hot excitement, was when she would reach down between my legs, under the water, and joggle around there vigorously, all the while keeping her eyes carefully averted, of course." He paused. "Pleasure is most intense when you don't understand the source of it."

Evelyn sipped again at the fragrant concoction in her cup.

"You are very—what is the word for quietly thinking?"

"Contemplative?" he offered.

"Yes. You are very contemplative, this evening. Quite the philosopher."

She lifted her eyes again, and they gazed at each other briefly, in a silence the significance of which neither of them could have explained. Then Quirke laughed, and shrugged, and held the whiskey glass aloft, like a chalice.

"Don't mind me," he said. "It's the drink that's thinking."

A tiny jewel of amber light glinted in the last drop of the liquor in the bottom of the glass.

7

He woke in the night, instantly alert, and prey to a nameless fear. Was there someone in the room? He lifted his head from the pillow and peered into the shadows, but saw nothing there, no narrow-faced fellow with mustaches and a dagger, and no slim-hipped, sloe-eyed dusky girl in a bar apron, either. The only movement he could detect was the slight stirring of the gauze curtain in the breeze at the open window.

With a sigh, he let his head drop back onto the pillow, and made himself listen to the hushed sound of that long wave outside falling, then gathering itself and falling again. Presently, the sense of alarm dissipated and his nerves quietened. He still didn't know what it was that had wakened him. Probably some fragment of a dream, already forgotten.

He thought again of the young woman at the café with the Irish accent. The table at which she and her gentleman companion had sat was quite far back under the stone arcade, and in the latening evening light Quirke had got no clear impression of her, except that she was thin and dark-haired, and seemed agitated in some way. He had guessed her to be in her middle twenties, perhaps a little older. It seemed to him that he had seen her before, a long time ago. But if so, where?

He turned onto his side, thrashing his legs against the constricting bedclothes. His imagination was overheated. Darkness played tricks on the mind. And he had been drinking, too, and drinking too much, as Evelyn had pointed out. She knew his long history on the bottle. "On the bottle"—it was from Quirke she had first heard the phrase, and had been much amused by it. "You were all—what is that saying?—you were all weaned too early, all you Irish men."

Fully awake now, he got out of bed, going quietly for fear of disturbing Evelyn, and went into the bathroom. Yes, he had drunk too much. Despite the bracing effects of the Jameson, the sticky aftertaste of Spanish brandy still lingered on his tongue.

At the handbasin he filled a tooth glass with water, but then recalled the awful warnings he had read on the dangers of drinking water straight from a Spanish tap. He crept back into the bedroom and felt his way about in the silvery gloom, and at last found a bottle of mineral water in a cabinet at his side of the bed. He uncapped it and drank from the neck. *On the bottle*, he thought, and grinned bleakly into the glimmering darkness. The water was tepid and had a slightly brackish taste, but at least it was wet, and probably could be trusted not to give him a dose of dysentery or something even worse.

That was another reason to stay at home, the possibility of falling ill in some unsanitary foreign resort and being forced to put himself under the care of non-English-speaking medics who wouldn't even understand what he was complaining of.

He sat in his pajamas at the desk beside the window, seeking solace yet again in the view over the bay. It was late, it must be four o'clock, but in the stillness he heard music playing somewhere, though it was so faint he thought he might be imagining it.

But no, there was music. It wasn't the palm-court orchestra, the members of which would have packed up and gone home long ago. Maybe it was a wireless playing in one of the rooms along the corridor. A woman's voice, was it, singing flamenco? He strained to catch the distantly tiny, wailing notes as they rose and fell, rose and fell. He must get hold of a translation of some of those songs, to find out what terrible tragedy it was they were all lamenting with such throbbing fervor. He wondered if there was any happy flamenco music. If so, he had not heard it. Unless they were smiling through their tears.

Still the distant music buzzed and wailed. He thought again he was imagining it. Maybe there were mosquitoes in the room. They made the same kind of thin, ethereal sound.

And then suddenly, out of nowhere, as it seemed, it came to him that when the young woman spoke the word "theater," it wasn't a playhouse she was talking about, but a theater in a hospital—an operating theater.

How could he know that? He couldn't say. Maybe he was more drunk than he realized.

In the old days, the wild old days of his friends John Jameson and Mr. Bushmills and Madam Gin and even, in times of desperate need, the odd shot of thin blue methylated spirit—a fellow toper had taught him how to strain it through a crust of bread clamped between his front teeth in order to rid the ethanol of its noxious additives—his fevered brain would come up with the most bizarre, the most amazing, fancies.

There had been a particularly bad bout of almost uninterrupted drinking, over the space of a week or more, when he had been convinced he was under the control of a horde of tiny, multilimbed creatures, a species of humanoid spiders that could speak and reason and issue directives in sharp, unmodulated voices that came to him as a high-pitched whirring, something like the sound of a dentist's drill, only thinner and more penetrating—or like the music he seemed to be hearing just now. Over days and nights he had stumbled through a phantasmagorical world in which jagged sunlight and luminous rain alternated with long stretches of overarching darkness and tomb-like silence. He had slept, or dozed, in strange beds, on sofas, on floors and in gutters, and for one entire night in a suburban front garden somewhere, imagining himself lashed to the spot by a tracery of silken threads, a groaning and demented Lemuel Gulliver. When he recovered, he had determined never again to find himself in that particular, nightmarish version of Lilliput. Never again.

Evelyn it was who had cut through the tethers and hauled him teetering to his feet. He would not force her, not ever, to repeat that exercise in forbearance, patience and fortitude.

He stood up from the chair at the window and moved toward the bed, then stopped and stood still, stalled in his tracks.

...*need me in the theater*—that was what he had overheard the young woman say, not just the one word, but a fragment of a sentence, it came back to him now. *You said you didn't need me in the theater...*

No actor would ever talk of being needed in a theater, any theater, anywhere. Only a doctor would say that. He knew a lot of doctors, though none that was female, and none in Spain. There had been one, in Ireland, a friend of his daughter's. But she couldn't be the young woman in the café, for she had died.

LONDON

8

It was all right for a while, after Terry Tice had moved into Percy Antrobus's third-floor flat in Fitzroy Square. The place was bigger than he would have expected. It had five or six big airy rooms and a nice view over Fitzroy Square Garden. The grass and the trees gave a greeny-gold cast to the light under the high ceilings, especially in the morning-time. But the place was a rubbish dump, with most of the furniture broken, and filthy carpets and unemptied ashtrays and unmade beds, and smeared glasses put down anywhere and left so long that any drop of wine remaining in the bottom of them crystallized and made them a bitch to wash.

Not that Terry did much in the way of housework. He left that kind of thing to Percy, who was too mean to hire a char.

Terry liked to lounge on one of the sway-backed sofas and watch the old geezer at his chores, hoovering the sticky carpets, or up to his elbows in suds at the kitchen sink, with his shirtsleeves rolled and wearing a little frilly apron, a cigarette stuck in the corner of his mouth and one eye shut against the smoke, listening to comedians like Ted Ray or Arthur Askey on the wireless and phlegmily chuckling.

All the same, the dirt and the squalor had come as a surprise to Terry. He had expected that Percy, with his cravats and his patent-leather shoes and his la-di-da drawl, would live in the grand style, with pictures and books, and silver cutlery, and little antique gilt chairs, all that kind of thing, like in films. He should have known better, if only from the permanent snowfall of dandruff on the collars of Percy's Savile Row suits, and the dirt under his fingernails. Also his breath had an awful, grayish reek, as if something had crawled down his gizzard and died there.

They ate out, mostly, at a little Italian place just around the corner from the flat. Terry didn't much like Italian food, but Gino's did a nice veal cutlet, and the ice cream really was ice cream, not the usual English muck. Sometimes he sneaked off on his own to the Feathers for a pint of Guinness and a bag of pork scratchings. The tarts that haunted the place would come and sit beside him at the bar and cross their legs and try to chat him up, but he would tell them to get lost. He didn't mind having it on with a bird now and then, when the fancy took him, but he had no intention of paying for it, ever.

Percy pestered him that way, too; it really was a pain. In time they came to a suitable arrangement, or one that suited Terry, anyway. He would let himself be sucked off, but that was as far as he was prepared to go. Percy groused, of course, and even offered Terry money to let him do more things to him, but Terry had drawn the line and there was no crossing it. Imagine allowing himself to be buggered by that smelly old brute.

He often wondered if Percy knew about him stealing from him. He would wait until Percy was asleep and slip his wallet out of the back pocket of his stale-smelling, shiny-arsed pin-striped trousers where they hung by their braces from the ward-robe door, and quietly extract a ten-bob note or even a pound or two. He only did it this way for the fun of it. He could have just taken the money and not cared about getting caught. What could Percy do, even if he were to catch him red-handed? From the start Terry made it his business for Percy to go in fear of him. It didn't take a lot of effort. Percy had about as much back-bone as a slug.

Though Percy, too, had his rules, unspoken ones, mostly. For instance, one thing he wouldn't do was let Terry mix with his fancy friends. He had quite a few of them, or so he claimed. One night he came home pissed from a dinner out somewhere posh and mentioned casually that Princess Margaret had been among the guests and he had sat opposite her. Terry didn't know whether to believe him or not. Percy, dining with royalty?

He said he used to be a Guards officer, which Terry defi-nitely didn't believe, until, to prove it, the old fraud brought out a moth-eaten scarlet tunic with gold buttons and gold pip-ing and a string of colored medals pinned on the breast. He had a sword, too, in a decorated scabbard. Sometimes, when Percy was out, Terry would play with the sword in front of the misty, full-length mirror in Percy's bedroom, slashing and feinting and stabbing imaginary opponents in the guts and cutting down hordes of imaginary darkies.

He was a strange cove, though, was Percy. You never knew with him. He had that hoity-toity accent, talking as if he had a potato in his mouth. On a couple of occasions he went out for the evening in a top hat and tails. True, the hat was a bit dented, and the tailcoat had some iffy-looking stains on it, but the outfit was definitely the real thing. "There's a world of dif-ference between a gentleman and the other sort," Percy would say. "Putting on airs to which you are not entitled is the height of vulgarity. Remember that, my boy." This was one of what he called the "life lessons" he "bestowed" on Terry, in an effort to "inculcate wisdom" in him and give him "a dash of style."

Terry didn't resent this kind of stuff. On the contrary, it amused him, and even made him feel a smidgen of fondness for the sad old poofter.

It was hard to know where Percy got his money from. He had his inheritance from his dead ma, thanks to Terry, but it had turned out to be nowhere near as much as Percy had given the impression it would be. He had no job, and certainly wasn't in business for himself, though he claimed to act as a sort of agent for chaps who were. That was as much as he would divulge. It was hard to get Percy to be specific, about anything.

All the same, he put some sweet jobs Terry's way, sweet jobs that paid sweet.

"Got a little task for you, Terence, my lad," he would say, rubbing his dry, bloodless hands together and doing his smoker's cough and turning puce in the face. "Met a chap at the club who has a bit of a problem—dear me, how breathless I am."

That was another thing he wouldn't specify, which club or clubs he was a member of.

"Oh, yes?" Terry would say, offhand, without bothering to look up from the copy of *Titbits* he was reading. "What sort?"

And Percy would giggle and say, "You mean, what sort of problem, or what sort of job?"

"Both."

Terry had a look that could wipe the smirk off Percy's face in an instant.

"Small problem, fair-sized job."

"Sounds like an ad for laxatives."

The giggle again, followed by another bout of juicy coughing.

"Tee hee. You are a card, Terence."

Percy loved this kind of jokey to and fro. He should have been a comic on the wireless, Terry thought; he would have been as good as the ones he listened to, with their catchphrases and cheeky banter—"Get yourself some stronger elastic, missus!"—and their ancient jokes that audiences howled at but which for Terry went down like lead balloons.

The jobs Percy came up with for Terry to carry out weren't hard. Mostly they just called for a bit of muscle, to put the wind up one of the chap-at-the-club's debtors, or discouraging the usually crowded raft of Percy's creditors—Terry was a past master at the menacing smile. The real, serious stuff was rarely necessary. Once in a while he had to bring out his well-worn army knife, or the dandy little pocket-sized Colt .38 Detective Special he had got from a Yankee sailor who had jumped ship at Tilbury Docks one rainy night and was broke, and who let him have it in return for a hand job. But he was sparing with the use of force, if for no other reason than that it took a lot of effort.

So far he had done only half a dozen terminations. Each one he remembered as if it was the first. The moment he squeezed the trigger he felt like he did when he came into Percy's slobbery cakehole, only more so. One of his targets was a sixteen-year-old kid who had knocked up a rich man's daughter. How he squealed when he saw the gun in Terry's hand. "Please, don't, I'll do anything—" and then *bang!* right into the left ear. The poor fellow's left eye had popped out of its socket, all the way out, and hung down on his cheek at the end of a bloodied string.

Terry worried sometimes about the gun. He knew he'd have to get rid of it sooner or later—by now the police were bound to have traced it back through all of the six jobs he had so far done with it, though they had no way of knowing it was his, since they didn't even know of his existence. But he loved the gleaming little weapon, loved the way the butt with the cross-hatched wooden sides nestled into the palm of his hand, while the trigger, as delicate as a fish hook, pressed itself with pent-up

eagerness against the soft inner side of his crooked index finger. He couldn't bear the thought of it lying amid the slops in
the bottom of a dustbin, or rusting in the purplish-gray mud of
the Thames. When the time came and it had to go, he would
take it home with him to Ireland and give it a decent burial,
under a rock in a sunny place, or in a hole between the roots
of a gorse bush on some unfrequented hillside high up in the
Dublin mountains. That was his intention, anyway.

People would probably say he had no feelings at all, to do the
kind of work he did, but they would be wrong. He had a lot
of feelings. Look at the way the fate he foresaw for the weapon
that had been his standby and his pal for so long brought him
almost to tears. He would heft the gun in his hand, playing with
it, spinning the chamber and squinting along the barrel and gazing fondly at the prancing pony embossed on the badge on the
side of the frame. He saw the weapon as the very emblem of
himself, skimpy-looking, a bit on the short side, but hard, cold,
deadly and unstoppable.

He came close to tears, too, on the evening when he shot
Percy Antrobus and let his weighted, rubbery corpse slip soundlessly into the darkly gleaming, oily water of the Pool of London, down into the narrow space between the looming bulk
of an oil tanker and the slimed side of the dock. He was sorry
to have to do it, he really was, but there was no avoiding it, in
the end. Percy had mocked him and slighted him and generally
annoyed him too many times, and Terry just wouldn't stand
for it anymore.

The opportunity to be rid of him once and for all presented
itself handily enough—you could almost say the thing was done
on a whim. Percy had to go down to the docks to see the captain of a freighter that had come in from Hong Kong, or maybe
it was Saigon, Terry hadn't paid much attention. Percy wouldn't
say what his business with the captain was, but the meeting was

at night and he brought Terry along for protection. As Percy said, you could never trust a Chink.

When they got to the wharf there was a mist on the water, and all was dark and quiet—a real B-movie scenario. Percy went on board the ship, but told Terry to wait on the pier.

He walked up and down for a while, watching the drifting, ghostly mist and thinking about nothing much at all. It was cold, and he turned up the collar of his light-gray overcoat. At times like this he was sorry he didn't smoke, since it would be something to do. Also, a cigarette would add to the Jimmy Cagney look.

In fact, it wasn't Cagney so much as Richard Widmark that he secretly imagined himself as, especially in the part of Harry Fabian in *Night and the City*, which he had seen four times and would go to again if it was reshown. The picture had been shot in London, in locations much like the place where he was right now, whiling away the cold minutes until Percy came back from doing whatever it was he was doing with the sea captain up there on deck. Of course, it was only the look of Widmark that Terry admired, not the part of the two-bit hustler that he played. Harry Fabian was slick, all right, but in the end he had no style. And if Terry had learned one thing from Percy, it was the importance of having style.

Percy was a good half hour on the ship, and came back in a jumpy mood, and snapped at Terry when he asked him what was up. There was something in Percy's tone, an edge of disdain, of dismissiveness, that made Terry lose his rag. For the first time in his life he understood exactly what that phrase meant, to "see red." A crimson mist came down in front of his eyes, like a wavery version of the curtain in a picture house, and for a second or two his chest tightened all across its front and he could hardly breathe.

All right, Percy, he thought, all right. That's it.

They walked along the wharf. Percy suddenly quickened his

pace and hurried forward, as if he had a premonition of what was about to happen. Terry waited until they had entered a low brick tunnel over the narrow-gauge rail line that the coal skips ran along. He would still see those bricks long after he left London, even though it was dark under there. He would smell the rancid air, too, and the stink of stale piss, and see the faint shine on the rails, and the cuffs of Percy's sagging trousers trailing in the mud as he slouched along—all of it, clear as anything.

He increased his pace, and, catching up with Percy, he brought out the pistol and jammed the barrel under Percy's left shoulder blade, against the thick material of his overcoat, and fired twice, a quick one-two. He had always admired the smooth, rapid action of the little gun.

The coat muffled the sound of the shot, but it was still very loud, and twanged off the bricks, so that for a second Terry was deafened. Percy whirled about and stared at him with an expression of astonishment and outrage. It was as if, Terry thought, he had badly insulted the old boy, or made a joke in what Percy would say was "unforgivably bad taste, dear boy." A ship somewhere nearby—it might have been the freighter Percy had just been on—sounded its horn, so loudly it made Terry jump and almost run for cover. Percy stayed upright for a second or two, swaying on tiptoe, doing a kind of pirouette. Then everything inside him seemed to crumple suddenly, and he collapsed onto the slimed cobbles, all the puff gone out of him for good.

He was dead—he had probably been dead when he hit the ground—and Terry didn't bother checking for a pulse. The image of the front page of a newspaper popped into his mind, spinning in a circle like in the movies and then stopping, and the line jumping out: *The victim died instantly*. But did he? Terry knew there was no such thing as an instant death—hadn't Percy been alive for the time it took him to turn around and stare at Terry in shock and indignation, even with two bullets in his ticker? How long would it take? A second? More? If you were about to die, maybe a second could seem an eternity.

Strange, Terry thought, how a person could be there one minute, alive like everyone else, and nowhere the next. He wasn't much given to that kind of morbid thinking, but just then, under that tunnel, in the darkness of the misty night, he felt a sense of awe before the mystery of the origin and the unavoidable end of all things. In dying, Percy had delivered to Terry his final life lesson.

It proved no joke, lugging the old man's amazingly heavy corpse to the edge of the dock and delivering it to Thames water, water that looked, just then, as thick and shiny as creosote. Terry hunted around and found some loose bricks and stuffed them into the pockets of Percy's Crombie overcoat to weigh him down. He didn't really think it would work—a few bricks wouldn't be enough, surely?—and old Percy would probably come bobbing up again in a matter of days. You can't keep a fat man down, Terry thought, and laughed—Percy wasn't the only one who had wit.

But if the body did come up, what would happen then?

Terry didn't stay around long enough to find out. That night he went straight back to Fitzroy Square and packed up his things. He didn't have much gear to take with him, for it had always been his rule to travel light.

He spent some time ransacking the flat in search of cash, but found nothing except Percy's collection of dirty photographs. Some of the pictures were hair-raising, even to Terry's less than innocent eye—no tarts, just fellows with enormous how's-your-fathers doing the most amazing things to each other. There was a space behind a loose skirting board in the kitchen where he used to hide some of his own things, and now he stuffed the snaps in there, he wasn't sure why—what did he care if the rozzers got their paws on Percy's grubby secrets?—and hammered the board back in place with his fist. His fingerprints were all over the flat, of course, but that didn't matter: it was a point of pride with him that he had never been nicked and his prints weren't on file.

In the morning he took the train to Holyhead, and that night got on the mail boat and sailed away to Ireland. Even if they did manage to stick him with Percy's killing, the Irish government would never extradite him—not to England, the old enemy. He was safe, he was sure of it. Or almost sure.

DONOSTIA

9

Quirke was hauled into hazy consciousness by the medleyed sound of what seemed to be—could it be?—a band of minstrels playing on flutes and drums and squealing bagpipes. He opened his eyes and was dazzled by splinters of morning sunlight. Evelyn was sitting by the open window, smoking a cigarette and reading a Simenon novel, in the original French. She had been down for breakfast already. He hadn't even heard her get up. Now she turned to him.

"Good morning, sleepyhead," she said.

"Is there really a band playing?" he croaked. "Or am I imagining it?"

"Yes, there is a band, going past. Traditional costumes, very gay and colorful. It must be a special day for the Basques, some festival. It's charming—come and see."

"I'll take your word for it."

He sat up, gathering all the pillows on the bed and making a mound of them at his back. At once he was overcome by a fit of coughing. He coughed like this every morning; it was a sort of ritual his lungs went through, their version of calisthenics.

"Jesus," he gasped, thumping a fist against his chest.

His wife shook her head at him.

"You smoke too much," she said. "In fact, you should not smoke at all."

"You're a fine one to talk."

"I smoke exactly six cigarettes a day."

"So do I," he said, with a straight face.

"Ha!"

He gave her a death's-head grin and reached defiantly for the Senior Service packet on the bedside table. He fumbled a cigarette to his mouth and lit it with the silver lighter that was one of the presents Evelyn had given him on the eve of their wedding.

The squealing and banging of the band was fading into the distance.

"Be careful, don't drop ash on the sheet," Evelyn said.

Quirke was looking past her to the window.

"I see the sun is shining again," he said. "We were promised rain."

"Yes, the warm sun is shining, people are swimming and lying on the sand, children are playing, and there is a man selling ice cream. And yes, we are on holiday."

He smoked moodily for a while, then said, "It was hot last night. I couldn't sleep."

"If you were not asleep, then you are the only person I have ever heard of who snores when he is awake."

He gave her a crooked smile.

"I do love you, *Liebchen*."

"Even when I nag you?"

"Even when you nag me."

He could never say the word "love" without flinching, a little, inwardly. Yet he made himself say it, and go on saying it, as if to shore up something that was in constant danger of collapse. It was a bit of mortar he applied to the edifice they had fabricated together, he and Evelyn. Both were well aware of the jerry-built nature of the thing, the little thin-walled structure that was the two of them together, huddled under the weight of the world.

Should he tell her about the young woman in the bar under the arcades, and how he had woken up in the night thinking about her? Should he say how he was convinced he knew her from somewhere in his past? Should he tell her how the notion had frightened him, and how it made him uneasy even yet to think of it? How was he to put into words feelings so nebulous they could hardly be called feelings at all?

He got out of bed, kissed his wife lightly on the fringe of hair where it lay on her broad brow and went into the bathroom. He looked at himself in the mirror above the handbasin and groaned.

"Does my breath smell?" he called back to her over his shoulder.

"Yes."

He began to brush his teeth vigorously. He had balanced his cigarette on the edge of the porcelain, between the taps. "Don't put your cigarette on the sink," Evelyn said sharply. How could she know he was doing something without seeing him do it? There was an uncanny side to his wife that Quirke felt it was best to leave uninvestigated.

"No ashtray in here."

"It took me many minutes to get rid of the yellow stain you left there yesterday. If you keep doing filthy things like that, they will ask us to leave this lovely hotel."

He rinsed his mouth, realizing too late what he was doing. He imagined a billion microbes invading the crevices between his teeth and lodging there. Death in the afternoon.

"But the place cleans itself," he said.

"What do you say?"

"I *zay*," he shouted, mimicking her, "that these rooms are self-cleaning. We go out, and when we come back it's as if we'd never been here. It's part of the general con trick that hotels play on us."

"You are a ridiculous man. *I* don't love *you*."

"*If equal affection cannot be, Let the more loving one be me.*"

Silence for a moment, and then her voice again, with that self-conscious, tentative note that always came into it when she encountered something she wasn't familiar with or didn't understand. "Who is that?" she asked.

"W. H. Auden."

Another silence. They could not see each other, but he could hear her smiling.

"Ridiculous man," she said softly.

"Who, me or Auden?"

"Ridiculous man!" she said again, more loudly.

"What's that in German?"

"*Lächerlicher Mann.*"

"Laker-licker-man? Ridiculous language."

He dropped his toothbrush into a glass and walked back into the bedroom. She turned her head and looked at him.

"You do love me," he said. "Why deny it?"

"Oh, love," she said. "This little word that causes so much trouble to people."

The pale curtain stirred at the window. They could hear the voices of children on the beach. She smiled at him in her demure, self-conscious fashion.

Let it last, he thought, not sure what he meant, only offering it as a kind of prayer into the void. *Please, let it last.*

10

Later that morning, she said, out of the blue—the cliché wasn't a cliché, down here in cloudless Basqueland—that he must have a hat, to protect his scalp now that the rains had passed and the sun was shining more strongly every day.

"But I have a hat," he said, showing it to her.

"Don't be ridiculous," she said. She had seen this hat of his all too often. It was made of heavy black felt and was, she pronounced, entirely unsuited to the Spanish climate. "Your big Irish head will boil."

"You promised me northern Spain would be southern Ireland."

"Not in the summer."

"It's not the summer."

"It's hotter than the summer is in Ireland. Much hotter. You should have brought the other one."

He had a straw hat but had left it at home. He hadn't expected to need it, with all he had heard of how much it rained, in these parts.

"I have hair to protect me," he said.

She sniffed. "Not as much as you think."

She liked to tease him in this way, saying he was going "thin on top." She had first heard this formulation from Quirke himself. It delighted her, and she never missed an opportunity of using it.

"You need a good panama hat," she said, "with a close weave, to shield you from X-rays, since you are going thin on—"

"X-rays?" he scoffed, interrupting her. "What do you mean, X-rays?"

"Well, whatever it is that is in sunlight. You want to get cancer?"

"No, I don't *vant* to get *concer*."

They found a hat shop not far from the hotel. It was called Casa Ponsol. A sign over the door announced with a proud flourish that it had been founded in 1838. It might have been an annex to the Londres. Quirke felt intimidated.

A young woman approached them, smiling, with her long, tapering, honey-colored hands joined before her. She was tall and slim, and wore a suit of cream-colored linen. Her gleaming, night-black hair was parted in the middle and drawn tightly back and wound in a knot contained in a thing like a little black lace net-bag at the nape of her neck.

"*Buenas días*," Evelyn said. "My husband requires a hat."

The slim young woman smiled and rapidly, with a conjuror's aplomb, produced out of their boxes a number of straw hats and laid them along the glass counter. Quirke brusquely tried one on, took it off and said he would take it.

"Don't be silly," Evelyn cried. "Try some of these others. We are not in a hurry, and neither is this young lady. Look at this one, with the wide brim. Or this—the red silk band is very nice, *ja?*" He gave her a terrible look, which she ignored. "What about this darker one, do you like it? Very dramatic, very *duende*."

The young woman smiled at her again.

Quirke snatched the second hat from his wife's hands and clamped it on his head.

The saleswoman said, "*Me lo permites?*" and reached out those graceful hands of hers and adjusted the angle of the hat, drawing it down at one side. Quirke caught her smell, milky and yet sharp—lily-of-the-valley, he thought, and for no good reason recalled Goya's *Maja desnuda*. But the *maja* was of a different type entirely, chunky, with hair under her armpits and cockeyed breasts, an ill-fitting head—the angle to the shoulders was all wrong—and lumpy, sallow flesh. The slender creature before him would be as smooth all over as oiled olive wood.

He said he would take the hat—he hated shopping almost as much as he hated holidays—without bothering to look at the price tag. When he saw the amount popping up on the cash register, he blinked twice and swallowed hard.

"It is a lovely hat," Evelyn said firmly, standing back to admire him in his dashing new headgear. "You look so handsome"— she turned to the saleswoman—"doesn't he?"

"*Sí, sí, ciertamente—un caballero.*"

That he understood. A *caballero*, eh? He felt ridiculous. He thought of his confirmation day and the scratchy new suit he had been made to wear. That was the year Judge Garret Griffin and his wife rescued him from Carricklea and took him into their home to be their second son.

He handed over a fistful of crackling notes. The saleswoman produced a capacious paper bag with straw handles. Quirke was about to drop the new hat into it, but Evelyn took the old one from him and put it into the bag instead.

"Wear the panama," she said. "See, outside, the sun is shining. That's what a hat is for, to protect you from the sun, and make you look like a true Spanish gentleman."

He took the hat from her and jammed it down on his skull again with both hands. This time it was Evelyn who reached up and tilted it at a rakish angle.

When they stepped out of the shop, a skittish breeze came swooping up from the ocean and snatched at the hat, lifting the brim of it and flattening it against Quirke's crown. That was all he needed, he thought, to be turned into one of John Wayne's comical sidekicks, Chill Wills, was it, or Smiley Burnette?

Evelyn was laughing at him. Her laughter didn't make a sound but he heard it all the same.

"I'm so glad I amuse you," he said.

"So you should be. Humor, as you know, is an essential part of the psychiatric project."

"And am I your project?"

This she let pass.

"Read Freud's book on jokes," she said. "You will learn much."

"Oh, yes?" he said, lobbing the ball swiftly back at her: "I seem to recall Mark Twain observing that a German joke is no laughing matter."

But she was at the net, ready to pounce.

"Freud was Austrian," she said, "not German. And so, please remember, am I." With an index finger she flipped down the wind-harried brim of his new hat. "Don't sulk, dearest one." She pursed her lips in a cajoling smile and pretended to tickle him under the chin. "You look just like Victor Laszlo."

"Who's Victor Laszlo?" he growled.

"In *Casablanca*, remember? He was the good-looking husband. I was always glad she stayed with him, rather than the other little fellow with the damaged lip and the funny way of speaking whom everybody loves."

"Poor Rick," Quirke said. "Imagine ending up with Claude Rains when you might have had Ingrid Bergman."

And in that way the rally petered to a close, with a score of love-all.

11

They went to the little bar on the square—by now it had become *their* bar, though Evelyn still insisted on calling it a café. They sat at a table outside, under the canvas awning. They drank the spritzy white wine and tried not to eat the complimentary nuts that came with it. Whenever Quirke reached out to the bowl, his wife slapped his hand away. "You will get fat, like me," she said, "and then I won't love you anymore."

"You said this morning you didn't."

"Didn't what?"

"Love me."

"*Ach, du Lügner.*"

"*Du* what?"

"Of course I love you, silly man—you said so yourself. Though why I should love you I do not know."

She touched his hand where it rested on the table. She often reached out to him like that, as if to make sure he was still there, still real.

The day was hot already. Quirke felt drowsy. He hadn't entirely recovered yet from his troubled night of anxious waking. Even when he had managed to fall back to sleep, something had continued to weave its way through his dreams, like a thin trail of oily, acrid smoke, something to do with the young woman on whom he had accidentally eavesdropped here.

Evelyn was speaking to him.

"What?"

"I said, I am so glad you chose that one." She pointed with her chin at his splendid hat where it lay before him on the table. The thing looked, to Quirke's eye, irritatingly smug and self-satisfied, in its polished newness.

"It's just a hat," he said.

"No, no, it's a *Ponsol* hat," Evelyn countered. "*Un gorro de Ponsol is muy especial*—that's what the girl in the shop whispered to me when your back was turned. *Muy especial*—very special."

"I always feel like a clown when I have to wear something new," he said. He squinted up at the clock over the building opposite, guarded by its rusty cannons and its pockmarked stone lions. "Did you know that an English gentleman always chooses a valet whose measurements match his own, so that he can break in his suits and his shoes for him?"

"Break in?"

"Wear them first for a while, to take the look of being new off them."

"Why?"

"Bad form, unscuffed shoes, or a suit without a wrinkle."

She gave him a grave slow stare from under her fringe, her plump top lip pushed out. "This is a joke, *ja*?"

"*Nein*. It is not a joke. It is the truth. At least it used to be true, when the English still had valets—and when there were still gentlemen, for that matter."

She shook her head slowly from side to side.

"Such a strange people, the English," she said. "How did they win the war?"

"They didn't—the Russians and the Yanks did. I thought you'd know that better than anyone."

"I wasn't there, when it was being won," she said gravely. Quirke wryly smiled—the last word, yet again.

They strolled about in the Old Town. In one of the squares they came upon an outdoor market. The stalls were set up under canvas lean-tos that flapped and rattled like sails in the sea breeze. Quirke was dazzled by the profusion and colors of the produce laid out enticingly on all sides. He found the rich fragrances of fruit and fish and poultry almost overpowering in intensity. What would home seem like, after all this? Gray, and stale. And yet he had a sudden, sharp longing to be back there, walking along a shining pavement in slanted April rain, with the scent of rained-on laurel in his nostrils. Home? Well, yes.

The odors from a fish stall made him think of sex. On one of their first nights in bed together, years before, as they lay side by side in the languorous afterglow of lovemaking, Quirke had expounded to Evelyn his theory as to the origins and purpose of sexual desire.

"It's nature's way of making sure we can overcome the natural revulsion we feel toward other people's flesh."

"What?" Evelyn had murmured sleepily.

"Think of it, and you'll see it's true," he said. "If it wasn't for blind lust, the species would have died out eons ago."

Evelyn had chuckled deep in her throat. "What a silly idea." Her hair gleamed darkly in the light of the bedside lamp. She hadn't a single gray hair—whenever she spotted one, she would pluck it out. He wondered what would happen when the day came that there was too much gray and she had to give up the struggle. "Animals feel no disgust of each other," she had said, "so what is the purpose of lust for them?"

"Animals are machines."

"Oh, so you are a Cartesian?"

"A what?"

He smiled into her face.

"A follower of the philosopher Descartes," she said.

"Oh. Right. I thought it was something to do with wells."

"Now you're teasing me."

"Tell me about Descartes."

"He's the one who said what you say, that animals are only animated machines." She had paused then, with a finger to her cheek. "Or was it Pascal? I can't remember. They were equally foolish, both of them. Very clever and very foolish." She smiled, drawing in that plump upper lip and biting on it lightly. "Like so many men."

He had made to reply, but she silenced him by turning in the bed and clambering on top of him, laughing. "*Mein geliebter Ignorant.*"

That was the night he had asked her to marry him. Or was it she who had asked him? He couldn't remember. It didn't matter.

Now, as they stood in the Spanish sunshine surveying the stall of wet and glistening fish, she asked him what he was thinking of.

"Why?"

"Why what?"

"Why do you want to know what I'm thinking?"

"Because I think you are thinking of sex."

It was uncanny, how she could read his mind.

"Then why did you ask?" he asked.

"To make sure."

"Isn't that what men are *always* thinking about?" he said, with a laugh.

He peered into the glazed gray eye of a fierce-looking fish

the name of which, unlikely as it seemed, was *rape*, according
to a sign pinned to its flank.

"Yes, almost always," Evelyn replied equably. "Someone in
America has made a calculation of it. A very high percentage,
I can't remember what it is. Though how you could find out
such a thing is mysterious, no? Men always lie, especially about
sex." He started to protest but she put a hand on his wrist and
squeezed it, saying, "As women do also, of course."

The young woman tending the stall was pretty. She wore
her hair in a thick coil that hung down at her left shoulder. She
had enormous eyes, the irises so deeply brown they were almost
black. She smiled at Quirke and pointed to his hat.

"Is very good," she said. "I know—I am from Ecuador."

He took off the hat and looked at the label inside the crown.
She was right—*Hecho a mano en Ecuador.* Even he could trans-
late that.

"Let's buy some oysters," Evelyn said. "Look at them, they
are enormous."

They went for lunch to a restaurant on the quayside just above
the Zurriola Bridge, across from the city's second, smaller beach,
after which the bridge was named, or perhaps it was the other
way around, he didn't know. They ate a dish that looked like
very pale mashed potato but turned out to be salt cod whipped
to a smooth paste. For their main course they had sole fried in
a great deal of sizzling butter, and sautéed potatoes and French
beans sprinkled with almonds.

Evelyn had asked for a green salad on the side. Quirke rarely
ate things that were green, and never in their raw state. There
were limits.

But the fish was excellent.

He had ordered a bottle of txakoli. Although this one, he
noticed, was called txakolina, with an added *n* and an *a*. He

wondered what the difference was, but couldn't summon up the nerve to ask.

Their waiter looked like a superannuated toreador. He was short and dark and slightly sweaty, with oiled black hair and a rigid, convex spine.

"Gypsy blood," Evelyn said, when he had taken their plates away.

Quirke said he supposed she was right. "Why do they all look so angry all the time?" he mused.

"You mean the Spanish?"

"Well, the ones like him. The way they scowl."

He watched the little man hurrying about at his tasks. He was top-heavy, with a cask-shaped chest, narrow hips and a ballerina's dainty, bowed legs.

"How would they not be angry?" Evelyn observed. "The civil war was terrible. I saw two men being—what is the word? Lynched? Yes, lynched. From a lamppost."

He gazed at her across the table, holding his knife and fork motionless in midair.

"Where?" he asked. "When?"

She shook her head. "Oh, here," she said. "Back then." She was looking down at her plate, with that mild, blank expression she put on when she had said more than she meant to and wished the subject to be dropped. What things she must have seen, Quirke thought, in those wartime weeks when she and her uncle were making their perilous way along this coast.

Given all that had happened in her life, it was a wonder that she slept so peacefully at night. Or so deeply, at least. For how could he know what was going on in her dreams? She would never tell him, that he knew. But a mind doctor's dreams, now— surely they would be worth hearing of. Or perhaps not. Perhaps she dreamed the same nonsensical stuff that everyone else did, except that to her and her revered Dr. Freud it all meant something other than it seemed. Wasn't it Freud who said no dream is innocent?

When they left, they forgot the bag of oysters, and the swarthy little waiter had to come running after them with it. Evelyn thanked him, bestowing on him her sweetest smile, but he turned away stony-faced. Quirke regretted what seemed now the much too generous tip he had tucked under the rim of his plate. So angry, all of them.

In the hotel they realized the mistake they had made in not buying a tool to open the oysters with. They could have got one at the stall, but Evelyn didn't know the Spanish name for it, and Quirke wouldn't let her point to it—they would be shown up as tourists.

"But we are tourists," Evelyn had said, laughing. "You think they don't see our gray skin and know we are from the north?"

Now she came out of the bathroom.

"Here is a nail scissors," she said. "That will do to open them with."

And that was how Quirke ended up in the hospital, and came face-to-face with the young woman whom he had heard at the café saying something about a theater.

12

Her name, she told them, was Lawless. Dr. Angela Lawless. She seemed to Quirke almost too convincing, like an actor playing the part of a doctor. She wore a white coat and flat-soled white shoes, and a stethoscope was draped around her neck in just the required fashion. She was older than he had taken her to be when he glimpsed her in the shadowy twilight at the bar Las Arcadas. He would put her now in her late twenties. She was small and quick, and watchful as a bird—he had the impression that at the slightest sudden movement she would fly off with a shrill cry and a clatter of feathers. She would have been pretty, perhaps more than pretty, if her features had been less angular and her manner less intense. Her hair was very black, and her skin was very white, despite the Spanish sun.

She addressed Quirke in what even he knew to be fluent Spanish. When he responded in English, she frowned, and turned to Evelyn.

"Are you Irish?" she asked, almost accusingly.

"I am Austrian," Evelyn answered. "But my husband, he is Irish, yes."

The woman blinked rapidly and glanced from one of them to the other with a look that seemed suddenly full of suspicion.

"You're Irish, too," Quirke said. "I spotted you at the bar under the arcades. I recognized your accent."

She said nothing. She had not so much as glanced at his injured hand, as if she believed it to be a deliberate and clumsy pretext for something or other and she was not going to be taken in by it.

"We're very busy today," she said. She seemed to be making urgent calculations in her head.

An orderly came with a large wad of cotton wool and Quirke took it and pressed it into his palm—the handkerchief that Evelyn had wrapped around his hand at the hotel was by now thoroughly blood-soaked. Quirke felt dizzy. The day was hot, which seemed to be making the pain in his hand worse. The point of the nail scissors had skidded on the hinge of the oyster and struck deep into the soft flesh at the base of his thumb. He had cursed himself for his maladroitness, and ordered a double whiskey from room service.

Evelyn had insisted he must go to the hospital.

"This is Spain," she said. "Remember what you told me about Hemingway, that he brushed his teeth only with brandy because there were so many germs in the water?"

"Ach, that's just another of Papa's myths," Quirke responded irritably. "Besides, this is seawater."

"But it was inside an oyster shell! Don't you know how dangerous that is?"

So he had allowed her to call the concierge and request him

to order a taxi at once. It had arrived with surprising prompt-
ness and sped them off to the San Juan de Dios Hospital, where
they were received without warmth by the inexplicably tense
and wary Dr. Lawless. Later, Quirke wondered why he hadn't
been more forcibly struck by the fact that of all the doctors that
there must be in all of San Sebastián, it should be this one to
whom he had found himself presenting his injured hand. It was
life's playful way to arrange these things, sometimes.

Dr. Lawless led him and Evelyn to a bench and bade them
wait, and went and spoke to the nun seated behind the reception
desk. The nun, in a gray habit and a sort of modified, minia-
turized wimple, gave her a quizzical look. Quirke watched the
exchange with interest. The doctor hesitated a moment, then
turned abruptly from the desk and walked swiftly away down
a corridor, without a backward glance, her rubber-soled shoes
squeaking on the polished floor tiles.

Evelyn turned to Quirke. "Where has she gone?"

Quirke shrugged.

"Don't ask me," he said.

They waited. There was no sign of Dr. Lawless returning.
The telephone at the reception desk rang.

Evelyn touched Quirke's swollen hand. "You look so pale."

"Don't worry," he said. "I'm not the fainting type."

"But you have lost so much blood." She looked along the
corridor down which the doctor had disappeared. "This is very
bad," she said. "We must do something."

She rose and crossed to the reception desk to speak to the
nun, who was on the telephone. Quirke watched as the nun put
a hand over the receiver and looked up at Evelyn and shrugged,
and spoke a few words and then lowered her head until it was
almost below the level of the desk.

By now the wad of cotton wool was soaked through with
blood. Quirke felt increasingly light-headed, and wondered if,
after all, he might be about to faint. One of his abiding fears

had come to pass—he had injured himself, and was in a foreign hospital seeking treatment from people who were either indifferent or hostile. Suddenly he had a childish longing to go home. Maybe he should? There was a direct flight from Madrid, but when did it fly? He seemed to remember it only operated once a week. And how to get to the capital quickly, from way up here in the north? Was there a direct train? Or maybe he could fly from Barcelona, or even somewhere across the border in France.

He was becoming increasingly agitated, and his thoughts raced. It was the effect of having lost all that blood, he supposed. And why wouldn't it clot? He seemed to have forgotten everything he knew about medicine.

Evelyn returned and sat down beside him on the bench.

"Another doctor will come," she said.

She was, he saw, uncharacteristically cross.

"Did that nun give a reason for the first one to walk off like that?"

"No."

He brooded.

"There's something familiar about her," he said.

"About that nun?"

"No—the woman, the doctor. What did she say her name was?"

"Lawless."

A crimson droplet fell on to the floor between his feet. The point of the scissors must have hit a blood vessel, he thought. But were there blood vessels in that part of the hand? He couldn't remember—he, who should know about these things. How many bodies had he dissected? He swore under his breath.

"Why won't the damned thing stop?" he muttered.

"You are the doctor," Evelyn observed mildly.

"I'm a pathologist," he snapped. "The dead don't bleed."

"Do they not?"

"They seep a little, sometimes."

She looked at him in silence for a moment.

"And sometimes I wish you had taken up some other profession."

"What would you prefer me to be?" he asked in a savage whisper. "A witch doctor, like you?"

He was in pain, his hand was throbbing and he was growing increasingly indignant. It was she who had handed him the nail scissors. It wasn't fair—none of it was fair. He had been persuaded to come to Spain against his will, or as good as, and was being required to be "on holiday," and now he had a gashed hand and was at the mercy of hospital doctors—a breed he distrusted and despised, having known a great many of them—one of whom hadn't even taken the time to examine his hand, but had walked off and abandoned him.

"I don't trust foreign medicine," he said.

The hospital smell was making him nauseous.

"We are the foreigners here," Evelyn said.

Quirke grunted. The last thing he needed was to be reasoned with.

Evelyn leaned her weight softly against his hostile shoulder.

"My poor Q," she murmured.

He thought yet again, as so often, how odd it was that this woman should have appeared in his life, a creature in need of shelter from the storms of the world, just as he was, and odder still that she was still with him. Would she leave him someday? If she did, at least she wouldn't do it out of disillusionment, since he knew she had no illusions about anything, including him.

One tawny autumn evening after rain, when they were sitting together in Evelyn's little mews house in Dublin, she had looked up from a thick treatise on psychiatry by some famous German doctor whose name Quirke thought he probably should know but didn't. She was smiling, in the vague, happily bewildered way of someone who has just made a momentous discovery.

"This wise Herr Professor," she said, tapping a finger on the page of the book lying open on her lap, "informs me that what persons such as I suffer from is a lack of affect. Isn't that interesting?" Quirke didn't find it so, but said nothing. He wasn't absolutely sure what an affect was. "A lack of affect—think of that! But I love you," she added, "and therefore it doesn't matter."

To this last Quirke had made no reply. The logic of her words was beyond him, as was so much of her—far, far beyond him.

13

Presently, a second doctor appeared. His name, Jeronimo Cruz, was handwritten in block capitals on a laminated badge pinned to the lapel of his white coat. Jeronimo Cruz. It sounded to Quirke like the name of a Mexican bandit in one of those fifteen-minute serials that used to be shown after the main feature in cinemas on Saturday afternoons when he was young.

Dr. Cruz had spoken to the nun behind the reception desk, who in turn had pointed them out to him, and he had come over to where they were seated, the large man with the bleeding hand and the soft-faced woman at his side who looked vexed.

"I shall not offer to shake hands," the doctor said in his almost accentless English, and his lips twitched at one corner. Quirke thought to point out, but didn't, that it was his left hand that was injured.

Cruz was tall and lean—were there no fat people in Spain?—with pale-blue eyes and thin pale lips and a neatly trimmed, sharply pointed, charcoal-flecked silver beard. He must be from the south, Quirke decided, for the skin on his face and the backs of his hands was so deeply tanned it appeared almost black in the creases at the corners of his eyes and mouth.

Quirke recognized him as the man Dr. Lawless had been sitting with outside Las Arcadas. It came to him, with certainty, that he was not her father, as that night he had taken him to be. He couldn't have said how he knew this. He had been wrong about the man's age, too, as he had been wrong about the young woman's. The man was in his fifties, and his hair was prematurely gray, or silver, rather, and probably had been so since he was a young man. His manner was courtly and remote. He wasn't given to smiling, being of altogether too serious a disposition.

He requested Evelyn to wait at the bench, while he led Quirke into a vast, crowded, noisy hall with makeshift cubicles closed off behind olive-green curtains. There were two chairs, and the two men sat down facing each other, their knees almost touching. Quirke was still indignant at having been abandoned by Dr. Lawless, and felt he should demand an explanation from this man as to why she should have departed so abruptly and without explanation. But he said nothing. A pulse of pain was beating dully in his hand. He had a dreamlike sense of everything gliding slowly past while he sat here, helpless and immobile. The body, he thought, is jealous of its lifeblood, and lodges protests at its shedding.

Dr. Cruz removed the pad of cotton wool and unwound the handkerchief underneath, on which the blood had stiffened to a kind of brick-colored sludge. He let Quirke's hand rest across both his palms, as if it were something dead that had been passed to him for inspection.

"How did you do this?" he asked.

"I was opening an oyster."

"Ah. Always a hazardous undertaking. I see the results of it often."

He stood up and swished his way past the plastic curtain and was gone. Quirke wondered if he would come back, or if he had been abandoned for a second time. He gazed before him blankly at a chart luridly illustrating the inside of the human chest, the epidermis slit and neatly folded back and the ribs removed so as to display the tightly packed organs within. What a thing it is, he mused, the human carcass. It never ceased to surprise him that within the sack of flesh that is a human being there should be pent up such a stew of lurid, squashy, quivering parts.

Presently Dr. Cruz returned, bearing a steel kidney dish in which lay a number of medical instruments, from which Quirke quickly averted his eye. He was not a good patient. He had no stomach for blood, not when it was fresh, and certainly not when it was his own.

The doctor sat down and set about inserting a plastic thread into the eye of a fine, curved needle. He looked as practical and homey as a seamstress at her work. Quirke would not have been surprised if he were to lick a forefinger and thumb and twirl the tip of the thread into a point prior to insertion in the needle's tiny slit.

"You are English, yes?" Dr. Cruz asked.

"No. Irish."

"Ah," the doctor murmured, indifferent.

"Yes, I'm Irish," Quirke repeated, and paused. "Like your colleague."

Cruz did not respond to this, only continued his preparations for the repair of Quirke's gashed hand.

It came to Quirke, and again he couldn't have said how, that Jeronimo Cruz and Angela Lawless were not only not father and daughter, they were also more than colleagues, probably much more. It was not by what they did but what they didn't do, Quirke reflected, that men betrayed their sexual secrets. Cruz was altogether too determined to let drop the topic of Angela Lawless.

He was probably old enough to be her father. Ah, yes. Daddy's little girl.

"This will sting," the doctor said. "Perhaps you would wish me to give you some local anesthetic?"

He might have been offering an aperitif. Quirke declined the offer with a shake of the head, and a moment later was sorry he had.

That evening, out of consideration for the sufferings Quirke had endured, Evelyn did not object when he decreed that there was to be no question of their going out to a restaurant—they would stay in and eat in the hotel's dining room, even if it did feel like a mortuary.

"You can take yourself off somewhere on your own, if you like," he said with morose vengefulness. He was feeling sorry for himself, and thoroughly enjoying it.

His hand, under the bandage that Cruz had applied, was throbbing like a tom-tom. How could a nail scissors, so small and seemingly harmless, have penetrated so deep into his flesh? The pain, too, though, was enjoyable, in a perverse way.

Evelyn remarked how fortunate he had been to have damaged his left hand. Quirke scowled.

"Fortunate?" he said, with lifted eyebrows.

"You know what I mean."

He did, but he would not be comforted. His brain felt fuzzy, as if his skull were stuffed with some warm, soft stuff, like the bloodied wad of cotton wool he had clutched in his palm at the hospital.

They went into the dining room and were shown to a corner table, by the window. Cod stew was the special of the evening.

Quirke spurned it with a disparaging snort—they had eaten cod for lunch, hadn't they?

"That was salt cod," Evelyn reminded him.

He ignored her, and ordered a steak, well done, and a bottle of, as he said, the filthy house Rioja. No txakoli for him, no sparkles tonight, thank you.

When the steak arrived, Evelyn had to cut it for him into manageable chunks. This was another of the many small humiliations he had not reckoned with. It made him even more incensed against his wife, his wound and the world. He counted it fortunate, at least, that they were seated at a corner table, where the rest of the room wouldn't see him being tended to like a child.

"Pity they do not serve bacon and cabbage," Evelyn said, widening her eyes in studied innocence. "I'm sure you would have preferred it." Even at times like this, or especially at times like this, when Quirke was in one of his dangerously petulant moods, she couldn't resist the urge to tease him.

"Very funny," he said, and she bent her face over her plate to hide her grin.

They ate in silence. Quirke had little appetite. His cut hand had sent his entire system into a state of low-key distress. All the same, he forced himself to eat, if only to spite himself. He felt foolish—who but a fool would attempt to open an oyster with a pair of scissors?—and dreaded the prospect of going about for days like a bear with a splinter in its paw. How was he to shave?—although he was right-handed in everything else, he used his left hand to wield the razor. And then there were all the other intimate procedures he would somehow have to negotiate. Of one thing he was certain—wherever else Evelyn might be allowed to minister to him, he would not suffer her to help him in the bathroom, even if it was only to trim his fingernails. He would gnaw them short, if necessary.

"I didn't like that doctor," he said, forking a square of steak into his mouth without relish.

"But you noticed how pretty she was, I could see that."

"What?" He stared at her, then shook his head. "I meant him, not her," he growled. "Geronimo of the Cross."

"It's Jeronimo," Evelyn corrected him. "The *J* is like an *H*." She was determined that if he learned nothing else of the language, he should be able at least to pronounce the Spanish alphabet. "You seemed to be very interested in the young woman," she went on. "Despite how rude she was, walking away like that."

Quirke made a face, in a show of exasperation.

"I was interested in the fact that she was Irish. That's all."

"Yes, when you heard her accent the tip of your nose sprang up like a—what do you call it?—like a retriever dog."

"That's 'what do you call it?'"—he smiled with ferocity, showing his teeth—"*laker-licker.*"

She would not be provoked.

"There is nothing ridiculous in responding to a familiar accent," she said. "We all miss our own place, when we are away from it." She paused. "You know, when I first heard the word 'homesick' I thought that it meant being sick of home, of wanting to get away from where one lives. And I thought how strange it was that the English should have invented such a word, considering how much they like to be at home themselves."

He felt the stirring of a familiar unease. She rarely spoke of home and homeland, of loved ones and the loss of them, and when she did, it laid down a darkness between them, like a shadow falling across an expanse of mud and ashes. This was a zone into which neither of them cared to venture very far. He, too, like her, had his losses, though his losses weren't at all like hers, and they both knew it. He had been orphaned early, and whatever he had been deprived of he couldn't remember ever having had. She, on the other hand, had lost a world and the people in it whom she had loved, and whom she could never forget.

"Let's drink some wine," he said shortly, snatching up the bottle. He began to pour the Rioja, then paused. "But you're having fish. I'll order you a glass of white."

She smiled her solemn baby's smile.

"You know, my dear," she said, "you are so very much nicer than you will admit."

The wine waiter came. He was the old fellow from the bar, he of the hairy ears and squeaky shoe leather. He pretended not to know Quirke, and Quirke did the same for him. There were the niceties to be observed. Quirke requested a glass of txakoli for his wife.

The old boy murmured something obsequious in Spanish, and shuffled off, creakingly.

Quirke had begun to feel a little better, unaccountably. It couldn't be the wine, he had hardly started on it yet. He looked across the table at his wife and made himself smile. She knew these wordless apologies of his. In return she drew her lips together into a kissing shape. He leaned back expansively on his chair, keeping his bandaged hand out of sight below the table edge.

"We should invite them to lunch," he said. "Dr. Cruz, I mean."

"You said 'them'"—she lifted an eyebrow—"do you mean both?"

He shrugged. He suspected he was blushing. How absurd.

"Yes, why not?" he said stoutly. "Chief Geronimo and Dr. Frosty Face, who refused to treat me."

"But you don't like seeing new people," his wife said, doing her innocent act.

Quirke shrugged again, and looked away from her.

"We're on holiday, as you keep reminding me," he said. "Let's make a grand gesture."

He heard afar the faint strains of last night's palm-court orchestra, but thought perhaps it was only in his imagination. Some
years previously he had gone through a period of suffering from
mild hallucinations. At the time, he feared he was developing
a brain tumor. Tests had been done, and it had turned out his
fantasies were the result of having been attacked and beaten by
a pair of thugs on the basement steps of a house in Dublin on a
winter's night long ago. Could all that be starting up again? he
wondered uneasily now. Well, what of it. He could think of far
worse things to be beset by than a ghostly melody on imaginary
strings. But no, he was not mistaken. There it came again, *The
Merry Widow Waltz*. The band must be practicing somewhere,
or giving a private performance, perhaps, in some gilded salon
upstairs.

He wondered if there were such a thing as a merry widower.
There was bound to be, of course, and bound to be many more
of them than the female kind. All the same, his heart quailed.
He had lost a wife, a long time ago. He couldn't, wouldn't,
imagine losing this one.

"All right, yes," Evelyn said, summoning him back from his
maunderings. "Let us have a nice lunch, and invite our new
friends. It is a good idea."

He was about to protest that Dr. Cruz and his girl could not
by any stretch of the imagination be considered friends, of him
or of her. But he didn't bother. She would only come back with
something else, and have the last word.

14

Of course, the organizing of the thing turned out to be no simple matter. Quirke was already cursing himself for having suggested it. And why had he suggested it, anyway? Because there was something about this Dr. Lawless, something that nagged at him, although he couldn't have said precisely what it was. She had laid a shadow over his mind, like the shadow that lingers after a nightmare, even though the frightful details of the dream are forgotten. Half the time he was convinced he knew her from somewhere, the other half he told himself it was all in his imagination. Yet if that was the case, why was she haunting his thoughts like this? She was on the tip of his mind, the way a sought-for word would be on the tip of his tongue.

He said nothing to Evelyn of any of this, and wondered why.

Why the secrecy, why what seemed to be the sense of shame of some kind? It was almost as if he were on the brink of a love affair and was afraid of being found out. None of it made sense. Yet when he pictured the young woman's face, something seemed to twang inside him, producing a dark tone that came out of the past.

The following morning, Evelyn telephoned the hospital and asked to speak to Dr. Lawless. The woman on the switchboard, that surly nun, no doubt, was hard to understand. Evelyn thought perhaps she might be a native Basque, and that her mangled Spanish was a way of spitting upon the language of the oppressor. What she seemed to be saying was that there was no one of that name on the staff. Evelyn reminded her of their visit to the hospital the previous day, when they had encountered Dr. Lawless herself, but it made no impression. In the end she gave up, and requested to speak to Dr. Cruz instead.

She had to wait for him for a full five minutes, and was on the point of hanging up when at last he came on the line. She asked him to hold on, and passed the receiver to Quirke. He made a point of taking it in his bandaged hand. She smiled. As if she could forget how grievously he was wounded, and that it was in part her fault.

When Cruz heard Quirke's voice, his tone became markedly guarded.

Indeed, he said coolly, he would be delighted to come to lunch with him and Señora Quirke—he pronounced the *e* in Quirke—but at present he was extremely busy. The tourist season was under way and there was much extra work in the casualty department—foreigners were accident-prone to an extraordinary degree, he added, and made a sound that might have been a chuckle. Quirke took the gibe. He thought of saying something about Spanish oysters being rockier and more resistant than those on offer elsewhere, but knew it would be childish. He didn't at all care for Dr. Cruz, that was certain; the fellow

was altogether too suave and self-assured. But in that case, why
was he suggesting the four of them should meet?

"All the same, surely you eat lunch," he said, with a degree of
truculence he hadn't quite intended. What was that old music-
hall song? *I'll raise a bunion on his Spanish onion if I find him bending
tonight…* Quirke grinned horribly into the mouthpiece, baring
his incisors. Evelyn slapped him on the wrist reprovingly.

"Certainly I take lunch," the doctor was saying, smoother
than ever. "But usually a sandwich is all I have."

"A *pintxo,*" Quirke said brightly, just to show he knew the word.

"Yes, sometimes." Cruz had sounded bored; now he began to
sound irritated. "There is a café here in the hospital. I go there."

Quirke sighed. This was hard work, and for what? He was
tempted to give up, say a polite *adiós* and put down the phone.
Cruz was making it perfectly plain that he had no real wish to
lunch with an Irish tourist and his Austrian tourist wife. However, there was something in the man's tone, a hint of bland superiority, that made Quirke grit his teeth and keep on.

"What about dinner, then?" he said, twisting a length of the
telephone cord into a miniature noose. There was a silence on
the line. Quirke held the phone away from him and made one
of his monkey faces at it, scratching under his arm with a flapping right hand. Evelyn frowned hard at him, shaking her head,
but laughing silently, too.

"My wife discovered a very nice restaurant," Quirke said
coaxingly. "It's just at the Zurriola Bridge, if that's how it's pronounced, in the Old Town. Perhaps you know the place. The
fish is very good there."

"The fish is always good in Donostia."

"Yes, I know. But it's especially good at this place."

Another pause, then: "When do you propose we should meet?"
Dr. Cruz asked. His tone by now had icicles forming on it.

"Whenever you like," Quirke said airily, and winked at his
wife. "What about this evening?"

Now the doctor made a humming sound, soft and tuneless.

"All right, this evening," he said at last with a pointed sigh. "But I should tell you I do not dine late, as most Spaniards do— my mornings begin early. Shall we say eight o'clock?"

"Wonderful. I'll ask the concierge here to reserve a table. You know where the restaurant is, at the Zurriola Bridge, yes?" No response. "So: four people, eight o'clock."

"Four?" Cruz said quickly, on a rising note.

"Well, yes. Us, you and your—your colleague, Dr. Lawless."

It came to Quirke that he was enjoying himself. He was spitefully pleased at having outmaneuvered this stuffy, silver-haired *hidalgo*. He did another of his simian faces, drawing his lips as far back from his teeth as they would go. Behind him, Evelyn dug an admonishing knuckle into the small of his back.

"Let me ask Dr. Lawless, then, if she is free this evening," Cruz said, and gave another, sharper sigh. "If you don't hear from me in the next hour, assume that we shall both meet you and Señora Quirke at the restaurant at eight o'clock."

Then he hung up, without saying goodbye.

"'Quirky,' he says," Quirke said. He laughed.

"They will come?" Evelyn asked from afar—she had gone into the bathroom. She hadn't closed the door and he could see her, standing before the mirror applying lipstick. It was the only makeup she wore, and even that she often forgot to put on.

"The frosty bugger didn't even inquire after my hand," Quirke said. "What are we thinking of, issuing this invitation?"

"It was your suggestion."

"Yes, I know, but all the same."

"Anyway, it's not him you want to see."

"What? Listen, do you really imagine I'm interested in Dark Rosaleen?"

"Dark who?"

"Dr. What's-her-name. I don't find her in the least attractive, in case you think I do."

"Oh, no, of course not." He heard her chuckle. "*Mein Irisch Kind, Wo weilest du?*" she sang, in her out-of-tune voice.

"What's that?" he asked. "Goethe?"

"*Tristan und Isolde.* It's quoted in *The Waste Land*, by Mr. Eliot."

"How literary we are this morning."

She came out of the bathroom, and leaned against the jamb of the door, smiling at him, her waxy scarlet lips compressed, the little swollen bead in the center of the upper one glistening.

"How transparent you are," she said. "I can see straight through you."

"You spy, with your shrink's little eye, is that it?"

"Don't call me that," she said, putting on an injured look. "Don't call me shrink."

He laughed, and she advanced on him with a pantomime glare and a fist upraised as if to strike. He caught her by both wrists and wrestled her onto the bed.

"Stop, stop!" she cried, laughing. "You will ruin my lipstick."

He fumbled at the buttons of her blouse. She looked down at an angle and watched him do it, her double chin showing.

"I'll ruin your lipstick for you," he growled with mock ferocity, waggling his big, bearish head.

An hour later they got dressed for the second time that morning, and Evelyn went downstairs to drink a coffee and read the newspaper. Quirke mooched about the room, smoking a cigarette. He stepped onto the shallow balcony and surveyed the bay. The morning was still. He listened to each successive long curved wave making its subdued crash as it collapsed.

A pretty girl in sunglasses and a black swimsuit, her skin delicately tanned, was lying propped on her elbows just beyond the white-painted wrought-iron balustrade at the edge of the seafront walkway. He looked at her for a while in innocent admiration. She seemed so relaxed, so self-absorbed, so confident of what and who she was. The young consider themselves a separate and invulnerable species. The thought darkened Quirke's benign postcoital mood. He stepped back into the room.

They were lovers, of course, the silvery Dr. Cruz and jangly-nerved Angela Lawless; he took it for a fact. Cruz's voice had assumed an unmistakably proprietorial tone when he spoke her name. Well, good for him, he thought, though he wasn't sure if he could say the same for her.

That name, Angela Lawless—somehow there was something wrong with it. It wasn't convincing, somehow. People grow into a name, until it ceases to be a name and they become synonymous with it. Angela Lawless wasn't an Angela Lawless. How did he know? He had only met her once, and only twice heard her speak. He knew nothing about her, except that she was Irish, and that her manner was abrupt to the point of being offensive.

He wondered if she would come to dinner, or if she would find some excuse to stay away. He had to admit, he would be disappointed if she wasn't there. What he had said to Evelyn was true, he felt no physical attraction to the tight-faced young woman, with her little sharp features and narrow, beady stare. He was curious, that was all. He wanted to know who she was, and why he was convinced he had some unremembered connection with her. It was as simple as that. But he knew it wasn't. It wasn't simple at all.

He came in from the balcony and lay down on the bed. After a while he fell into a doze for what he thought was no more than a few minutes, but when he woke and looked blearily at his watch, he was surprised to find that almost an hour had passed.

Dr. Cruz had not called back. Dinner was set, then.

Picking up his cigarettes and the door key, Quirke walked along the corridor to the lift. Instead of going directly down, he pressed the button for the top floor. The iron cage around him juddered and clanked as he ascended. He felt both exhilarated and sheepish. Evelyn was right, part of him would forever be a child. It was at least in part her fault, he told himself. She had made him happy, or so it seemed, and where happiness was con-

cerned, seeming was the same as being. But it was a dangerous
thing to do to a man of Quirke's saturnine and bodeful temper.
Laughing will end crying, he thought, trying to remember the old
nun's name. Sister Cataclysma, let's call her, he thought, and
grinned at himself in the framed looking glass on the back wall.

Christ never laughed. Who was it had told him that? Nowhere in any of the accounts of the Evangelists does the Mes-
siah allow himself even a chuckle. But then, he had a lot on his
mind. The certain prospect of crucifixion would hardly be con-
ducive to the belly laugh.

In the bar, he ordered his first glass of wine of the day, while
Evelyn went and requested the concierge to book a table for four
at the Restaurante Zurriola.

She was puzzled by Quirke's uncharacteristic insistence on
dining with these two doctors, but she had made no objection.
She was happy to go out to dinner to a nice restaurant. She
smiled to herself. Jealousy, according to Herr Professor Zwingli's
big fat book that she was reading, was one of the affects that she
lacked. Secretly, she considered Doktor Zwingli something of a
Scharlatan. It did not matter. Even frauds had some wise things
to say, despite themselves.

And what of herself? Was she entirely genuine? She thought
of her life, when she bothered to think of it, as something like
a ramshackle caravan, with camels, and swaying wagons piled
high with baggage, and music and drumming, and men in tur-
bans riding on elephants, and wild animals in wheeled cages,
and, oh, *alle möglichen Dinge*, yes, a caravan that had emerged
out of deep night into the sunlight and soft shadows of what,
for now, was the present, and that one day, when she was old,
would be the all but forgotten past.

She was not normally given to such ruminations. It must be,
she decided, the effect of the south.

"Yes," she said to the earnestly smiling young man seated behind the desk, "for four people, at eight o'clock. So kind. *Gracias*."

15

It was clear from the start that the evening was not going to be easy. Quirke and Evelyn had been at the table for a full half hour before Dr. Cruz arrived. He was alone, Quirke saw, with a twinge of disappointment. The doctor seemed preoccupied and distinctly cross, and made no apology for being late, but sat down brusquely at his place, snatched up his napkin and cracked it like a whip and laid it on his lap. Quirke and Evelyn glanced at each other. So far there had been no mention of Dr. Lawless. Quirke, in the end, having been kicked twice under the table by Evelyn, cleared his throat and inquired with a show of polite concern if everything was all right with the young woman. Cruz stared at him, perplexed.

"All right? How do you mean, all right?"

"Well"—Quirke glanced at his watch—"it's almost eight forty-five."

Cruz shrugged.

"Oh, she's always late." He frowned at the menu. "She will be along soon. We should perhaps order, without waiting for her."

Quirke and his wife exchanged another, larger look. By now it was plain, to Quirke at least, that there had been a row between Cruz and his girl, and a serious one, at that. Quirke surmised that Angela Lawless had been furious at Cruz for accepting the Quirkes' invitation without having consulted her. Thinking this, he settled down to derive what pleasure from the evening that he might. He enjoyed occasions of social awkwardness, though he tried to hide it. The glassy crash of brittle surfaces shattering was sweet and intricate music to his ears. People revealed so much of themselves in distressful circumstances, and tonight had more potential than he would have dared hope for. A lovers' quarrel was always good fun, sometimes even for the lovers. Evelyn, from whom he could conceal nothing, was eyeing him reprovingly, though not, he saw, without sharing a little in his sense of happy anticipation. After all, she was a shrink—that forbidden word—and here, potentially at least, was strife aplenty. He rubbed his hands and suggested a bottle of champagne. Cruz, ill-temperedly picking at crumbs on the tablecloth, frowned more deeply and gave his head a swift, dismissive shake, as if at a breach of good manners.

"But you'll drink some wine, surely?" Quirke persisted.

"Yes, yes," Cruz answered shortly, to get the business out of the way.

Quirke summoned the waiter—it was the retired toreador again—and ordered the most expensive bottle on the list. When the waiter had gone, Quirke showed the list to Cruz and pointed out the vintage he had ordered, asking his approval, but really to make sure he would see the price. But Cruz hardly looked up from the little cone of crumbs he had built beside his plate.

Quirke grinned. Things were shaping up nicely. Evelyn gave his knee a warning with a fingertip under the table. She knew these playful moods of his, and how often they ended not in laughter but tears.

A plate of fried sardines and a basket of bread were brought, to keep them occupied while they awaited the tardy Dr. Lawless. A silence settled on the table, which the arrival of the wine relieved only a little. Quirke invited the doctor to perform the ritual tasting, but he made a sharply dismissive gesture with his hand, and said he knew nothing about wine, his tone implying that those who did were of an irredeemably trivial cast of mind. Quirke signaled brusquely to the waiter to fill the glasses.

Evelyn was asking Dr. Cruz if San Sebastián was his hometown, and if he spoke the Basque language. The doctor pushed himself back in his chair and, lifting his head, peered at her along the side of his finely chiseled nose, his eyebrows raised high, as if such a question verged on the insulting.

"I am from Cádiz," he announced, with heavy emphasis. "In the south."

"Ah, yes, the white city," Evelyn murmured. "I have been there."

Quirke glanced at her, startled. It was news to him that she was familiar with other places in Spain besides this northern coast. She would never cease to surprise him, he thought, and for some reason his darkly cheery mood was further cheered. He pictured Evelyn, younger, slimmer, in khaki britches and a broad sombrero, astride a donkey and negotiating the tortuous passes on some far inland mountain range.

He sipped his wine and looked surreptitiously about the table. Was there not something entertainingly comical in their absurd predicament, sitting here like caricatures of themselves, waiting more or less expectantly for the arrival of Dr. Cruz's rude and inconsiderate inamorata?

The wine was cool and soft, with the tiniest hint of a fizz on the tongue. Quirke's glass was empty already.

Conversation, such as it was, quickly petered out, and another large and weighty silence settled on the table. Cruz's glance kept flicking to the doorway, in what seemed to Quirke a mixture of impatience and apprehensiveness. However, he was forced to endure another twenty minutes before the missing guest arrived at last.

She entered in a flurry, as if she were fleeing from something or someone in the street and had plunged into the first open doorway she had come upon. She wore enormous dark glasses, the bulging lenses of which were gleamingly opaque—they looked to Quirke like the magnified eyes of a monstrously overgrown insect—and a mantilla of heavy black lace that covered her hair entirely. Her frock was a silvery silk sheath, with long sleeves buttoned at the wrists, and her shoes had four-inch heels. Her mouth was a wide slash of scarlet, the lipstick somewhat crookedly applied. Evelyn wondered afterward why she had got herself up as Audrey Hepburn—all that was lacking was an ebony cigarette holder and a diamond tiara. She was to keep the mantilla on throughout dinner, and only lifted the sunglasses, and then by no more than half an inch, when she had to deal with something on her plate. Her perfume was intense. Like Cruz, she didn't smile. They were a serious couple. Quirke had the impression they weren't entirely present, but were listening instead for the sound of something that they knew was about to start up elsewhere.

The waiter came with his pencil and pad. It was not the toreador this time, but a lazy-eyed young man with an insolent droop to the side of his mouth and oiled black hair that was molded smoothly to a strikingly bulbous skull.

Quirke scanned the menu in some desperation—he worried he might by mistake order something that he would have to have Evelyn cut up for him. He had been trying to keep his injured hand out of sight under the table. Dr. Cruz had not asked him how it was. Indeed, Quirke suspected it had slipped from his mind.

In the end, Quirke settled on a rice dish with shellfish and something called *carabineros*, which made him think of firearms, but which turned out to be nothing more than oversized prawns. He lifted the wine bottle preparatory to pouring, but Cruz and the young woman simultaneously put their hands over their glasses, both with faintly scandalized frowns. He filled his own glass to the brim, and signaled for a second bottle. He felt like getting drunk, if for no other reason than to match himself to the comedy of the occasion. The effort of keeping himself in check was making his head feel as full and weightless as a balloon. But he mustn't get drunk, really, he mustn't. It would be grievously unfair to leave Evelyn alone to steer them through whatever was left of what had turned into a ghastly if grimly entertaining evening. After all, he was the one who had proposed this fiasco in the first place.

16

From the outset, Angela Lawless had made it plain that she had no wish to be here, in this restaurant, with these people, who were strangers to her and, if it were up to her, would remain so. She made no effort to hide how cross she was. But there was something else, too, something deeper than mere impatience at being compelled to take part in an occasion that was none of her making. Quirke got a sense from her of agitation and deep-lying anxiety. He watched her out of the corner of his eye. Why was she anxious, why agitated? And why had she come in this absurd disguise that would fool no one, and that, on the contrary, only served to draw attention to herself—a number of people at tables round about had stared at her when she came in, and some of them even yet had their heads together and were plainly discussing her. She must really have thought she would be taken for some famous international film star traveling incognito—wasn't there an annual film festival in San Sebastián?

Evelyn, determined as a cross-channel swimmer breasting a sluggish sea, tried repeatedly to keep the conversation going. She spoke of the beauty of the bay, of which she and Quirke had such a wonderful view from their hotel room. She exclaimed at the greenness of the countryside, here in the north. She mentioned the tortuosities of the Basque language. Each topic she offered hopefully around the table, but each one fell into silence.

Dr. Cruz, spurred by his hostess's efforts, and aware of his position as a man of consequence and a native Spaniard, made a wan attempt to breathe a little life into the table talk. He bemoaned the annually swelling number of tourists coming to Donostia—a number, it was tacitly though pointedly indicated, that Quirke and his wife were this year adding to—and the resulting seasonal increase in the price of everything. This was followed by yet another interval of silence. He tried again. General Franco, he said, kept a holiday home here, over in the western hills above the bay. It wasn't that he loved the place, however—he came only to make the point that the Basque country was as Spanish as any other part of Spain. The doctor chuckled dryly.

Evelyn, encouraged, mentioned the two Basque rebels whose lives the Generalissimo had refused to spare.

"Yes," Dr. Cruz said, with smooth unconcern, "they were to be executed on Sunday, but the Church stepped in, complaining that it would be an insult to the Sabbath, so it was put off for a day."

He was eating, and did not look up from his plate.

Angela Lawless seemed to pay not the slightest heed to any of this. She had ordered nothing but a salad, which she didn't eat, only pushed the greasy leaves about the plate listlessly with her fork. She had developed by now the defiantly sulky demeanor of a spoiled and rebellious daughter surprised by her parents in some rash and compromising situation. Toward Cruz she displayed no sign of affection, or even, Quirke thought, of interest. He might not have been there, for all the attention she gave him.

Quirke asked her where in Ireland she was from. She turned to him with frowning incomprehension, whether real or otherwise it was hard to say. She appeared to be affronted, not by the question, but by the fact of his having dared to address her at all.

"Oh, Dublin," she said dismissively.

"Yes, I guessed that," Quirke said. "But what part of Dublin, exactly? North? South?"

She went on staring at him—at least, he assumed she was looking at him, for he couldn't see her eyes behind those bulging lenses—with a kind of concentrated indifference, like a princess regarding an insistent footman. Evelyn and Dr. Cruz stopped eating and turned to her, waiting for her to speak. Something seemed to thrum above the table, like a stretched piano wire.

The young woman stirred herself at last.

"I haven't lived in Dublin for a long time," she said, and went back to fiddling with her salad. And that, it appeared, was that.

Abruptly she rose and without a word to anyone at the table walked swiftly off in the direction of the ladies' room. Cruz watched her go, then turned back to his plate. No one spoke. The minutes trickled past. Then she appeared again, moving more slowly now, it seemed, and sat down and smiled about her blurredly.

"I stopped to look at the river," she said, smiling, then blinked, and frowned. Quirke regarded her with interest. Cruz caught his eye and quickly looked away.

The waiter returned. Coffee? No, they would not take coffee. A digestif? Shakes of the head on all four sides of the table. Quirke cast a glance at Evelyn. What now? Hardly half an hour had passed since Angela Lawless's arrival, but plainly the evening was at a close. Quirke had the sense of himself, of his entire being, opening in an irresistible, crackling, jaw-breaking yawn. Under the table, his bandaged hand ached. He turned

once more to Angela Lawless. She looked away quickly, then
down at her plate, and even ate a leaf of lettuce.

He was more than ever convinced that he knew her, somehow, from somewhere. Was there something about him that
struck an answering echo in her? Was that why she had got herself up in this ridiculous disguise, afraid that he would recognize her? But why afraid? What harm did she think he might
do to her?

She put down her fork and fumbled in her handbag—a dingy
thing of pink leather with a broken clasp—and brought out
a packet of Spanish cigarettes and lit one. As she smoked she
seemed to feel cold suddenly, and drew her shoulders in around
her hollowed chest like a pair of bony, bedraggled wings. She
murmured something in Spanish to Dr. Cruz. The doctor nodded, in some annoyance, Quirke thought, and placed the fingers of both hands flat on the edge of the table, preparatory to
rising from his chair. He managed a smile, though it was hardly
more than a stretching of his lips at one side, and said that they
must be going, and thanked Quirke and his wife for a wonderful, wonderful evening.

Quirke, still seated, watched the young woman as she un-
folded her scrawny wings and stood up, clutching her bag to her
chest, not looking at any of them.

Outside, in the cool stillness of the night, none of the four
knew quite what to do. There seemed to be a vaguely distress-
ing recognition of something, of everything, having been left
unfinished. Angela Lawless adjusted her mantilla, arranging one
frilled edge of it across her shoulders. Along with the sunglasses,
which she had still not taken off, it gave the look of a fantasti-
cally rarefied and probably poisonous creature, displaced here
from some far-off and hardly inhabited tropical zone.

Quirke was glad to be free of the restaurant, the four walls
of which had seemed to be drawing steadily closer throughout
the evening. He called out now a spuriously cheery, loud fare-

well, and pressed a hand firmly into the small of Evelyn's back, preparatory to both of them making their escape, telling himself *never, never again.* Cruz, however, seeming belatedly to feel that the proprieties had not been fully observed, said that he and Angela would walk with them to their hotel. At this the young woman gave a start, and seemed about to object, but said nothing, and lapsed back into a sulky silence.

They crossed the street. The river flowed silently beside them, sprinkled with shivery lights. The footpath was narrow, and the two women moved ahead and walked on side by side. Quirke lit a cigarette. He was tired. In the night air the good effects of the wine were dissipating rapidly, and his hand had begun to pain him again, badly.

Cruz spoke of the history of San Sebastián. In the Napoleonic Wars, the city had been razed to the ground by undisciplined and marauding British and Portuguese troops. Quirke's thoughts drifted. His eye was on the young woman walking ahead with Evelyn. He wondered what they had found to talk about.

Angela Lawless. No, that name wasn't right, it just wasn't.

Once, in the past, another young woman with the same initials, A. L., had briefly loomed large in Quirke's life. She had died, violently, at the hands of her own brother. A tragic and ugly business.

Recalling this other A. L., Quirke suddenly remembered that he had promised to telephone his daughter in Dublin this evening, to say hello and to tell her how much, supposedly, he was enjoying the holiday. She would be amused to hear of the ghastly evening he and Evelyn had just endured, all of it his fault for having suggested it.

Cruz had come to the end of his history lecture and, after a pause, suddenly asked, "How did you find her?"

Quirke was startled.

"My daughter?" he said. Cruz looked at him in perplexity. "Sorry, I was thinking of my—I was thinking of something else."

He thought of mentioning the other A. L., and the fact that Phoebe, his daughter, had been her friend.

Cruz was still looking at him, still frowning.

"Come, Dr. Quirke," Cruz said, "you don't expect us to believe that you are here in Donostia by chance? Do you think us so naive?"

Quirke stopped. He was baffled.

"Dr. Cruz, I have to tell you I don't know what you're talking about."

Cruz smiled coldly, as they stood face-to-face under the night's glistening dome.

"Who are you, exactly, Dr. Quirke?" he asked.

Quirke gave a helpless, spluttering laugh.

"Who am I, 'exactly'? That's a question I often put to myself, but get no answer."

Cruz dropped all pretense of politeness.

"This is not a joke," he said. "Tell me why you are here, and what it is you want."

Quirke assumed an expression of large surprise and puzzlement.

"I don't think I understand you, Dr. Cruz," he said. "What do you mean, who am I, and why am I here? I'm a medical man, like yourself, and I'm on holiday with my wife in this lovely city. What else do you need to know?"

Cruz took a step back and made himself smile.

"Forgive me," he said, and paused a moment, scanning the pavement at his feet. "Angela has had some troubles in her life. It would not be good for her if—if the past were to come back." He lifted his eyes. "You understand?" His smile this time was ruefully complicit.

Quirke shrugged. "It's none of my business," he said easily. "I hope I haven't done anything to upset your—your friend."

A lightning flash of pain from his wounded thumb sped along his forearm to the elbow. He was remembering a rainy night in

Dublin. Some hotel. The Russell, was it? No, the Shelbourne. Splinters of light in the panes of the revolving glass door, the rain shining on the conical breasts of the twin statues of the Nubian slave girls holding aloft their lamps at either side of the door. He was drunk, as he so often was in those days. He had got into an altercation with the top-hatted doorman. *Why don't you go home, sir, and sleep it off.* The glass door revolved, two young women came through, one looking back and saying something, the other unfurling an umbrella. The one facing back was Phoebe. Now she turned, and saw him, his bleared eye, his sodden coat. Her smile died. Behind her, the black umbrella sprang fully into bloom. A thin pale face, a pair of dark eyes regarding him.

Dr. Cruz was speaking to him, but he wasn't listening. He looked along the pavement. His wife had stopped, and so had Angela Lawless, so-called. She was lighting a cigarette. The match flame flared briefly, buttercup-yellow, identical in each of the black lenses.

Could it be possible? he thought. A dead young woman not dead at all, but here, just here in front of him, tapping her foot on the pavement and looking impatiently away? Yes, it was more than possible. It was what he had known all along, without knowing, that he had been right, that Angela Lawless wasn't who she said she was, that there was no Angela Lawless, in fact, or if there was, as there was bound to be, somewhere, this was not she, but another A. L. altogether.

April, he thought, and almost laughed at the sheer unlikeliness of the thing, at the sheer astonishment of it. April Latimer. April in Spain.

DUBLIN

17

Phoebe Griffin stood at the big plate-glass window of the viewing deck in Dublin Airport, worrying about the weather. Thick mist, ghostly gray, pressed itself against the tall panes before her. It might have been trying to get inside, out of the cold.

When she was little, her father used to bring her here, on Sunday afternoons, to watch the airplanes taking off and landing. It fascinated her how the propellers made a circular silvery blur until the engines stopped and they began to slow down. Strange to think of them, in the heights of the sky, beating through the blued air, hour after hour. Such speed, such frailty. The aircraft looked so small, from up here, small and sturdy and brave.

At that time, in her childhood, she still thought Quirke was her uncle, and it would be many years before she discovered otherwise. When they came here together, to watch the planes, he would leave her alone for twenty minutes or more and return with a glossy look in his eyes and a funny smell on his breath. She remembered the moment when she realized that while he was away, he had of course been in the bar. The bar was open all day, because it was in the airport, and she was his pretext to come here and that way circumvent the Sunday licensing laws in town. She wondered how many whiskeys he managed to lower in twenty minutes. She thought of him there, furtive and urgent, lifting glass after glass and trying not to catch his own eye in the mirror behind the bar. She felt sorry for him. She supposed he thought that at the airport, with all the comings and goings, no one would know him or pay him any attention. He would be safe.

She didn't mind that he had used her in this way. It hadn't done her any harm, after all. Of the two of them, Quirke would have been the one in distress.

He was always kind to her, in his awkward, overcheerful way. He bought her ice creams in summer, and chocolate bars in winter. In the wintertime there weren't many airplanes—tourists didn't come, when it was cold and wet. Sometimes, when Quirke was away at his furtive drinking, she would go down and wander around the airport by herself, looking at the people. Once, a little black girl of about her own age had smiled at her. The girl was with her parents. Phoebe had never seen black people before.

She was here to meet Paul. His flight from Zurich had already been delayed by an hour. She wondered if it would be allowed to land at all. If not, where would it be diverted to? Shannon, most likely, or even somewhere in England. If Paul were here, and not up in the sky somewhere, he would touch her elbow with his fingers and tell her, smiling, that she should go home and wait for him there. Paul was the soul of considerateness. She should have been glad of it, but instead his unflagging thoughtfulness annoyed her a little.

And was it thoughtfulness, anyway? Was it not something else, something that assured him of being always in control?

She had already drunk three cups of tea and eaten two sausage rolls. The first roll had tasted all right, probably because she was hungry, but the second was a serious mistake. It had given her a stomachache, and there was a horrible, mucus-like scum coating the inside of her mouth.

The metal line of numbers on the arrivals board high up behind her clattered through a new set of changes. She turned expectantly, but no, the Zurich flight was still due to land late, at noon. She looked out at the mist again. When did mist stop being mist and become full-blown fog? In the hour that she had been waiting so far, not a single flight had taken off or landed. She was torn between the wish for Paul to be here, now, and the worry that the pilot would run out of patience and decide to risk coming down, and would lose his way because of poor visibility and the plane would crash.

She looked at her watch, and thought it must have stopped. But it hadn't—the spear-shaped second hand was sweeping around the dial with what seemed to her infuriating smugness. It was only five minutes past eleven. If there was another delay, she would go to the bar and have a drink, and let the people, especially the women, glare at her in disapproval if they wanted to. Unescorted young ladies weren't supposed to sit on high stools in airport bars with their legs crossed, drinking gin. Only certain girls did that kind of thing.

Paul had been attending a conference in Zurich on the campaign to stem the spread of smallpox in the Horn of Africa.

Waiting for him, she had a sense, only slightly guilty, of her superiority over the people around her. There were businessmen's doll-like wives, in white gloves and pillbox hats, and couples up from the country, seeing off their emigrant sons or daughters, and rough-faced fellows returning to their jobs on building sites in England, cardboard suitcases at their feet, their wives beside them with red-rimmed eyes and five or six screaming kids hanging on to their coattails. They would all look so dowdy, even those pampered wives, compared to her boyfriend.

He was a man who went to international conferences and gave talks to distinguished audiences on important topics. He wore sober suits and a homburg hat and carried under his arm a slim black briefcase. Also, he had a very slight Austrian accent that sounded like a lisp, and gave her a tingling along her spine when he held her in his arms and put his face into her hair and murmured endearments, even when the inanity of his words made her shut her eyes and feel embarrassed for him. Paul was a very serious young man who nevertheless could be remarkably silly at times, without meaning to, and without his being aware of it.

Her father had telephoned her late the previous night. The recollection of what he had told her was a small dark cloud of dread hovering over her heart. She had assumed he was drunk—she hoped so, though he hadn't sounded as if he was. The thing he had called to tell her about was mad, utterly mad.

She sat down on one of the peculiarly uncomfortable tubular metal chairs that were set out in a line, facing the observation window. She had no time for Scandinavian design, however fashionable it was nowadays. Something about the angle the chairs leaned back at made her think of people seated in the front row of a cinema, gazing up mindlessly at a blank screen.

It made her feel slightly dizzy, sitting in front of that unreal-looking big blank square of glass with the mist pressing against it. She stood up. She remembered the sausage rolls, and her stomach seemed to flop over like an ailing fish in a muddy pond.

She heard a faint droning sound outside, and glanced at her watch again. Not quite half past eleven. It couldn't be his flight, not yet. She waited, standing at the window, and presently she saw a plane coming in to land. It looked like a metal dragonfly, as it emerged abruptly out of the mist and skimmed down and alighted in clumsy haste on the runway. The wheels threw up behind them twin parachute-shaped clouds of spray that was whiter than the surrounding mist.

Downstairs, in the bar, a man was loudly sobbing out a verse of *Come back to Erin, Mavourneen, Mavourneen*. He sounded very drunk. She thought of her father. At least he didn't sing, drunk or sober. That would be the limit.

The board behind her clattered again.

18

Paul emerged from the baggage area, striding swiftly forward in his black overcoat and his black scarf, holding his hat in one hand and his briefcase in the other. He glanced about the arrivals hall, and when he saw her, she couldn't prevent herself from waving eagerly, though she knew he disapproved of public displays of affection—of displays of any kind, really. He was smiling, all the same, she saw. It was a thing he didn't often do, not because he was dour or ill-tempered, but because he portioned out everything carefully, even smiles.

She had wriggled her way through the waiting crowd and was standing right up against the metal barrier. Now she stopped waving and lowered her hand uncertainly, experiencing a lurch of misgiving. It was a trick of perspective, she knew, but she had the peculiar and unsettling impression that, even as he advanced toward her, he was at the same time hanging back somehow. She couldn't make it out, the sensation she had—it was as if he were sending a wave of some kind ahead of him, a palpable qualm of doubt and unwillingness, so strong it made her falter for a moment, stalled in uncertainty.

It was the effect of the sausage rolls, surely, or of the three cups of horribly strong tea. She should have had that drink; it would have steadied her nerves.

Paul skirted the barrier and came forward quickly and put an arm around her, the stiff brim of his hat pressing into her back between her shoulder blades. He kissed her lightly on both cheeks. She wasn't having that, and, whether he disapproved or not, she clasped him to her and put her mouth, fairly squashed it, in fact, against his. Why were men always so stiff and reserved when they came back after being away? Was it shyness? She could never understand it.

"The thing, the board, showed your flight was delayed," she said, breathless and laughing. "What happened?"

"Oh, we were supposed to circle until the fog cleared. There was no announcement, just suddenly we were descending and a minute later we were on the ground. So here I am."

They were walking toward the exit. She linked her arm in his. Then she halted. "But where's your suitcase?"

"A porter is bringing it. He will be waiting at the taxi rank."

She felt momentarily deflated. It would never have occurred to her to engage a porter. Paul was accustomed to clicking his fingers and summoning porters, taxis, waiters, barmen. He saw nothing remarkable in being instantly attended to. Would she ever achieve that level of sophistication? And yet, strangely, she felt that in ways she was more advanced than he was. Advanced—it was a word her late grandfather, Judge Garret Griffin, would have used. Disapprovingly. Girls weren't supposed to be advanced. It was almost as bad as being "fast."

They were at the exit.

"Should we stop for something?" she said. Paul turned on her a frowning smile. "I mean, a drink, or something." She faltered, seeing his look. "Or just a coffee, maybe. I've been waiting an age."

His smile had switched itself off, leaving only the frown.

"I'm sorry, my darling," he said, in that sweetly condescending way that he spoke to her sometimes. "I wasn't in charge of the plane, you know, or of the fog, for that matter."

She nodded, compressing her lips. She hated when he spoke to her like that, as if she were a child, or a stupid person. She wasn't stupid. She was as clever as he was, in her way. He had been gone only a week, and yet, now that he was back, he seemed changed, in some way. Had something happened, that he should find her more provoking and annoying than before? But no, she told herself, no, she was imagining things.

"It doesn't matter," she said lightly. "Let's go to the flat, shall we? I bought a cake."

They walked out to the taxi rank. The porter was waiting with Paul's modest suitcase—how did he manage, being away so many days with so few things? He pressed a coin into the man's hand and the man saluted and, turning away, glanced at Phoebe and back at Paul, and smirked. She had a name for that look—the Irish innuendo. She felt like putting out her tongue at the fellow. If she did, what would Paul say? Nothing, probably. He probably wouldn't notice her doing it, and even if he did, he wouldn't understand. And when Paul didn't understand something, he took no interest in it.

The taxi driver, a black-haired, slightly rat-faced fellow, was stowing the little suitcase in the trunk. He came and opened the rear door for Phoebe. As she was climbing in, Paul said to her across the roof of the car, "Actually, I must go straight to the Institute."

He worked in—or, as he would say, was attached to—the Institute for Advanced Medicine, on Merrion Square.

"Oh, I see," she said, and climbed into the taxi and sat down with her handbag on her lap and gazed straight ahead. She hadn't missed the forced casualness with which he had said it. She felt a fool for having bought that cake.

They set off for the city. The mist had turned to a fine, soft rain. Phoebe thought she could hear the tiny drops whispering against the window beside her. She was biting her lip. Nothing of significance had happened between her and Paul just now, nothing she could point to or identify, yet she was afraid she might be about to cry. It was as if a door had flown open suddenly and a gust of cold air had blown straight into her face. Was he planning to leave her, as others had done? If so, there had been no warning, no inkling.

Or had there been, and she hadn't noticed? Maybe he hadn't known before he went away. Maybe he had met someone, in Zurich, at the conference, someone bright and serious, like himself.

She tightened her grip on the strap of her handbag. She mustn't cry. Paul would be shocked if she did, shocked first, and then annoyed. A woman weeping, he had once assured her, made him feel only impatience. Women when they cry are crying only for themselves, that was what he had said. He seemed to have forgotten, when he was saying it, that she was a woman. Or maybe he hadn't forgotten. Maybe he knew exactly what he was saying and to whom he was saying it.

"Quirke telephoned last night," she said, and heard herself give an unsteady, brittle laugh. When she spoke of her father, she always used his name. It was left over from the days when she didn't yet know he was her father.

Paul was looking out of the window on his side, stroking his chin with a finger and thumb, as he did when he was lost in thought. And what was it, she wondered, that he was thinking about?

"Your father?" he said then, vaguely. "He's in Spain, isn't he, with Tante Evelyn?"

"With?—oh, yes." She often forgot that the woman Quirke was married to was Paul's aunt. In fact, she often forgot her father was married at all, and had been for years, so unlikely a thing it seemed to her, even yet. It also slipped her mind on occasion that she had once worked for Paul's Tante Evelyn, as a receptionist at her consulting rooms in Fitzwilliam Square. How things changed, in the run of time. "They're in San Sebastián," she said.

"Are they enjoying it?"

"Yes, I think so. Hard to tell."

"Your father was drunk, I take it?"

How could he say it like that, in that coldly impersonal way? He might have been asking how the weather was, down there in Spain. He knew Quirke's history of self-destructive drinking, and knew also how much Phoebe worried that he would fall again, at any moment, into that terrible spiral, which each time drew him deeper, and in which one day he might finally lose himself.

"He told me he had seen April."

"April?"

"My friend April Latimer."

"But isn't she dead? Didn't her brother murder her?"

Again, that cold, detached way of speaking, as if he were taking a question from the floor at one of his international gatherings. Even Quirke, the pathologist, didn't talk like that.

"Yes." She turned away, and looked at the rained-on city passing blurredly by in the window. "But her body was never found."

Could it be? she wondered. Could April be alive? Phoebe did not know what to think, what to feel. It seemed impossible, and almost too painful to think of. She had considered April Latimer to be her best friend, though she had never been sure if April would have felt the same toward her. After Quirke's phone call, she had stayed awake half the night, turning what he had told

her over and over in her mind, examining it for all its implica-
tions. As far as she was concerned her friend was dead, actually
and, to her, metaphorically—would she now have to dig her up
again, not metaphorically at all?

No, no, Quirke must be mistaken. April couldn't be alive.
Could she?

April had been a troubled soul, obsessed with, among much
else, her older brother, as he had been with her, except that his
obsession had deepened over the years, to the point that he had
felt he had no choice but to murder her. But had he?—had he
murdered her? He had confessed to the killing, had confessed
it to Quirke and to herself, one dreadful, dreadful morning, in
a motor car high up on Howth Head.

Yet there the unavoidable fact remained—there was no body.
April had vanished, but her corpse was never found.

Paul was regarding her with a skeptical eye. His soft, silky hair
was the color of wet straw. A lock of it tended to topple down
over his forehead, giving him a boyish look.

It came to her suddenly that she was a little jealous of him.
Probably she always had been. It was a shocking thought, but
one that wouldn't be dismissed. He had only qualified eighteen
months ago, and already he was publishing papers in learned
journals, and going around the world to important meetings and
conventions and giving advice to governments. Her brilliant
boy, which was how she used to think of him. But he wasn't a
boy, not anymore.

His field was immunology. She had only the vaguest notion
of what immunology was—she had checked in Quirke's copy
of *Black's Medical Dictionary*, but the word wasn't even listed. If
she asked him to tell her about his work, which she used to do,
he would only smile, in his annoyingly arch, remote way, and
smoothly change the subject. She was doing first year medicine
herself. Should that not be enough to earn her even a modicum
of his respect?

"Quirke wants me to come down there," she said.

That, at least, caught his attention.

"Down where?" he asked suspiciously, staring at her.

"Spain. San Sebastián. It's in the Basque country, on the coast."

"I know where San Sebastián is," he informed her stiffly.

"Sorry." She made an exaggeratedly contrite face. "You've probably been there lots of times."

"Really, Phoebe, I don't have to have been somewhere to know where it is." He paused, and then went on, "He wants you to come there, you say? He cannot be missing you that much, surely."

She decided not to respond to this. Paul believed he had the measure of Quirke, and never missed an opportunity to show his disdain for him. Not only did he know about Quirke's drinking, he also knew that Quirke had pretended for years that Phoebe was not his daughter. And besides, he was a pathologist, which in Paul's unspoken opinion—unspoken to her, anyway—was hardly more than being a butcher.

"He wants me to see this woman that he met, and tell him if it could really be April. He has only the haziest notion of what she looks like—or looked like. He met her just once, with me, years ago."

"Was he drunk then, too?" She said nothing, and Paul smirked. "Why on earth does he think this woman is your friend?" he went on indignantly. "What put the thought into his head?"

"I suppose he must have remembered her. And then there are her initials."

"Her initials?"

"She told him, this woman in Spain, that her name is Angela Lawless. You see? Angela Lawless—April Latimer. A. L."

Like Quirke, she didn't think the name sounded genuine, somehow. Just as, she reflected, the word "father," for her, didn't sound quite right when applied to Quirke.

Paul was shaking his head. "This is so far-fetched as to be laughable."

"The woman is a doctor," Phoebe said, "and so was April. Two coincidences is one too many, Quirke says."

"Well, there's no such thing as a coincidence," Paul said. "It is like believing in fairies. These chance things happen all the time, only we don't notice."

He had spoken in the lofty, superior way that she had got used to, though there were times, and this was one of them, when it made her quietly furious.

"You believe in atoms, don't you," she snapped, "even though you've never seen one."

He chuckled. "If you are trying to start a fight, my dear, you are going to be disappointed."

Dr. Blake—his "Tante Evelyn"—used to call her "my dear" in just that way, though without the sarcasm.

"Whatever you want to call it," she said, turning her face away from him and staring angrily out of the taxi window, "it's still strange, that he should come across a person with those initials and be convinced straight off that it's April Latimer. Quirke is not fanciful, and he certainly doesn't believe in fairies."

Paul leaned back against the seat and folded his arms.

"And so you are going to join your father on his wild-goose chase," he said, amused and incredulous.

In truth, she hadn't intended to go, but at that moment she decided that she would. What right had he to patronize her and disparage her father? She would phone up the airlines as soon as she got home. There was an Aer Lingus flight to Madrid, she knew, and an Iberia one to Bilbao, twice a week, and Bilbao wasn't far from San Sebastián.

Despite her irritation—how was it that Paul always managed to have the last word?—she felt a stirring of excitement. What would the weather in Spain be like, at this time of year? Already in her mind she was going through her wardrobe and deciding which of her things would be suitable for a sunny climate. For it was bound to be sunny, in April, in Spain.

19

Paul had instructed the taxi driver to drop him at Merrion Square, outside the Institute. He asked Phoebe if he could leave his suitcase with her. She could take it to the flat and he would collect it that evening. He was living at his Tante Evelyn's tiny mews house off Northumberland Road. He had moved in with her in the last year of his medical studies, and was still there. Phoebe had suggested that he might come and live with her, in her place in Baggot Street, but she could see he found the notion shocking. In many ways, he was a deeply conventional young man. However, his nice sense of propriety didn't prevent him from spending nights with her at the flat. Whenever she alluded, lightly, of course, to this contradiction—she would never utter the word "hypocrisy"—he would avoid replying, and she was always discreet enough to drop the subject.

He was, she had to admit it, a tiny bit of a cold fish. He made love deftly, in an exploratory sort of way, like a doctor searching for the source of an obscure malady. He was circumspect in many aspects of his character and behavior. When he was leaving her flat, always he would make a detour to pass by the window and scan the street outside with a quick glance, as if he thought there might be a task force from the Legion of Mary or something posted out there, waiting to collar him and afterward denounce him for moral turpitude in the columns of the *Irish Catholic*.

True, he was considerate—respectful, he would probably have said—but his scrupulous considerations always left her dissatisfied and slightly cross. It wasn't that she expected him to be a Heathcliff or a Lord Byron, but all the same she wished he would on occasion drop the restraint and let himself go, even if only by a little. A show of heedless gaiety now and then would be nice. She wouldn't have minded a bit of rough stuff, even, in bed, once in a way. But no. Where Paul Viertel was concerned, the traces would remain safely unkicked over.

When she arrived at the flat, the rain was still drifting down. It was so soft and fine it seemed no more than exploratory, the prototype of rain.

She paid off the taxi, and used her key to open the front door, and climbed the stairs, carrying Paul's suitcase.

The inside of the flat felt as damp as outdoors. She struck a match and turned on the gas fire. She liked the little *whoomp!* the gas gave when it caught, and the feathery way it danced along the as-yet-unheated filaments. Strange, how companionable such ordinary things could be, in their humble, uninsistent way.

She heated some beef broth and poured it out and sat down by the big window in the kitchen, both of her hands wrapped tightly around the mug for warmth. She had tried to put out of her mind last night's phone call from her father, but now, as she sat here alone, it pressed in upon her irresistibly.

Quirke hadn't sounded drunk. Tipsy, maybe, but not drunk. He had sounded, in fact, like a little boy who had discovered a rare species of insect, or a particularly repellent bright-green toad, a prize he was eager to show to anyone prepared to look at it.

"As soon as it occurred to me that it might be April, I knew it was her."

He had pressed her to describe April to him in detail, but what good would a description be, no matter how detailed? "What about a photo, then?" he urged. "Have you got one of her?"

She was sure she had, but even if she could find it, it would take a week for her to get it to him, even by airmail. He told her to send it, anyway.

"How did she seem, this woman?" she had asked. "How did she behave? I mean, there must have been something, besides her initials, that made you think she was April. You only had a single glimpse of her, that night outside the Shelbourne, and even then, you were—" She broke off.

"I was drunk, yes, I know," he said, brushing the fact aside. "But I remember what she looked like then. The trouble is, I don't know what she would look like now."

"Then what good would a photograph be? She would have changed."

She heard him lighting a cigarette, without putting down the receiver. It was a knack he had, one of a number, which he liked to show off, with a casual air, whenever the opportunity arose. There was something of the ageless boy about Quirke, for all his darkness. And now here he was, in Spain, on the track of a girl who was supposed to have died. It was an adventure straight out of the *Boy's Own Paper*.

"She was nervous," Quirke was saying, "nervous, and agitated. In fact, she seemed scared out of her wits. She didn't take her sunglasses off, not once, all through dinner."

"Maybe there's something the matter with her eyes."

"And she left her veil on, too."

"Her veil?" Phoebe gave a delighted squeal of laughter. "She hasn't become a nun, has she? If so, then it's definitely not April."

"No, not a veil, but that Spanish lace thing, what do you call it?"

"A mantilla?"

"That's it. Left it on the whole time, covering her hair. At first I thought she must be afraid of being spotted by someone—a husband, maybe, though how she could imagine her own husband wouldn't recognize her, even in that get-up, I don't know."

"Didn't you say her husband was there with her, at dinner?"

"No, not her husband. Fellow by the name of Cruz, also a doctor; she works with him at the hospital. Sleek-looking fellow, quite a bit older. Altogether too plausible, I'd say."

"Too plausible for what?"

"To be plausible."

"Is he her—her lover, do you think?"

"Something like that, I imagine, yes. I don't know what kind of arrangements they make, down here. They're all Catholics, but not like at home."

"Oh, yes, those Latin lovers," she said dryly.

"The point is," Quirke said, lowering his voice, and she pictured him hunching more closely over the phone, "the point is, it was us, or me, anyway, that she was trying to keep from getting a good look at her. She was afraid I'd recognize her, if she let me get close enough. All the same, she knew I knew it was her."

"But why would she come to dinner with you?"

There was a pause. She heard him taking a draw at his cigarette. He said, "Maybe to find out if I *had* recognized her."

"But you said—"

"I know, I know."

Another pause, and Quirke's breathing.

"This is all crazy, you know," she said. "The heat must have gone to your head."

"It is her, Phoebe. I know it is."

It had taken her an age to get him off the phone. At one point she had pretended that Paul had arrived and that she would have to go down and let him in, but Quirke kept on. In the end, while he was urging her to come down to Spain, she had hung up on him.

She looked out now at the gray spring rain slithering down out of a grayer sky. At least, she thought, the food and the wine down there were bound to make the trip worth doing.

She stood up from the table and went into the living room, carrying her mug of broth with her. The air in the room was laden with the flabby fumes of the gas fire. She stood by the window, sipping her drink and remembering her lost friend.

What if what Quirke had said was true and April wasn't dead? What if it were she whom Quirke had stumbled on, by the merest chance? She could as well be in Spain as anywhere else. It would be like April to go off, just like that, without telling anyone, to start up a new life. April was strange. She had been Phoebe's friend, but Phoebe had no illusions about her. There was something missing in April Latimer, some emotional connection to other people, and to the world.

Her brother had been the same. Oscar Latimer was a successful obstetrician—best baby-puller in town, Quirke used to say of him, and laugh. Then April had disappeared, and Oscar had confessed to her murder, before taking his own life. The whole ghastly business had been more or less hushed up, and even Quirke had been unable to find out all the facts. And April's corpse had never been found. Curiously, this fact had never struck Phoebe as particularly significant. At the time, she had assumed it had been spirited away by the family and buried in secret somewhere. As time went on, however, her doubts had grown. What if April's murder was a fantasy dreamed up by Oscar Latimer, for who knew what mad reasons of his own?

There had been some kind of awful, sick thing between April and her brother. When they were children they had both been sexually abused by their father, the famous Conor Latimer, hero of the 1916 Rising and, later, the country's most successful heart specialist. It had left both of them horribly damaged, of course, Oscar more so than April, as it turned out. Indeed, it could be said of poor Oscar that he had died of a broken soul.

April, when she was still hardly more than a girl, had earned herself a bad reputation around town. People said she was a nymphomaniac. Certainly, she had slept with many men, and not a few women as well, or so rumor had it. Yet Phoebe had been fond of her, for all her faults—perhaps more than fond, she sometimes thought, with a twinge of unease, when she looked back on that never-less-than-fevered friendship.

She hadn't known about the history of abuse until the day of Oscar's death, when he had revealed his family's darkest secret to her and Quirke, up on Howth Head, before driving himself in Quirke's car over a cliff into the sea.

Outside, the half-hearted rain had intensified into the real thing. On days like this when she was little, she used to love to sit by the window in her Grandfather Griffin's house in Rathgar and watch the big drops bouncing on the tarmac. She imagined them to be tiny ballerinas making superquick curtsies and then dropping through little trapdoors hidden in the stage.

What would happen, if Angela Lawless really was April Latimer? Quirke wouldn't let a thing like that go, his daughter was certain of that. But what would he do? Would he tell her family? April's uncle, William Latimer, was in the government—he would have to go down to Spain and try to get her to come back with him. If he did, and if April went with him, would all that awful stuff be raked up again? A scandal this time, of that magnitude, would not be so easy to suppress. Somehow,

April's return to life would cause a bigger commotion than her supposed death.

As Phoebe pondered these things, she was aware of a growing sense of unease, an unease tinged with, of all things, embarrassment. It was as if she had been told about her friend having done some horrible, shameful thing and then run away from the consequences.

And all this, when she was supposed to have been safely dead.

Safely.

The word brought Phoebe up short, with a guilty start. But she had to admit it, she did not want to have to deal with her friend, not now, not after all that had happened, or that she had believed to have happened. April was too much part of a painful past. Let it stay that way.

She closed her eyes and leaned her forehead against the cold, clammy windowpane.

Poor April.

20

She searched for a photograph with April in it. She had gone through drawers, and rummaged in the bedside chest where she kept odd bits and pieces. She was about to give up the search when she remembered the old shoebox in the wardrobe. She hadn't looked in it in years. It was on a high shelf, and she had to stand on a chair to reach it.

She blew the dust from the lid—how lovely dust could be, when it lay like that, like a smooth coating of fur, dull-mauve and almost too soft to touch—and sat down on the side of the bed and set the box on her knees. In it were spools of thread and samples of dress material, and a hatpin with a garnet set in it that was the only thing she had kept from the days when she had worked for Mrs. Cuffe-Wilkes at the Maison des Chapeaux on Grafton Street. And there, at last, underneath all the other stuff, was what she had been searching for.

It was only a snap. The print was of the fancy, deckle-edged kind that used to be all the rage at one time. A corner of it had been torn off, and a jagged, whitish wrinkle ran athwart it from top right to bottom left.

She wondered who had taken it—she supposed it must have been Jimmy Minor. He was dead, too, now. He had been a reporter, and had got caught up in one of Quirke's "cases."

The photograph showed April and herself posing in the shade of a tree beside the duck pond in St. Stephen's Green. The tree had white blossoms on it—chestnut, was it?—so the photo must have been taken in late spring or early summer. The sunlight glared, and she stood in the angle of the tree's shadow with one shoulder lifted and her cheek pressed against it, in the catlike way that Phoebe remembered so well. Dark hair cut short, the pale, sharp little nose, the wide thin mouth and pointed chin. A striking face, the expression withdrawn and enigmatic. April had never been a beauty, but no one seemed to notice, certainly not those who had desired her, and there had been many of them.

What the camera could not catch, of course, was the sleek, slightly sinister aura with which April surrounded herself, and which played about that sharp little face of hers like foxfire. Nor was there any trace of the dark humor, the taste for mischief-making and, above all, the sense of a deeply hidden, ineradicable pain.

Yes, April was unhappy, always unhappy, for all the brittle brightness of her manner and the quickness of her wit. And cruel, too, in the way damaged people so often were, in Phoebe's experience.

A sudden thought rose up and became caught in her mind, like a broken fingernail snagging in silk. If April was alive, who had she meant to deceive by the trick she had played of being dead? Perhaps there had been no choice for her but to disappear.

Perhaps she had been under mortal threat, and had fled for her life. But who would have wanted her dead, and why? And for what reason would her brother have pretended he had murdered her, before taking his own life?

None of it made sense, none of it. Quirke was either drunk, or dreaming. Or—?

She returned to the front room, taking the photograph with her. It reminded her of the little cards of remembrance that families sent out to relatives and friends when someone had died.

Quirke wasn't drunk when he phoned her in the night, she was sure of that—she knew when Quirke was drunk, from bitter experience—but he had a way of becoming fixated on things, to the point of mania, sometimes, especially when he was bored. And he was bound to be bored, on holiday. And Quirke bored was almost worse than Quirke drunk.

If April wasn't dead, then the years that had elapsed since her disappearance would have to be run backward, like a film, and adjusted to accommodate her invisible presence in them. It was a dizzying prospect.

One night, when she was a child of four or five, Phoebe had suffered through a nightmare so terrifying that the memory of it had stayed with her ever since, with awful immediacy. In it, she was wandering through a cemetery on a dark, wintry afternoon. Even yet she could clearly see the graves and the moss-grown gravestones, and the bell jars with bunches of flowers under them rotted to slime, and blurred and wilted photographs of the person who was buried underneath. She could see the yew trees standing like shrouded sentinels, and the narrow pathways running along and crossing each other at right angles. She could even hear the crunch and squeak of the damp gravel under her tread.

Eventually she had come upon a grave, newly dug, with a high mound of wet, yellowish clay, and a little white cross with a name printed on it, to identify who was buried there. She stopped—in the dream she could clearly see herself from outside, halted there, a child in a belted overcoat and thick woolen stockings and laced-up bootees—and a creeping horror came over her. Sprouting at an angle out of the grave, like a withered branch or the thick stalk of a dead flower, was an arm, a bloodless arm with a clawlike hand dangling at the end of it.

She knew the source of the awful vision. In school, she had been taught that girls who told lies would end up like that, buried in a dank wet grave with one arm sticking up, so that everyone would know they were sinful little deceivers. Now, suddenly, that image of the dead arm flashed again into her mind.

Could it be? Could April be at once dead and alive?

Outside, the rain had lost heart again and was slowly ceasing. She put on her coat and took up her handbag and her gloves, found an umbrella leaning against the wall behind the door and hurried down the stairs.

In the hall, a coin-operated telephone was mounted on the wall above the big, scarred oak table that stood stolidly on four thick legs, like a retired beast of burden. She delved in her purse and came up with three single pennies. She liked the dull, brownish smell of the coins; it reminded her of Saturday morning trips to the sweet shop with her pocket money warm in her palm.

She consulted the tattered telephone book chained to the wall, and dialed the number of April's uncle, William Latimer, at his home in Blackrock. The maid answered. Phoebe thought she remembered her, a tubby little redhead with a supercilious manner. She said Dr. Latimer was not at home but in the Dáil. Her tone implied that only a simpleton wouldn't know where the Minister would be in the middle of a weekday afternoon.

Phoebe found more pennies and called Dr. Latimer's parliamentary office. In the last election, he had kept his seat with an increased majority and had been appointed Minister of Defense. It was common knowledge that this had been his goal since he had first entered politics. The Latimers were a warlike clan, who, after independence came, had taken on the mantle of bourgeois respectability. Bill Latimer was still well known for—indeed, thrived on—his uncompromising republican opinions.

"He's in the Chamber," his secretary said brusquely, when, after a long delay, Phoebe was at last put through to her. "There's an important debate going on."

"Please give him a message," Phoebe said. "This is—" She hesitated. She was probably the last person in the world Bill Latimer would care to hear from, given that she had been in the car with Quirke and Oscar Latimer that fateful morning on Howth Head, the morning when Oscar killed himself. She took a deep breath. "My name is Griffin," she said, "Phoebe Griffin."

"Will the Minister know who you are?" the secretary asked, sounding skeptical.

"Yes, I'm sure he will. Would you tell him I wish to speak to him urgently?"

"Oh, yes?" The voice on the other end of the line sounded more skeptical still. "May I ask what the matter is you wish to speak to him about?"

"His niece, April Latimer."

Silence, and then, "Please call back in an hour."

21

Phoebe entered the tea lounge in the Shelbourne Hotel and was shown to a small table below one of the three broad sash windows that looked out on to the railings of St. Stephen's Green on the other side of the road. A few other tables were occupied. The clientele here was composed mostly of weather-beaten, tweedy gentlemen and delicately preserved elderly ladies with skin like faded, rosy-pink parchment.

She ordered tea and cakes.

The soft spring rain had gathered its forces and started up yet again, and was gently graying the trees behind the black railings over there.

Phoebe was nervous, and kept smoothing a hand over the pair of calfskin gloves she had set down beside her on the table. She felt she was in a dream from which she couldn't wake. Before April's disappearance, the word "incest" had been for her no more than that—a word. The thing itself was something that happened in the Bible, or in the old sagas, not in her own time, not among people she knew. Then had come that day in Howth, in the car, when Oscar Latimer had undone the leather clasps and opened before her the big lurid book recording the childhood horrors that he and his sister had endured under their father's abusive rule. Now she didn't know what to think.

The waitress came with the tea tray. Authentically dented silver teapot, milk in a silver jug, a dainty pair of tongs for the sugar cubes, a folded linen napkin plump and white as a snow-drift. The little multicolored cakes were impossibly fiddly, and made her fingers sticky. She was sorry she had ordered them.

The Minister spotted her at once. He strode across the room and stopped by her table and stood looming over her.

"Are you going somewhere?" he demanded, in a tone of truc-ulent jocularity.

Phoebe was puzzled for a moment, then realized she hadn't taken off her street coat or even unbuttoned it.

"Oh, no, not at all," she said, flustered. Should she stand up to take off the coat? No, it would be too much fuss. She undid the buttons. "I hope you didn't mind my phoning," she went on, trying not to stammer. "I'm sure you must be very busy."

"I'm always very busy," he said curtly, and sat down opposite her on a small gilt chair that could hardly accommodate his bulk.

He was a big, forceful, impatient man with a thick shock of reddish hair and small, pale-blue, watchful eyes. There were broken veins in the skin over his cheekbones. He had a reputa-tion for ruthlessness and guile, but was regarded nevertheless as the most able figure in government, one of the "new men" who were reshaping the country. Her father considered him shallow and self-serving, and so did she.

"Bloody weather," he said, brushing at the speckles of rain on the shoulders of his heavy black overcoat, which he shrugged himself out of now and passed to the waitress hovering behind him, without looking at her. He wore a dark-blue three-piece suit, a white shirt and an emerald-green tie. Pinned in his lapel was a little gold ring, a *fáinne*, the badge by which he announced himself a fervent Irish-speaker. He sat down, plucking at the knees of his trousers. His bushy eyebrows were so pale they were almost invisible.

"Well, young lady," he said, with a feral grin, "what can I do for you?"

The waitress brought another cup. Latimer seized the teapot from Phoebe's tray and poured out tea for himself, ignoring Phoebe's own three-quarters-empty cup.

She opened her handbag and brought out a packet of Passing Cloud.

"What class of a yoke are they?" Latimer demanded disparagingly, as she selected a cigarette from the packet. "I never saw them in that shape before. Oval, by God! What next."

Phoebe clicked a little silver lighter into flame. She could clearly sense his disapproval of what she was doing—it wasn't respectable for girls to smoke in public. He brought out a packet of his own—Player's Navy Cut—and lit one.

"My father telephoned last night," Phoebe said. "From Spain."

"What's he doing there?" Latimer asked, with a derisive snort, as if the idea of anybody being abroad were inherently ridiculous. He selected one of the little cakes and popped it whole into his mouth and, munching, showed her again his awful grin.

This man's reputation as a bruiser was well known. All the Latimers had something of his bullish, mocking manner—even April had it, if in a less aggressive, or at least a more subtle, form. The men of the family, and some of the women, too, had fought in successive wars against the British. Now the British were gone and the Latimers and their like had taken over, and lost no opportunity to let everyone else know it.

Phoebe took a deep draw on her cigarette. She was angry at

herself, and was having a hard time not letting it show. She bitterly regretted having contacted this big, brash man, who had
swaggered in and sat now in complacent triumph among the
relics of an Anglo-Irish class that had been the rulers of his
country for centuries. She felt like a swimmer on a high diving
board whose nerve had failed.

"I'm told you've something to say to me about my poor unfortunate niece," Latimer said, picking up her napkin and using
it to wipe the cake crumbs from his fingers. "What has Dr.
Quirke to do with that?"

"My father," Phoebe said, her lungs contracting as she took
the plunge regardless, "my father believes he has seen April. In
Spain."

He stared at her, and blinked once, slowly. Then he licked his
lips and glanced quickly around the room. She was reminded,
disconcertingly, of Paul Viertel's way of casting a furtive glance
out of the window as he was quitting her flat.

"Christ almighty," Latimer breathed. "April—our April? Sure,
how could he have seen her?—she's dead this four year and
more." He did again his grin that wasn't a grin. "I'd say now,
my girl, your da must be dreaming."

22

Had his political hide been less tough, had his hold on the support of the party faithful been less strong, William Latimer would have suffered grievous professional damage from the successive tragedies that had befallen his family. In the latest of these, his nephew Oscar Latimer had confessed to the murder of his sister and then taken his own life. It would have been enough to destroy the career of a lesser figure. But Bill Latimer was not a man to be brought down by adversity.

The scandal had been contained, of course; that went without saying. The family had let it be known that poor Oscar, despite being the country's most respected obstetrician, was never quite right in the head, and on that terrible day had suffered some manner of a brainstorm—the word was his uncle's—and lost his reason entirely. And though he claimed to have done away with April, her body had never been found, so that the coroner had no choice but to close the case. It was all very sad and unfortunate, and best forgotten about as quickly as possible. The country had weightier matters to occupy its attention.

The Archbishop himself had attended Oscar's funeral, which was seen as the official wiping away of the taint of sin from Dr. Latimer's demise.

In the end, the Minister's political advisers, with their accustomed cunning and skill, had turned the whole incident to their boss's advantage, winning widespread sympathy for him as the survivor of a double tragedy, and showing up the fortitude of this scion of a legendary dynasty of patriots and revolutionaries, the living embodiments, for many, of Yeats's "indomitable Irishry."

Indeed, it could be said, Phoebe reflected, that the Minister had done well out of his family's woes. The Oscar business was only the latest in a series of misfortunes to have struck the house of Latimer. Hadn't this man's brother, Conor Latimer, the clan chieftain himself, also taken his own life, some years before, in a fit of noble despair? The country had failed him, it was said. The Ireland he had fought for was a shining dream that had given way to an ashen awakening, and it broke his heart. That was the legend. Few were aware of what Phoebe knew, that the late hero was the very one whose years-long abuse had blighted the lives of both of his children and led directly to the destruction of one of them, at least.

The Minister was watching her now through narrowed eyes, in each of which a spark of deep suspicion glinted—she thought of a weasel crouched in the corner of a yard and facing a pack of hunting dogs.

"Would it be the case, I wonder," he said, "that Dr. Quirke is back on the booze?" He smiled. "Sorry for asking."

He had adopted the voice he used on the hustings, the singsong, folksy tones of a doughty Connemara man, denizen of the

mountains of the far west. In fact, his family had been Dubliners
for generations.

"He was perfectly sober," Phoebe said, giving him a cold stare.
"He's certain the woman he met is your niece." The more dismissive this smugly smiling man became, the more convinced
she was that her father was right, that April was alive. "He saw
her, he met her, he spoke to her."

Latimer shrugged, making a ruminant's chewing motion with
his lower jaw. His eyelashes, like his eyebrows, were pale to the
point of translucence, which gave to his face a stark, raw aspect,
as if he had been exposed overlong to the elements and the sun
and the wind had left him bleached and bare.

"Has he confided his great discovery to anyone else?" he
asked.

"Of course not," Phoebe snapped.

Latimer sat back on his chair and eyed her coldly, still making that rotating grimace with his lower jaw.

"He's known to be a great talker, is Dr. Quirke," he said. "Especially from the bottom of a bottle." He signaled to the waitress. "A Jameson," he said to her, "and a glass of plain water on
the side."

Phoebe reached out and touched again the cool smooth stuff
of her gloves. She was surprised her hands weren't shaking.

Latimer fixed her with a bloodshot stare. For all his time
spent in the high places of public life, what he most closely resembled, she thought, was an irascible schoolmaster. He took
a swig of whiskey and shifted his heavy haunches on the little
bow-legged chair.

"It would be a very bad thing if April's mother was to hear of
this"—he paused a second—"this sighting, shall we say, of poor
April that your father claims to have made."

She studied him. All politicians were actors, more or less,
and William Latimer was a particularly skilled performer.
All the same, she wasn't convinced. He was playing the part

of the shocked uncle, yet he wasn't shocked—he wasn't even surprised—by what she had told him. He had known all along, she was suddenly convinced of it, that April was alive.

"I can assure you again, Dr. Latimer, my father wouldn't have spoken to anyone else about this."

Latimer gave a vague growl, glancing about the room again.

"And a good thing, too, for it's all wild stuff, anyway," he said, in a tone of vague rancor. His attention had lapsed, but still he was thinking hard. She could almost hear the weasel thoughts turning and turning in his brain. He gave her a soiled, sideways look now, his eyes narrowed again. "Wouldn't you say it's wild stuff?"

"No, I wouldn't," she answered. "My father is convinced."

"Anyway, I'd forget about it, if I was you," Latimer said, with what she clearly recognized as an edge of menace in his voice. "I'll have a word with Dr. Quirke when he gets back."

"Yes," she said, not sure what it was she was assenting to.

She had no doubts, any longer, none. April was alive, and this man knew it, for all his scoffing denials.

What had made April abandon everything and flee, letting everyone think she was dead? Had her family made her go, terrified of the scandal there would have been if word had got out about the child, the one she had aborted, hers and her brother's child? For that was the last, terrible secret Oscar had confided to Phoebe and her father that day in Howth, the secret of the child, April's impossible child, that April herself had aborted. And when it all went wrong, and April was dying, it was Oscar, the father of her child, who had found her, and saved her, and then, for reasons only he knew, pretended he had murdered her.

Yes, it must have been the family who forced her to flee to a new life elsewhere. Her uncle was in the government, he could easily have arranged it, could have got her false papers and found a place where she could live, in Spain, and a hospital where she could work.

But how did they persuade her? She had already cut herself off from her family—what sway would they have had over her? And her mother—would she have agreed to her daughter's banishment? What kind of mother would she be, to countenance such a thing? Maybe she wasn't allowed to be part of it, maybe she wasn't told. Maybe Bill Latimer and whoever else was involved had let the poor woman believe, like the rest of the world, that April was dead and lost to her forever.

She gazed at the man before her in a kind of slow amazement. Could even he have been so wicked, so cruel? She closed her eyes briefly. In her life she had seen enough of people to know what they were capable of.

But how strange it was to think, again, of April being somewhere, now, at this moment, doing something, going about her day, sitting in a café, or walking down a hospital corridor, or making love in a white room, her clothes thrown over the back of a chair and the sun striking through a louvered window above the bed. A thing that for years Phoebe had believed to be the case was not the case, and all at once the past, or a part of it as she had thought it to be, was undone.

Yes, she had loved April, had been in love with her, even, a little. She could admit to herself now what she couldn't have when she still thought April was dead.

She came back to herself with a start. Latimer was turning the whiskey glass in his fist and gazing into it with a frown. He was still thinking, calculating, scheming. He looked up suddenly and caught her eye.

"I'm trying to figure out what's the best thing to do," he said. "I suppose I will have to break the news to April's poor mother—if Quirke is right, that is, and April is alive, which I still don't believe."

"Maybe I shouldn't have told you."

"Aye, maybe you shouldn't."

Suddenly Phoebe felt a twinge of fear. He was right, she

should have kept quiet, or if she had to speak, she shouldn't have spoken to this man, of all people.

He brooded for a time, chewing on air, then burst out again, angrily. "I thought we were done for good with that bloody girl. She was nothing but heartache to her poor mother, and to the rest of us, from the time she got up out of the cradle and started to make trouble for us all. And of course, there was no talking to her—anything anybody said only made her dig her heels in deeper. To think of how her father treasured her—" He broke off, giving Phoebe a sharp, measuring glance. She saw him seeing from her look that she knew all too well the extent to which April's father had treasured his children. "Treated her like a princess, he did," he went on, challenging her to object, "and what return did she give him, only to scald his heart with her scandalous carrying-on? God forgive me for saying it, but she was a brazen bitch."

He set down his empty glass and squared his shoulders and sighed deeply. He had assumed the role now of a man regretting having allowed himself to be pushed beyond his better judgment by sorrow and righteous anger. Contempt for him rose in Phoebe's throat like bile.

"April was my friend," she said, lifting her chin and fixing him with a blank, cold gaze. "She still is."

23

Latimer ordered yet another whiskey. He was watching Phoebe with a speculative gleam. He was trying to calculate—she could see it plainly—the depth of her knowledge of his family's secrets, and how much April might have told her. She returned him an unflinching gaze. She was no longer afraid of him. In fact, she wondered if it might not be that he was afraid of her.

"How well did you know our April, would you say?" he asked, forcing himself to smile; she could see him struggling with it.

She shrugged. "How well is well?"

This angered him, and the smile disappeared; his brow flushed dark red and he clenched his fists in his lap. Oh, yes, he was dangerous.

"I'll thank you to keep a civil tongue in your head, my miss," he said quietly, making that grinding motion with his jaw again. "I didn't come here to get smart answers from the likes of you."

She was calm. It was easier to face up to him when he stopped pretending to be the hearty man of the world instead of the bully that he really was.

"April was my friend," she said again, simply. "I thought I knew her better than anyone did, but I realized afterward I must have been wrong, and that I didn't know her at all."

Latimer pounced. "Afterward? After she died?"

He was hunched forward, his head drawn down between his big shoulders.

"After she was supposed to have died, yes," Phoebe said evenly. "After she disappeared and left her friends no word of what had happened or why she had gone." She couldn't keep the bitterness out of her voice. "Because I knew in my heart she wasn't dead. I knew it."

Latimer shrugged. He had relaxed. She could see he had decided she wasn't the threat he had feared she would be. What of it, if her father had seen his niece alive? She was still far enough away to be as good as dead.

"Tell me, who, besides yourself, were these friends of hers?" he asked. "Was there a gang of them?"

"There was Jimmy Minor—"

"The reporter fellow, that was killed?"

"And Isabel Galloway."

He put his head back and flared his nostrils in disdain. "The actress one, from up at the Gate Theatre?" Now he grinned. "Wasn't she your father's—?" He made a pantomime show of interrupting himself. "Oh, pardon me, what shall I say? Didn't her and Dr. Quirke go out together, for a while?"

Phoebe knew better than to take him up on this.

"And Patrick Ojukwu," she went on.

This provoked a sour chuckle.

"The black lad, the Nigerian? I knew about him. He was

deported, as I recall." You would know it, she thought, since you were in the government then, too. Latimer shook his head, chuckling. "That's a fine crowd for her to be going around with. A showgirl, a scribbler for the papers, a buck nigger—"

"And me."

"And you," he said, with a kind of smirk. He looked her up and down with cold amusement, taking in her plain black dress with the white lace collar, her styleless hairstyle, her scuffed black handbag and sensible shoes. "You'd have been the odd one out, I'd say, among that gang."

He picked up his cup and poured tea from it into the saucer and lifted the saucer to his lips with both hands and drank, making slurping sounds. She watched him with distaste.

"That will be cold," she said.

"I'm used to it," he answered, sucking in another mouthful of the tea. "You should taste the stuff they serve us in that place over there"—he jerked his chin in the direction of Government Buildings—"'twould make a jennet blench."

He laughed. He had slipped again into his hustings voice, the one usually reserved for "his people." He put down the saucer, looking around the room to see who among the genteel clientele he had offended, and lit another cigarette.

"I really must go, Dr. Latimer," Phoebe said.

She felt dispirited suddenly. She wanted to be away from this terrible man. That morning she had received a letter from David Sinclair, her former boyfriend, who had left her when he emigrated to Israel. It had given her a jolt, to be unexpectedly addressed out of the past, and from so far away, farther even than Spain. Most of what David wrote was a bland account of his day-to-day doings, but the closing paragraph had deepened into something more unsettling.

You should reconsider and come over here. Life means something in Israel, and in every moment there is both danger and opportunity. We're building a country from the ground up. You would love it.

Reading that, she had smiled sourly. This wasn't how he had spoken when he was leaving her. Oh, yes, he had asked her to go with him, but she had known very well he didn't mean it.

The letter was signed, *Love, D.* She had read it twice, standing in the hall beside the big square table, then had gone back upstairs to the flat and sat by the window and read it again.

Danger and opportunity—what did he mean? Mortal danger, she supposed, the possibility of being killed at any moment—the country was menaced on all sides by hostile states and people seething with hatred—but what opportunity did he imagine he could offer her, out there in the desert?

She hadn't kept the letter. She had crushed it in her fist and thrown it into the kitchen bin. She wasn't angry. But she was puzzled that he should have chosen to write to her now, after all this time. It was four years since he had gone. He had been born in Ireland, and probably he was homesick, and feeling sorry for himself. Yet those words stayed in her mind: *danger, opportunity.* They were both troubling and alluring, like the "impure thoughts" the nuns in the convent used to warn about. Deep inside her there lurked always the urge to break free, to make a life elsewhere. As April had done.

She would go to San Sebastián, as Quirke had urged, and find there her beloved lost friend, brought miraculously back to life, like Hermione in the Shakespeare play she couldn't remember the title of. Despite all the horror and deceit, despite everything, a certain romance attached to April's tale.

Latimer summoned the waitress and ordered, this time, a glass of Guinness.

"I shouldn't," he said, giving the waitress a roguish wink, "but I've had a shock, so I have." He laughed, and coughed, and turned back to Phoebe. "And the dead arose and appeared to many, eh?"

Again he laughed. Phoebe gazed at him in fascination and disgust. His laughter wasn't laughter, but a kind of humorless crowing. How did such a man live with himself?

The waitress brought the glass of Guinness. Latimer's mood had shifted again. He was silent, brooding over his drink. Phoebe made a show of gathering up her gloves and her handbag, but the man seated opposite her seemed not to notice. His thoughts were again turned elsewhere.

"I used to take her to the zoo, you know, when she was little," he mused, rubbing at his chin. "She loved the elephants. She said they were like animals from another world. I can see her saying it—'creatures from another world, Uncle Bill'—in that funny little voice she had, so prim and proper. She was strange, even then, a strange little girl." He stopped, and regarded Phoebe with sudden malevolence. "I never knew about all that stuff, you know," he said harshly, "about my brother doing things to her and Oscar, or about the two of them, Oscar and herself, later on. I only found out about it long after. If I'd known, I'd have done something." He drank, and sighed. "Oh, Lord, what a terrible tragedy."

She eyed him with a shiver of disgust. She knew that lachrymose stoop, the droop of the eye, the sad shake of the head. Her father had made a way of life out of feeling sorry for himself.

"If April is alive," she said, "and I'm convinced she is, then her going away must have been to do with her brother, and her father, and what they did to her—all that 'terrible tragedy,' as you call it."

Latimer gave her a quick, sharp glance. He could see she had the measure of him, and he didn't like it.

"If she is alive, after all this time," he said, "I'll have a thing or two to say to her, when I see her."

"Are you intending to go down there, to Spain?" she asked, unable to keep the note of alarm out of her voice.

He shook his head. "Too much on here—there's an election threatened, God help us." He grinned bleakly, showing a set of surprisingly small, even teeth. "I'll get on to the ambassador, or the consul, or whoever. I imagine we have someone to

represent us there, in—what do they call it? The Basque coun-
try? Though what I'm supposed to ask him to do I don't know.
I suppose he should get in touch with Dr. Quirke, for a start.
Where is he staying?"

She was instantly wary.

"At a rather grand hotel, I believe," she said, purposely vague.
"On the seafront, somewhere."

"Aye, he does himself well, your da."

He finished his drink and stood up. She caught a whiff of
his flattish, slightly sour odor—it was the smell of a man who
had spent too many hours in smoke-filled committee rooms,
and who didn't send his suits to the dry cleaners often enough.

"If your father calls again, let me know," he said, thrusting his
arms into the overcoat the waitress was holding up behind him.

"Yes, I will," Phoebe said.

She was lying. She wanted no more dealings with William
Latimer.

When he had gone, the waitress looked at her timidly, showing her the bill.

"He forgot to pay for the drink," she said.

24

Terry Tice checked himself into a kip on Gardiner Street that grandly called itself the Gardiner Arms. He could have afforded something better. It wasn't a question of money—he had plenty of that, from the jobs Percy had put his way during the six months they knew each other. But he might attract attention to himself if he put up at the Gresham or the Shelbourne. Stick among your own, Reggie Kray used to say, it's the best camouflage there is. Reggie should have heeded his own advice, instead of mixing with the toffs. A great snob, was Reggie.

The old guy behind the desk in the Gardiner Arms had the look of a walrus, with fat shoulders and a sloped back and a tired mustache drooping at the tips. He was almost entirely bald, yet there was dandruff on the collar of his greasy uniform. He shoved the register across the desk and watched with indifference as Terry signed his name. He said there would be a five-quid deposit, and swiveled a slack-lidded eye in the direction of Terry's expensive suitcase—pigskin, Harrods—but made no comment. A cigarette with an inch of ash at the end of it was stuck in the corner of his mouth. He didn't take it out even when he was talking—which he didn't do much of—and the ash stayed in place. Well, everybody has a skill, Terry reflected.

In a good mood, he was. Nice and relaxed. Yet he had a feeling, too, of—what was it? Expectation, it seemed to be. But expectation of what? A few days in Dublin wasn't that exciting a prospect.

His room, on the first floor, looked down into a yard with dustbins in it. A mangy cat with orange fur sat on top of a soot-blackened brick wall, flicking its tail. There had been rain earlier but it was stopped now, and the day was blustery, with high clouds scudding across a clear blue sky. Spring. That must be why he had that fizzy feeling. On days like this, something always seemed about to happen. Something good.

He washed his face at the tiny sink in a corner of the room, wondering how many traveling salesmen had pissed in it over the years. Then he changed out of his suit into a navy-blue blazer with brass buttons, and fawn slacks with a crease you could cut your finger on. The black shoes he had been wearing wouldn't go with the light-colored trousers, so he put on a pair of brown leather casuals with gold buckles on the insteps. Penny loafers, Americans called them. He wondered why. He had always been a sharp dresser, since he started earning real money and could afford decent clobber. He took his shortie overcoat from the hook on the back of the door, but instead of putting his arms into it he draped it over his shoulders, for the casual Parisian look. He surveyed himself in the full-length mirror in the door of the wardrobe. Someone had said he looked a bit like Tommy Steele. He couldn't see it, himself. More the Frank Sinatra type, he would have thought. Frankie was a short guy, too.

He walked up to O'Connell Street and had a gander at Nelson's Pillar. It wasn't as tall as the one in Trafalgar Square, or at least it didn't seem so to him.

It was a long time since Terry had been in Dublin. The orphanage he had spent his childhood in was way over in the west, in a place called Carricklea. A couple of times a year he and half a dozen others would be brought to the city on the train for a treat, accompanied by one of the Brothers—Harkness, usually, the biggest bastard in the place.

Those were the days, Terry thought bitterly. Oh, aye, those were the days. He'd got so sick of it all he tried to cut his throat. Made a botch of it, of course. Blood everywhere. A week in the infirmary with a bandaged throat, and on the day he got out, Harkness took him around behind the boiler house and beat the shit out of him.

He crossed the road to see if the ice-cream parlor from the old days was still there. It was. The Palm Grove. It looked smaller and drabber than he remembered. Harkness would leave him and the others there for an hour and take himself across the street to Wynn's Hotel. There were always priests or Christian Brothers there to drink whiskey with and talk about whatever it was the buggers talked about. Wynn's was the place the clergy went to, their exclusive watering hole. The booze didn't cheer up Harkness; in fact, it made him even more surly and vengeful than—

Stop! Terry told himself. Stop thinking about it—Carricklea, and Harkness, the bruises under his eyes, the blood on the bathroom tiles, all of it. That was then, this was now. He had five crisp tenners in his wallet, and another wad back at the hotel, sewn into the lining of his suitcase. He looked spiffy in his blazer and his buckled shoes. He was young, he was cocky and he was a killer. And he had no Harknesses to bully and bugger him anymore.

He couldn't keep himself from wondering if he might still be around, Harkness. He hadn't been that old. Be nice to meet up with him by accident down a dark lane some night. That would call for the knife, no question, a bullet would be too quick. Yes, a job for the shiv, nice and slow.

He had contacts in the city, he might look them up. There was a fellow who bought and sold horses in Smithfield. What was his name? Connors, that was it. Joey Connors. A tinker, of course, all the Connorses were tinkers, but Terry didn't hold that against him. And there was a London bloke who'd legged it over here after a bank job went wrong and had never gone back. Ran a pub, the Hangman, up the river by Kingsbridge railway station. It was a rackety place, that place. A lot of queers went there, on the lookout for rough trade. Plenty of that available at the Hangman. That wouldn't put Terry off.

One thing you could say for queers, they livened things up. Some of them were funny, a real scream, when they weren't too busy trying to feel your leg or get a hand on your arse. The one time he was there he had amused himself by sending out false signals, and when anyone approached him he put on his special stare that made people turn white and back away as if they'd just seen their granny's ghost.

The Hangman would be the place to get himself a replacement gun.

It had broken his heart to get rid of the Colt, but it had to be done. He had abandoned his plan to bring it here and give it a decent burial on some heather-clad hillside. Too risky, smuggling a piece through customs. An hour out from Holyhead he had gone on deck when no one was around and let it slip down the side of the boat, the way he had let what was left of Percy slide into the Pool of London. If it made a splash, he didn't hear it. Just when he was letting go of it, a seagull came sweeping out of the twilight and passed him by so close he had felt the swish of its wings. Huge bloody thing it was, and gave him a fright, too. He wasn't superstitious, but still.

Now he couldn't get the image out of his head of that sweet little weapon half-sunk in the sand at the bottom of the Irish Sea.

A Belfast bloke he had met in one of the Soho clubs had given him the name of a fellow here who dealt in the kind of hardware he was looking for. Lenny something was the fellow's name—Terry had the information written down on the back of an envelope at the hotel, his full name and a telephone number where he could be contacted. He would go back in a while and give him a call, arrange a meeting at the Hangman, for old times' sake, if the place was still there. But first he felt like a drink.

He wandered over to Wynn's—this was turning into a right old stroll down memory lane—and sat in the front bar and ordered a pint of bitter. The barman wore a crisp white shirt, dicky bow and tartan waistcoat. Terry liked the people serving him to be properly dressed. This fellow was no genius, though. Didn't know what pale ale was.

"Pale ale?" Terry said, with a disbelieving laugh. "It's beer. Whitbread. Fuller's London Pride."

The lummox nodded and grinned, but still couldn't understand. Terry was beginning to have serious doubts about Dublin. Maybe he should have gone to the Isle of Man, or Jersey, or somewhere like that—Canada, even. He had the funds, he could have gone anywhere, but home sweet home had called to him. He grinned to himself. Home—this place? Nowhere was home. Footloose and fancy-free, the world his oyster, that was how he liked to keep it.

In the end, he settled for a half-pint of Smithwick's. It had a soapy taste, but it was ale, and it was pale. He lit a Capstan, and looked around the bar. Lots of mahogany and brass—the usual. Reminded him of a place near the Seven Dials, out the back of which one night he had shot a fellow in the face. A gyppo, he was, and had been putting the squeeze on one of Percy's pansy friends. Nice quiet pub, though, decent clientele, not your usual crowd of spivs and five-bob tarts. Pity he wouldn't see it again, not from the inside. He would never go back into a place where he'd done a job. It was another one of his rules.

Two priests were sitting at the far end of the bar, each with a tumbler of whiskey in his fist. No change here, then. Red-faced, well-fed and half-crocked already. He thought again of Brother Harkness, but made himself stop. Didn't want that curtain of red mist coming down again inside his head. Shooting priests was frowned on, over here. Anyway, no gun, remember? Felt half-naked, he did, without a piece in his pocket.

He left the beer half-finished and got down from the bar stool and put on his coat. No sooner was he in the street than a shower of rain started up, fat drops spattering on the pavement like flung handfuls of coins. He stopped and took shelter in a shop doorway. Rain wasn't good for his shoes, or his lightweight overcoat, which had cost him twenty guineas in Harrods. Had cost Percy, actually.

Poor old Percy. Free with his money, he was, when the mood took him. A regular fairy godmother. Terry cackled softly. That was a good one. An image popped up in his mind of Percy in a little red flouncy skirt and a sparkly tiara, fluttering in midair and waving a magic wand.

Then, suddenly, his mood darkened. What was he doing here, in this gray, godforsaken, rained-on city? He leaned his head out of the doorway and peered up. The clouds were breaking, and a blue sky was shining through in ragged, pale patches. He would call the fellow about the gun, tell him to meet him in the Hangman, do the business and head back to the Smoke. What if Percy's body had been found by now? There was nothing to tie him to the killing. He didn't exist, as far as the rozzers' records were concerned. He was the Invisible Man, was Terry.

He turned up the collar of his coat and set off in the direction of Gardiner Street. To hell with the shoes—they could look after themselves, or he could buy another pair, or go barefoot.

Go barefoot? Sometimes the weirdest notions came into his

head. He pictured himself, walking along this city street, in his expensive coat and natty slacks, his hair wet and nothing on his feet. No shoes, no socks, just those two pale, blue-veined things flapping along at the ends of his legs like some sort of sea creatures dragged up out of the deep. But why not? Who was to stop him? If people laughed at him, he would plug them on the spot, without a moment's hesitation.

Except that—yes, yes, all right!—he hadn't got a gun.

He wondered what Percy's feet were like by now, and his hands, and his pouchy old face. He'd look like a sack of corn tied around the middle with a rope, bulging and sort of shiny and ready to burst. Terry had seen drowned corpses. Terry had seen a lot of things.

In the hotel, he shook off his coat and hung it on a hanger over the bath, then toweled his hair dry and combed it carefully. He avoided meeting his eye in the mirror. In mirrors you couldn't hide from yourself, no matter what sort of face you put on. He thought it must be something to do with your reflection being reversed. Once, in a Mayfair restaurant—Percy's treat, needless to say—he had been seated facing a corner where two glass walls met at right angles, so that somehow he was able to see his face the right way around. Some shock that was. Hardly recognized himself. His eyes were all at the wrong level, his nose was crooked and his mouth looked as if he'd had a stroke. Left him feeling queer for days. It was as if there was someone else, the man in the mirror, still lurking inside him.

There was no telephone in the room, of course, so he had to go downstairs and squeeze himself into the wooden booth opposite the reception desk. The air inside was thick and musty, as he imagined the air in jail would be, and smelled of cigarette smoke and sweat. He took up the receiver and wiped the mouthpiece carefully with his handkerchief. Teeming with germs, telephones. The pennies jangled as they dropped into the box.

"This is Mr. Percy," he said—it was the first name that came into his head. "Mutual friend gave me your name. I need to order an item of hardware." He waited, listening. "What? That's right, an indoor model."

His mind wandered back yet again to thoughts of the late Mr. Percy Antrobus, Esq. He had never given much consideration to the old boy, not really, but now, when it was too late, his head was full of him.

Who was Percy, exactly, and more to the point, what was he? He claimed to have fought in the war, in some hush-hush outfit. "Special ops," he would say, letting one eyelid fall shut like a window blind and tapping a finger to the side of his nose. One night in his cups he told Terry all about a German sentry he had killed with his bare hands—that was how he said it, "with my bare hands," widening his watery eyes and nodding solemnly. From the way he spoke, Terry could tell he was making it up. Terry knew all about killing, how it looked, what it felt like— how it smelled, too. And he knew Percy had never killed anyone. The next day, when Terry pressed him, he had admitted it, with a giggle. All made up, the terrified look in the Jerry's eyes, how he called for his *Mutti* and pissed in his pants—the whole bleeding thing. Terry was disgusted.

See? Everybody wants to be a tough guy, even pudgy old Percy.

The fellow on the phone agreed to meet that night in the Hangman. Said he'd bring the gadget with him. Thirty quid, no questions asked. Terry got him down to twenty-five.

"No, not for anything in particular," he said. "I just like to keep one on me, in case someone needs a ventilation job done."

That had given them both a chuckle.

25

Phoebe was furious at herself. What had possessed her to go to William Latimer, him of all people, and tell him about Quirke's phone call? She felt shaken, and when she lit a cigarette her hands were shaking so much she could hardly keep the match flame alight. After paying for the tea, and for Latimer's drinks, she had fled the Shelbourne and come to the Country Shop, which was nearby—she needed somewhere quiet to sit and think. She hurried down the basement steps and into the café and went straight to her usual corner table.

She had a fluttery sensation in her chest, as if dozens of butterflies were trapped in there and panicking.

The plump waitress with a wen at the side of her nose gave her a friendly smile. A lapel badge said her name was Rosita, which seemed unlikely—she didn't look at all like a Rosita,

Phoebe thought. She had worked here at the Country Shop for longer than Phoebe could remember—certainly since the days when she and Jimmy Minor used to meet here. Jimmy had been a born newspaperman, a newshound to the tips of his correspondent shoes, as he used to say. Jimmy was a great moviegoer, and knew how they talked in the pictures—though she suspected he had never even seen a pair of correspondent shoes. A story he was following, that involved Quirke, as it happened, had been the death of him. Phoebe remembered the day, remembered the very moment, when she heard that his body had been found floating in the canal at Leeson Street Bridge. He had been beaten to death and thrown into the water, like a dog, she had thought at the time. Like a dog.

Now for a moment she closed her eyes, steadying herself. She had known too much violence in her life. It was because of Quirke, because of being his daughter. He was a good man but a carrier of wickedness, like Typhoid Mary.

"Are you all right?" the waitress asked solicitously.

"What?" Phoebe said, lifting her eyes to the girl's kindly face. She made herself smile. "Oh, yes, yes, I'm fine. Thank you."

She looked around the room. She had come here with April, too, a few times. But the Country Shop, the clientele of which consisted almost exclusively of housewives up from the country to do a day's shopping, was far too dull for the likes of April—if there was anyone like April, which Phoebe was inclined to doubt.

Spain, though, Spain would suit April. Surely that country would be lively enough even for her, with its bullfights and its flamenco dancers. People used to say of April that she was "wild." Had she been tamed by now?

The tea at the Shelbourne had been straw-pale, but here it was the color of only slightly diluted molasses. Phoebe wasn't sure she should drink it. Didn't they say tea had more caffeine in it than coffee? A stimulant was the last thing she needed, she was so agitated already. All the same, the tremor in her hands had stopped, and the butterflies in her stomach had begun to fold their wings.

A thought came to her. Quirke's friend Hackett, Detective Chief Superintendent Hackett—he was the one she should have called on, not William Latimer. Why hadn't she thought of him? It was he who had led the investigation into April's disappearance. When weeks passed and her body wasn't found he had shut down the case, no doubt with relief. He would surely have been glad to be free of the Latimers. They were the kind of people, powerful and dangerous, a policeman would wish to avoid.

She smoked a cigarette, then stood up, and paid for the tea and for the bun she had eaten only half of, and climbed the steps into daylight. She crossed the road to a telephone box that stood under the shade of a chestnut tree. She had no more pennies, however, and had to go back to the café and ask the friendly waitress for change of a sixpence. The waitress, counting out the coins from the till, blushed scarlet and suddenly said, "It's lovely to see you in here again, after so long."

Phoebe was startled. But yes, it was a long time now since she had been here, with Jimmy Minor, with April, even with Isabel Galloway, though Isabel was a night bird and often didn't get up until the middle of the afternoon, and hence preferred the Shakespeare or the Bailey. Goodness, how long ago was it? They seemed so simple now, those days, simple and innocent, when she looked back on them.

"I'm not around these parts much, nowadays," she said to the waitress, slipping the pennies into her purse.

But why had she said that? She lived in Baggot Street, and was around these parts all the time.

The waitress smiled again. How kind people could be, and yet young men got beaten to death and disposed of like dogs, and young women were abused by their families and forced to flee abroad. Phoebe smiled, and bit her lip. It was hard to think of April Latimer being forced to do anything she didn't want to do.

She hurried across the road, and stepped into the phone box again, and dialed the operator and asked to be put through to Pearse Street Garda station.

Hackett's voice reminded her of the tea in the café, strong, brown, warm and bittersweet. She found herself smiling again, into the receiver.

"Miss Phoebe!" the detective exclaimed. "Is it yourself?" It amused him to exaggerate his Leitrim accent when he spoke to her, playing the country hick that he wasn't. "And what can I do for you, at all?"

She told him of Quirke's telephone call, and of her encounter with William Latimer. Hackett was silent for a good ten seconds. She could almost hear him thinking.

"I'm sorry," she said, "I hope I haven't—"

"Come down here to the station, will you?" he said, shifting to his official voice. "I'll tell them at the desk to expect you. Just tell them your name and they'll let you through."

He hung up without saying goodbye.

Phoebe stood for some moments with the receiver in her hand, listening to the disengaged tone and frowning through the small square panes of the phone box into a tangled clump of greenery behind the railings of the square. She felt let down. It was plain, from the way his tone of voice had altered, that Hackett was no more pleased with the possibility of April being alive and living in Spain than William Latimer had been.

She felt as if she were stumbling through a barrier of thickets and thorns. She shouldn't have called Hackett, any more than she should have called William Latimer. But then, maybe Quirke shouldn't have called her, in the first place. Maybe the dead were better left in peace—even if they weren't dead, but had chosen to seem so. After all, just how delighted had Lazarus's family been, after Jesus restored him to life and he came home rubbing his hands and shouting for his dinner?

The afternoon light had turned to a shade of pearly gray, and above the trees big heavy silver clouds were trundling across the sky. Before leaving the phone box she fixed a hat pin in her hat to keep it from flying away. Everything seemed to be in motion, and nothing seemed content to stay still. The world itself was suddenly volatile.

26

She went along pensively by the black railings. She was in no hurry. Shaken by her confrontation with Bill Latimer, she was chary of another possibly troublesome encounter, even though it was she who had just now requested it. Chief Superintendent Hackett, for all his appearance of avuncular good cheer, could be unpredictable.

As she walked, she ran her fingertips along the railings beside her. Their ancient paint was pitted and shiny, like wet coal. The spring wind shook the boughs of a sycamore tree above her and sprinkled her with a flurry of drops, which made her think of funerals, and the priest dipping the little drumstick-shaped silver thing into the container of holy water and shaking it over the coffin. She had long ago given up religion, and hadn't been to Mass since—oh, she couldn't remember when. All that seemed so far off now, the ceremonial and the sacraments, the Communion of Saints, the kneeling and praying and repenting. The only part of it she had ever really believed in, as a child, was the doctrine of Hell. Since then, she had seen enough of mortal life to know that we do not need to wait for the hereafter to have our fill of horrors.

On Grafton Street, her attention was caught by a slight, narrow-faced young man standing outside the Eblana Bookshop, surveying the books on show in the window with a bitterly contemptuous half-smile. He wore a pale-colored neat little overcoat with all the buttons done up, well-pressed fawn trousers, the legs of which hardly reached below his ankles, and light-brown loafers with gilt buckles. There was something about him, she didn't know what—perhaps it was those buckles, or the sharp creases in his trousers—that provoked in her a sudden, brief outrush of pity. He looked so cocksure, standing there sneering at the display of books he would never read, that her heart went out to him. It was plain he wasn't what he imagined himself to be, and didn't dream the rest of the world only had to look at him to know it.

When she got to Pearse Street Garda barracks she stopped, as she always did, to look up at the miniature stone models of policemen's heads set into the mortar above the doorway. They were from the old days, under British rule, and were supposed to represent vigilance and stern resolution, as they peered off frowningly to right and left. They were, in truth, too small and too naively fashioned to be anything other than endearing and faintly comical.

She gave her name to the desk sergeant, as she had been instructed, and he lifted the flap in the counter and waved her through.

Hackett's office was on the top floor. It was cramped and wedge-shaped, with a window at the narrow end that gave on to a view of steeply slanted rooftops and grimy dormer windows.

The detective sat behind his cluttered desk with his back to the window. The air in the room was blue with cigarette smoke. His hat hung on a nail in the wall, beside a flyblown calendar that was a dozen years out of date. The rank of Chief Superintendent was a recent promotion, which he had accepted reluctantly and with bad grace, to the surprise and annoyance of his superiors. He had protested that he was perfectly happy as he was, but in the end had agreed to the new position, on condition that he could keep his old, pokey little office, where for so many years he had been happily perched, like a sailor in the crow's nest.

He rose to greet her, giving her his wide-mouthed, froggy smile. She noticed flecks of gray at his temples, but otherwise he seemed not to have changed at all since she had last seen him— four years ago, was it? His shiny blue suit looked very like the one he used to wear then. The tie seemed the same, too. Across the top of his forehead there was a hat-wearer's narrow band of babyishly pale skin. It pleased her, more than she would have expected, to find him much as she remembered him.

"Sit down, sit down," he said, shuffling his feet and doing his snuffly chuckle. "I'd offer you a cigarette, except I suppose you still smoke those fancy ones that you used to." He pressed a bell push on the corner of his desk. "Will you have a cup of tea? Nice cup of Garda barracks 'tay'?"

"Yes, that would be lovely." She smiled, and groaned inwardly. More tea.

"Did you get drenched, on your way here?" he inquired solicitously.

"It's not raining."

"Is it not? It was, a minute ago." He turned about in his chair with a grunt and looked out of the window. "April," he said, the name giving Phoebe a start, until she realized it was the month and not her missing friend he was speaking of. He went on, "An undependable time of year—you wouldn't know what it's going to do," and she understood her mistake. Her nerves were so much on edge that everything seemed a sign or portent. Hackett turned back from the window. "Tell me," he said, "how is that father of yours, at all? I haven't spoken to him since I don't know when."

"He's very well. He's married—did you know?"

"So I heard, indeed. He sent an invitation to the wedding, to me and the missus. Very thoughtful, very kind."

"But you didn't go."

"No, no. Too busy, altogether."

"Ah. I see."

She was sorry she had asked. He fiddled with a stack of papers on the desk. He was shy of social occasions. Quirke's wedding he would have considered altogether too grand an affair for the likes of him. Hackett and his missus—a famously elusive entity—kept themselves to themselves.

"Mind you, I do miss seeing him around, the bold Dr. Quirke," the detective went on. "We used to have the odd drink together, in the old days."

They were silent, both thinking of "the old days." They had always been easy in each other's company, or almost always. Hackett leaned back on his chair. He shifted his legs under the desk and his boots squeaked.

"So," he said, "you tell me Dr. Quirke believes he spotted the late Miss Latimer down in Spain somewhere?"

"Yes. In San Sebastián. It's in the north. Maybe you—?" She stopped herself, and winced.

"No," he said blandly, "no, I've only ever been to the south. Málaga. Maybe you—?" Now she smiled. Touché! "And what," he went on, "was she doing with herself, down there, the ghostly girl?"

He was regarding her with a skeptical twinkle.

"She's working in a hospital," Phoebe said, a shade too loudly, conscious of sounding defensive. "That's to say"—she hesitated—

"the person my father met is a hospital doctor. He cut his hand and had to have it stitched. She—April, or whoever—treated him. In fact, she didn't, in the end—treat him, I mean. Someone else did—another doctor."

She touched a hand to her forehead.

"I see," Hackett said, though plainly he didn't see at all. He was taking none of this seriously, or seemed not to be, at least—one could never tell, with Hackett. All at once her confidence deserted her, and she felt foolish.

There was a tap at the door, and a uniformed Garda entered. He was young and ungainly, with big hands and bigger feet. Hackett eyed him darkly.

"You took your time," he said. "We'll have a pot of tea, and a plate of ginger snaps." The young man bobbed his long, large-eared head apologetically, and withdrew. As he was shutting the door, he gave Phoebe a quick glance and shyly smiled. Hackett, watching him go, clicked his tongue. "I don't know where they're getting them from these days," he said darkly. "Straight out of the cradle, it seems like."

Phoebe looked past him through the window to the airy view outside. Sunshine and cloud-shadow chased each other across the rooftops.

Hackett brought out a packet of Gold Flake. "Do you mind?" he asked.

"Please, go ahead."

The detective struck a match and lit the cigarette and inhaled deeply. Phoebe thought of lighting one of her own "fancy ones," but didn't.

"How did he sound, your father?" the detective asked, lifting his eyebrows and scanning various objects on his desk, pretending to be shortsighted. She had the impression he was trying not to laugh.

"Do you mean, was he drunk?" she asked. "No, he wasn't—

at least, not drunk drunk. He doesn't do that anymore, since he married."

"A reformed man, then."

She smiled. Hackett's raillery was never more than mild.

"He's quite convinced, you know," Phoebe said, "that the woman he met at the hospital was April Latimer. He's sure of it."

Hackett nodded, still looking down, still with his eyebrows lifted.

"What name is she going under?"

"Angela Lawless. I think it was the coincidence of the initials that struck him first."

"The initials?"

"A. L.—Angela Lawless, April Latimer."

"Ah. I see." Hackett was nodding. "That would be a coincidence, all right." He rolled the tip of his cigarette on the edge of a tin ashtray, and cleared his throat. "There must be a lot of people in the world with the same initials. Alvar Liddell. Annie Laurie."

She knew he was teasing her. Behind him, on the window ledge outside, a seagull alighted and folded its wings, bobbing its head in that peculiar way gulls did, as if it had something stuck in its gullet.

"Dr. Quirke must have known your friend already, then," Hackett said, with a tone of dreamy mildness, contemplating again the objects on the desk before him.

"Yes, he saw her with me," she said, and she, too, looked down. "We were leaving the Shelbourne one evening, April and I. It was getting dark. My—my father was coming in. We didn't speak. He was—"

Hackett waited, stroking his lower lip with a thumb and forefinger.

"A bit under the weather?" he gently suggested.

"Yes." She clicked open the clasp of her handbag and clicked it shut again. "I believe he's right, you know," she said. "I believe it was April he met."

"I see," Hackett said. He straightened an untidy pile of papers on the desk, then extracted another cigarette from the packet, but noticed the half-smoked one he had set down on the edge of the tin ashtray. He sighed.

"You've put me in a pickle, Miss Griffin," he said. "What you're telling me is 'mere conjecture,' as the barristers like to say."

"I know," Phoebe said, "I know." She unclasped her handbag again and this time took out her cigarette case. Hackett advanced the box of matches, pushing it along the desk with the tip of a finger. "You know, I never really believed she was dead, and when my father said he had seen her, it was like a light going on inside my head. *Of course*, I thought, *of course it's her, it has to be.*"

Hackett, his face half-turned away, was watching her aslant. His gaze was the same as that of the bird outside on the windowsill, at once blank and measuring.

"But her brother confessed that he had killed his sister—"

"Yes, but—"

"—and that he had buried her body in a place where it would never be found. Isn't that so?"

"That's what he said, yes. But he wasn't in his right mind. It was all a fantasy, don't you see? The poor man was sick in the head. A minute after confessing, he drove the car over the side of a cliff into the sea and drowned himself."

"But since he knew he was going to do that, why would he tell you lies about having murdered her?"

"It's what I've said—he was mad."

Hackett flicked ash from his cigarette toward the ashtray, and missed.

"Would even a madman make up something so outlandish?"

"Of course he would. That's what being mad is, you imagine mad things and think they really happened."

At that moment there came another tentative tap at the door, and the tall young Garda entered, bearing a tray with tea things and a plate of biscuits. With his forearm, Hackett swept aside the jumble of papers on his desk, half of them tumbling onto the floor. The Garda set down the tray and made a hasty retreat, not risking a glance at Phoebe this time.

"Will I be mother?" Hackett said.

He poured the tea, and leaned far back on his chair, cradling the cup and saucer on the ledge of his little high round belly. Phoebe took a sip from her cup. The tea was lukewarm, and tasted like leather. If Hackett managed to spill it on himself, at least it wouldn't scald him.

"But would she go off like that, without a word to anyone?" he said.

Phoebe looked past him again to the window. The seagull had departed without her noticing. Raindrops pattered against the glass, though the sun was shining. She had never understood the fuss people made about springtime. For her it was the season of ill-content, of unassuageable agitations. In this, as in other things, she knew herself to be her father's daughter.

"He asked if I would come down to Spain," she said.

Hackett let the front legs of his chair fall forward and himself along with them, still managing not to spill the tea. He stared at her. "What for?"

"Well, to verify that it is April."

Hackett set the cup and saucer on the desk before him with slow deliberation.

"And will you go?" he asked.

She pretended to consider. She had already made up her mind. Though Quirke had offered to buy her an air ticket, she would pay for it herself. She always paid for herself. She had her own money, left to her by her grandfather. She had spent hardly a penny of it. It sat in the bank, increasing year by year. She never thought about it, sometimes forgot it was there. It was only money, and besides, it was tainted with the darkness of the time out of which it had come to her.

She straightened her back, and held her head upright. "I will go, yes," she said.

Chief Superintendent Hackett hooked his thumbs in the pockets of his waistcoat and rocked himself back and forth slowly, with his lips stuck out. The rain flung a final handful of drops against the window and abruptly ceased. The shadow of another cloud skimmed the rooftops, swift as a bird. Phoebe put the cigarette case into her handbag and made to rise. Hackett lifted a hand.

"Hang on there a second," he said. He picked up the receiver of the big black phone on his desk, dialed a single digit, waited. "Hello, Strafford? Come up here a minute, will you? Yes, now. What?" He winked at Phoebe. "You're going to go on a little holiday. What?" He winked again, enjoying himself. "Abroad, my lad. Abroad."

27

Detective Inspector Strafford entered the room and closed the door gently behind him. His manner was abstracted, as if he had wandered in by accident and hadn't quite realized yet where he was. Phoebe regarded him with candid interest. He was thin to the point of gauntness, with pale, bony wrists and peculiar, pale soft hair. His face was so narrow it seemed that if he turned sideways it would collapse into two dimensions and become a fine, straight line. He wore a three-piece tweed suit. The chain of a fob watch was looped across his concave midriff. He didn't look in the least like a policeman. He might have been a university don, or an unfrocked priest.

Hackett introduced him. "And this is Miss Phoebe Griffin."

Strafford's handshake was unexpectedly firm, and his hand

was smooth and cool. Phoebe couldn't begin to guess his age—he could be anywhere between twenty-five and fifty.

"Miss Griffin," he said. "How do you do?"

His accent was another small surprise. Protestant, Phoebe knew at once, landed gentry, though come down in the world—why else would he have joined the Garda? Hackett was watching her with eager amusement.

"You'll no doubt know her father," he said to Strafford. "Dr. Quirke, State Pathologist—he used to be at the Hospital of the Holy Family."

"Ah, yes," Strafford murmured, nodding. "Dr. Quirke. Yes, of course."

Phoebe saw him glancing at her left hand, looking for a ring, no doubt, on the third finger. Women often did that, men rarely. Since she was Quirke's daughter, no doubt he was puzzled by her surname. She wondered if she would get to the stage, always a delicate one, when it would be appropriate to explain to him why she was called Griffin and not Quirke. She rather hoped so. She liked the look of this oddly emaciated, diffident man, with his slight stoop and lean face and pale-gray eyes. An image came to her mind of the two of them together in the Shelbourne Hotel, sitting over drinks at a table by the windows in the lounge, her speaking and him listening, while the sunlight inched across the floor, and the trees on the far side of the street leaned down as if to catch what she was saying.

She blinked, and drew herself upright on the chair, and straightened her shoulders. She didn't often indulge in daydreams. She thought of Paul, and what she saw was his neat little lightweight suitcase.

There was no chair for Strafford, so he leaned against the wall beside the empty fireplace, with an elbow on the mantelpiece and the fingers of both hands laced together and his ankles crossed. She noticed his shoes, and looked more closely at his suit. These items hadn't been bought on a detective inspector's salary. Old money, then, though not a lot of it—the suit was close to threadbare.

Hackett was still rocking himself back and forth on his chair, almost hugging himself, delighted with everything, it would seem, with Phoebe and her sudden alertness, with the singular creature leaning at the fireplace, with himself, even. His granny had been the village matchmaker.

"Miss Griffin is going down to Spain," he said, "and is in need of an escort."

Afterward, she was surprised at herself that she had fallen in so readily with Hackett's devious plan. He had been so brisk and practical-sounding that it had seemed the most natural thing in the world that she and this detective should travel together to Spain. There were questions that might have occurred to her, for instance as to what Paul Viertel would have to say about it, but they didn't. Or if they did, she ignored them. She hadn't realized how fiercely she had been longing for something to happen in her life, for something to change.

She left the Garda station in a state of not unpleasant confusion. She was about to embark on a probably foolhardy and potentially disastrous adventure. All the same, an adventure it would be. When was the last time she had felt such a buzz of excited anticipation?

Then she stopped, struck by an obvious, and awkward, possibility. What if Paul were to offer to come with her? She saw herself sitting on a plane with her boyfriend on one side of her and Detective Inspector Strafford on the other. It was a prospect at once dismaying and ridiculous, a scene out of a farce. But then, wasn't there a touch of farce to the thing in general? Certainly, there would have been, if it weren't literally a matter of life and death—of life *or* death. The thought of April brought a pang of guilt. She had quite forgotten about her.

In Westmoreland Street, the pavements were drying in big

gray patches. For her, the smell of spring rain always brought with it a sense of vague yearning. She was due to attend a lecture this morning, on diseases of the spleen, but decided to skip it. The spleen could look after itself, for now.

At the doorway of the airline office she hesitated. If she crossed the threshold, she would have committed herself irrevocably, and there would be no going back. She could see people standing at the high counter, and the salesgirls in their uniforms, and the clerks at the back, bent over their desks.

She pushed open the door and stepped inside.

28

William Latimer's secretary wondered if the boss was coming down with something, he was that distracted. She had to ask him three times, no less, to sign a chit for the office's monthly pound of Bewley's tea and tin of Jacob's assorted biscuits. He had snapped at her, too, when she asked him how she should reply to the French Ambassador's invitation to a Bastille Day dinner at the embassy. She was used to his gruffness—in fact she secretly admired it as a manly quality—but this kind of bad-tempered treatment she didn't think she should be expected to put up with. The fact that there was nothing she could do about it wasn't the point. She had been with him through two ministries, and deserved better. It must be that he was feeling under the weather. There was a dose going around.

At four o'clock he rang through from the inner office and

barked at her to bring him his coat and hat. She was on the point of telling him what he could do with himself and his coat and his hat, too, but she kept her temper, contenting herself with putting on a sweetly sarcastic tone when she said "Yes, Minister" to him, and slammed down the receiver with a bang. She should have said, "*Sea, a Aire*," but had spoken in English instead, just to show him.

Latimer had registered none of this, and stood, distracted, with his arms out behind him while Miss O'Reilly slipped the coat on him and handed him his hat. He was thinking of Phoebe Griffin, and of what she had reported that bastard Quirke saying to her on the phone the night before. Christ almighty, but would that fellow never stop popping up in front of him, like one of those bottom-heavy toys that won't stay down no matter how hard they're knocked over? Quirke had meddled when poor Oscar did himself in, and now here he was again, claiming to have found April, when to all intents and purposes April was dead and buried. Quirke was the proverbial bad penny.

"Where's my umbrella?" he growled, and was startled when the secretary said nothing, only marched out of the door and then marched back in again and unceremoniously thrust the thing at him, looking as if she would rather have walloped him over the head with it. What had got into her, for the love of God, to put that face on her? Women! he thought, and made a champing motion with his lower jaw.

On the stairs he paused to light a cigarette. He had already told Miss O'Reilly to phone the Taoiseach's department, on the private line. Whenever trouble reared its head, especially the kind of trouble he was facing into now, there was only one man Bill Latimer would think of turning to.

He went out through the side gate onto Merrion Street. The Garda on duty tipped a finger respectfully to the brim of his cap, and the Minister gave a quick nod of acknowledgment. The trees in Merrion Square were dusted with spring's first green shoots, not that he noticed. He turned right and walked the short distance to the Taoiseach's office, and climbed the steps. Another Garda, another salute.

"Good afternoon, Minister," said the old fellow in the glass booth just inside the door. Pink bald spot the size of a half-crown, gray mustache tinged yellow at the fringes, a small stain on the front of his waistcoat that looked like dried egg yolk. What was his name? Murphy? Molloy? Moran? He couldn't remember. Bad, that. Always get the names into your head and be sure to remember them, that was one of the first rules of politics, or one of his first rules, anyway.

He was making for the lift, then changed his mind and took the stairs. Had to let out his belt a notch this morning. Middle-aged spread, he thought grimly, and then had to remind himself, more grimly still, that he could hardly consider himself middle-aged any more. How long could he keep going before he began to slow down? In his secret heart he half hoped his crowd would lose the coming election. Bowing out would be less of a blow to his pride if the party was in Opposition.

On the first landing he stopped again, dropping the butt of his cigarette on the stair carpet and treading on it with his heel. Bloody Quirke and his stuck-up bitch of a daughter. He had thought all that business with April was over and done with, but now here it was again, rising up and bursting like a big soft bubble, giving off a horrible and all too familiar stench.

Ned Gallagher's secretary informed him that Mr. Gallagher was in a meeting.

"Is he, now," Latimer said, in a menacing purr. "Miss O'Reilly phoned you not ten minutes ago and you told her he'd be here."

"The meeting ran over."

He looked at her, grinding his jaws. She was the image of the dried-up spinster in his own office—they were all out of the same mold.

"Tell him the Minister needs to see him now," he said. "Who-ever he's meeting can hang on a few minutes."

The secretary hesitated, but he did that thing with his eyes,

letting them go cold and dead, that frightened all underlings, especially of the female variety. The woman tightened her mouth
and picked up the phone and said something into it in a voice
too low for him to hear, and hung up.

"Mr. Gallagher will be with you in a moment."

"*Go raibh maith agut*," he said, not that she merited thanks.

Her display of resentment had amused him. Yes, they were all
the same. Two things in particular they had in common. They
were hopelessly in love with their bosses, and ever on the lookout for slights. He paced the floor in front of her desk, knowing it would annoy her. She bent over her typewriter, poking a
pencil into its innards. He whistled a tune thinly between his
teeth and batted his hat against his leg.

The door behind the secretary's desk opened and a little pale-
faced man in a pinstriped suit came out, with Ned Gallagher
behind him.

"Good luck, now, Francis my lad," Gallagher said briskly to
the little man, putting a hand on his shoulder and propelling
him forward. "We'll renew our discussions another time."

The little man cast an anxious glance in the Minister's direction, nodded to the secretary and was gone.

"Bloody old woman, that fellow," Gallagher said to no one
in particular, making a face at the door through which the little man had made his getaway. Then he turned to the Minister, extending his hand. "Bill, how are you, and what can I do
you for today?" The Minister did not return the greeting, only
gave a curt nod. He didn't care to be addressed in so familiar
a fashion by a civil servant, and certainly not in front of a secretary. "Isn't the weather a tonic?" Gallagher went on blandly.

The Minister grunted.

They went into Gallagher's office, and Gallagher shut the
door behind them.

29

Ned Gallagher resembled some big-shouldered forest-dwelling creature, Latimer thought, one of those apes, say, with over-hanging brows and a patch of white fur on their chests, that swung themselves on their knuckles along the jungle floor. However, there was nothing apish about him when it came to handling whatever clown happened to be the Taoiseach of the day. There wasn't a poli-tician in the House Ned Gallagher didn't have a file on. Ned kept a count of all the bodies and where they were buried, and could order an exhumation at a moment's notice. Bill Latimer despised him, but he had a grudging respect for him, too. He knew how useful he could be. Ned Gallagher was the fixer's fixer.

Gallagher walked around his desk and sat down, crossing an ankle on a knee and lacing his fingers together across his belly.

He wore a blue serge suit and a waistcoat, a white shirt and a dark tie. Bill Latimer hadn't taken off his overcoat.

"Ned, I have a problem," he said.

Gallagher smiled, though a Gallagher smile was never quite a smile.

"Sure, what else would bring you up here to stand before the seat of earthly powers in the middle of your busy afternoon?"

The Minister registered the taunt, but let it go. You didn't start a sparring match with Ned Gallagher unless you were prepared to take off the gloves and use your bare fists.

"Sit down, man, sit down," Gallagher said now, "make yourself at home." He flipped open the lid of a silver cigarette box on his desk. "Here, have a coffin nail."

Latimer took a cigarette and brought out his lighter. Wreathed in smoke, he stood up from the chair and took off his coat and threw it down on a sofa and dropped his hat on top of it. He felt weary suddenly. There were times when retirement didn't seem such a bad option. He returned to the desk and sat down again.

Gallagher regarded him with a lively eye. Gallagher derived much quiet satisfaction from other people's troubles.

"So, Minister, what's up?"

Latimer hesitated, framing in his mind the request he had come here to make. He eyed the man at the other side of the desk. To look at him, with that big square head and those massive shoulders, you'd never think he was a queer. But one foggy night not all that many years ago the Guards had caught him in the gents' convenience at the top of Burgh Quay, on his knees in front of a young lad with his trousers around his ankles. Why they hadn't locked themselves into one of the cubicles was a mystery to all concerned, including, presumably, Gallagher himself. The danger was part of the thrill of the thing, the Minister supposed. All the same, for the highest civil servant in the land to take such a risk was madness, without a doubt.

In the end, though, he got away with it. The Garda that had

caught him servicing the bumboy had taken him to Pearse Street barracks, where Detective Inspector Hackett, as he was then, had chosen not to press charges. Not long afterward, Hackett was promoted to Chief Superintendent. Was there a connection? Hackett was said to be as straight as a die. All the same, at the time Bill Latimer had thought of directing that the matter be looked into. It wouldn't have done him any harm at all to have exposed a blatant instance of corruption in the upper echelons of the Garda Síochána. He dropped the idea, however, after poor Oscar drove himself over that cliff in Howth and caused such a rumpus. Hackett had been in charge of the case, and had kept it low-key, and after a few follow-up headlines on the inside pages the story fizzled out, to the great relief of the Latimer family.

Until now, when it seemed quite possible it would flare up again.

How in Christ's name had Quirke got on to April's trail? Had Quirke's daughter somehow known all along that April wasn't dead? Maybe April had got in touch with her. When the girl came to him this afternoon, she had claimed not to have known a thing until that phone call from Quirke in the middle of the night. But could he believe her? Maybe it was she who had asked Quirke to go down to Spain in the first place, to talk to April and persuade her to come home.

The Minister leaned forward and tapped ash into the ashtray. His mind was in a whirl. He didn't know what to think.

"I've had word," he said hesitantly, "I've had word that a— that a person I believed, that everyone believed, was dead is in fact alive."

Gallagher waited for more, but the Minister just sat looking at him, with desperation in his eyes. He felt like a rat being backed into a corner.

"This person, now," Gallagher said, going cautiously, "would it be someone you know, or knew, personally? Someone close to you? A relative, say?"

The Minister narrowed his eyes. What did this fellow

know?—had he heard something about Quirke, and Spain, and his niece? Word got around fast, in this city, and Gallagher had a gundog's nose when there was the faintest scent of scandal in the air. Few things gratified Gallagher more, the Minister knew, than the spectacle of a politician in a fix. He sighed, and took the plunge.

"It's my niece," he said, "April Latimer. You remember—?"

He let his voice trail off. Gallagher leaned back and set his elbows on the arms of his chair and made a steeple of his fingers and nodded slowly, solemnly. He was like a priest, Latimer thought with disgust, like a bloody priest in the confession box.

"Oh, of course I remember," Gallagher said, in a tone of unctuous sincerity. "A terrible business, terrible altogether." He lowered his head, as if to offer a silent prayer for the dead. Bloody hypocrite. He looked up again. "The poor young woman's body was never found, isn't that so? It struck me as odd, at the time." Oh, but he was enjoying himself, Bill Latimer could see. He clenched his fists in his lap. "And now," Gallagher said, crushing the stub of his cigarette into the ashtray, "now you tell me it may be she didn't die at all. Is that right?"

"It can't be her," Latimer said brusquely. "Somebody has made a mistake."

"And who, may I ask," Gallagher purred, "might this somebody be?"

Latimer was in the corner now, trapped there by a large, slow-moving and inescapable cat.

"Quirke," he said, through clenched teeth.

Gallagher fairly threw himself back on his chair in exaggerated surprise and shock.

"Dr. Quirke? The State Pathologist?"

"Yes," the Minister said, as if he were spitting out a stone. "He's in Spain, on some sort of a holiday. Last night he phoned—he phoned someone here and claimed to have seen my niece, to have met her, in fact, and spoken to her."

"And did she admit to him who she was?"

Latimer leaned forward and crushed his cigarette into the ashtray with an angry turn of his wrist.

"No. She gave another name. Lawlor, Lawless, something like that. I can't remember. First name Angela. The same initials, though—A. L."

"The same initials?" Gallagher said incredulously, doing his impression of a smile. "Is that what has Dr. Quirke convinced it's your niece? The same Dr. Quirke who, as is well known, is subject to—well, to seeing things, shall we say. I presume he's still—?" He made the motion of lifting a glass to his lips.

"Ach, I don't know whether he's on the drink or not," Latimer said with savage dismissiveness. "God knows he was a martyr to the booze, and I imagine he still is. There's no cure for being an alcoholic."

"And yet I hear he got married," Gallagher said smoothly. "To some foreign doctor, I believe, on a promise to mend his ways."

They exchanged a look, and Gallagher snickered.

"From what little I know of him," the Minister said, "I can't see that bucko reforming himself, wife or no wife."

A cloud passed abruptly, and a shaft of sunlight struck down at an angle through the big window at the far end of the room, bright and swift as a javelin.

"So anyway, tell me," Gallagher said, "do you think it might be your niece that he came across?"

The Minister looked aside, pursing his lips.

"It could be her," he said quietly, through clenched teeth. "It could be."

Gallagher, he saw, was having a hard time of it to contain his glee, though of course he was putting on a great show of concern and sympathy, the two-faced bastard.

"But wasn't there an inquest, and didn't the coroner pronounce the poor girl officially deceased?" said Gallagher, all innocence. The Minister made no reply, and kept his eyes turned angrily in the direction of the sunlit window. "Ah, so she's not dead, then," Gallagher murmured, nodding slowly. He sat forward eagerly. "What happened, at all? Was it that she had to be sent away? There was that business of the black fellow she was going around with, I remember—"

"That's got nothing to do with it," the Minister said sharply, turning his head and fixing Gallagher with a glare. "It was because of a—a family thing."

A short silence followed. Gallagher lifted his hands and joined his fingers at the tips again, gazing up at a far corner of the ceiling. He was contemplating with pleasure the hardly credible prospect of the final downfall of the mighty Latimers.

"I see," he said. "Family business. Yes." He watched Bill Latimer fumbling to light another cigarette. "And tell me, Minister," he said, lowering his voice further and adopting the hushed tone he usually reserved for funerals, "what can I do to help, at all?"

The Minister shifted in his chair, wincing as if at a twinge of pain somewhere low down. Gallagher looked away—the state of Bill Latimer's nether parts was a thing he didn't wish to contemplate.

"Something will have to be done, Ned, whatever it is," the Minister said. Gallagher noted the use of his first name. Things must be serious, all right, when a Latimer lowered himself to that level of intimacy. "If it is my niece," Latimer went on, "and Quirke has found her, then it will have to be dealt with. You know what that man is like, always sticking his nose into other people's business."

A heavy stillness fell, as if some stealthy thing had entered soundlessly and settled itself in a shadowed corner of the room.

"Dealt with in what way, exactly?" Gallagher softly inquired.

Latimer pushed himself up from his chair with a violent movement and paced the floor, three tight steps forward, three tight steps back.

"God damn it," he snarled, "how do I know? It'll just have to be dealt with, that's all. That girl can't come back here. There's too much—" He clamped his mouth shut with an almost audible snap. He stopped and stood still, his troubled glance darting here and there about the room and taking in nothing. "I thought it was all over and done with," he said, the words grating in his throat. "I thought it was finished. And now—"

Again that stillness, at the heart of which something seemed to stir itself, with a crackling of brittle wings.

"And now it's all starting up again," Gallagher finished for him, giving him a heartfelt look.

Latimer, drooping suddenly, made a sound like that of a limp balloon expelling the last of its air. He sat down, joining his hands and clamping them between his knees. A big man, he looked suddenly small.

"I tell you, Ned"—his voice trembled—"it could be the end of me." He shook his head, and cast about the room again with a look of desperation.

"Oh, come on now, Bill—" Gallagher began, cajolingly, but the Minister rounded on him.

"And I'll tell you this," he said in a hoarse whisper, "I'm not the only one who'll go down. There are others—plenty of others."

Gallagher returned him an unflinching stare. Is it to be threats now? he thought.

"What do you want me to do?" he asked, in a voice become suddenly hard and businesslike.

The Minister looked away.

"It's what I say," he said. "It will have to be dealt with, that's all."

"Yes, but dealt with how, Minister?"

"I told you, I don't know! You're the one who's supposed to be up with these things and how to sort them out. Suggest something."

Gallagher assumed his mandarin's blank mask.

"I'm a civil servant, Minister," he said primly. "I act at the directive of others."

The Minister put a hand to his forehead. Sweat glistened on his upper lip.

"Send someone down there," he said. "Send someone to deal with her."

"To deal with her?" Gallagher repeated, lifting an eyebrow.

"Aye—to get her away from there, away from Quirke, away from—whoever." He leaned forward heavily and set his fists on the desk, his big shoulders hunched. "To send her"—he lowered his voice to a whisper—"somewhere else."

Ned Gallagher again echoed him.

"Somewhere else?"

"That's right. To some other place."

They looked at each other in silence for a long moment. Then Gallagher said, "That's a tall order, Minister, if I understand rightly what it is you're saying."

Bill Latimer saw with satisfaction the look of alarm that had settled on the other's face. At last it had dawned on the numbskull what exactly it was he was being told to do.

"And aren't you a tall man, Ned," the Minister said briskly, pushing himself up out of the chair. "Tall enough for any task."

They parted then, with a cold handshake, Gallagher looking queasy and the Minister, suddenly, grimly cheerful. On his way downstairs, Latimer encountered again the pale-faced little man in the pinstriped suit whom Gallagher had earlier dismissed. He was standing in a corner of the ground-floor hallway, pretending to read the notices pinned to a green baize board on the wall. He glanced at Latimer going past, with what seemed to Latimer the ghost of a slyly knowing smile. Christ, he thought, is everyone in on the Latimer family's secrets?

30

Paul Viertel was not by any measure a vain or self-regarding man, or so he believed, but there was one thing he prided himself on, and that was his tolerance of the shortcomings of those around him. He had grown up an orphan—his father had died young, his mother, Evelyn Quirke's sister, had perished in the camp at Theresienstadt—and so he had been left to make his own way in the world.

He was a man of science, and, as such, a rationalist. He had every right to bear a grievance, against the Nazi rulers and their lackeys, indeed against the entire German nation, but also against the world in general and the people in it who had stood by and allowed his mother and millions of her fellow Jews to be murdered. However, he would not have dreamed of indulging in such a waste of emotional energy. He followed the motto his Tante Evelyn lived by, that the past was the past, and that in the present all one could do was observe, think, bear witness and work to alleviate the sufferings of those less fortunate than oneself.

Some people saw him as sanctimonious, he knew that. In his heart, however, he thought himself to be simply a good man. Not a saint, or anything like it. Just as he believed that goodness weighed more in the moral scales than evil did—which was a truism, of course—so, too, he considered it not immoderate to place himself on the side of the good.

His attachment to Phoebe Griffin he regarded with a certain bemusement. On the face of it—and although her face was quite a pretty one, or so he considered it—she was not his type, not really.

He had met her first at a dinner at his Tante Evelyn's house. He recalled that rainy night with a high degree of warmth, yet also with a faint sense of misgiving. By now, Phoebe and he had been "going out," as the Irish said, for nearly four years. When he looked back over that time, he could find nothing substantial to regret or be resentful of, in Phoebe's behavior or his own. Phoebe was a modern young woman, and made no excessive demands on him, in terms of his time or of his emotions. She never used the word "love" to describe what she felt for him, and he was grateful to her on that account. Which need not mean that she didn't love him, or that he didn't love her. But he set great store by restraint, in word as much as in deed.

The way he put it to himself was that they were together but free. He assumed Phoebe would agree with this formula, and therefore he had not deemed it necessary to test her on it. She was his girlfriend—another word that embarrassed him, but he could find no acceptable substitute—and he was fond of her. However, his work came first. He knew she knew that, because she had assured him of it. Or at least, he had assured her it was so, and she had not disagreed or raised an objection.

On the whole, then, he was content with the relationship, and
saw no reason to alter it. Yes, there was that lingering question
as to whether he should have waited in hope of finding someone more suited to his temperament. But he was not so naive as
to imagine that there existed somewhere a person who would
be for him the exact "Miss Right."

He supposed he and Phoebe would marry, one day, but that
day was still a hazily long way off. The fact was, he gave no
more thought to the future than he, and his Tante Evelyn, did
to the past. As a medical researcher, as a scientist, he saw himself
as living wholly in the present. He often put it this way, in his
talks with Phoebe—"I'm a being of the present tense"—and her
usual response was a smile. It didn't trouble him that the smile
at times struck him as enigmatic, or that it might, if he exam-
ined it closely enough, contain a trace of mockery. She was not
difficult to comprehend, since she was driven by what drove
everyone else, and how could he be mocked for characterizing
himself as a man of the moment?

However, one day she had asked him a peculiar question, the
peculiarity of which made it lodge in his mind. The question
was, did he ever entertain self-doubts.

It was autumn, and they were walking in Fitzwilliam Square,
to the gate of which his aunt had a key, since she was a semi-
resident by virtue of having her consultation rooms in one of
the houses on the square. The fallen leaves were at their most
glorious—Phoebe came up with the fanciful suggestion that it
was like wading through giant flakes of hammered precious
metals—and they were both in what he judged to be a mood
of muted happiness.

Her question was not remarkable in itself, but her tone was.
He could not have said why it was so, but, for whatever reason,
it infused her words with a significance that the words themselves would have seemed not to merit. For a moment he had
the discomfiting impression that she was laughing at him, gently

enough, but laughing all the same. He told himself that he was imagining it, and tried to dismiss the notion from his mind. It clung on, however, and raised itself anew each time he thought back to that day in the square, in the pallid sunlight, among the profligate abundance of yellow, red and russet leaves.

"You mean you actually intend to go?" he said now, peering at her with a startled frown.

They were in her flat, sitting at the kitchen table. They had just finished tea—on weekdays, when Paul came to visit her at four o'clock, at the end of one of his "short days" at the Institute, they had, instead of dinner, what it amused Phoebe to describe as a "meat tea," with bread and tomatoes and squares of sliced ham from the Q & L down the street.

"Yes, I do," Phoebe replied matter-of-factly. "I've decided."

"But it's mad—a mad idea."

She said nothing.

He went on gazing at her. When he looked at her like that, so she had told him once, she felt like something in a petri dish. Now she would not respond, and went on eating in apparent unconcern. He shook his head, then sliced a piece of ham neatly and conveyed it to his mouth.

"There's a detective who'll be going, too," she said, looking away and frowning.

His eyebrows shot up.

"A detective?"

"I went to see Quirke's old friend Chief Superintendent Hackett. He's sending a man down."

"To do what?"

"To investigate, I suppose. Isn't that what detectives do, investigate? April was murdered, you know. Well, not if she's alive, she wasn't, but you know what I mean. And a person did die."

"What person?"

"April's brother."

He stared at her. He might have been a hypnotist intent on putting her into a trance.

"But what good will it do?" he asked.

He sounded genuinely baffled.

"What good will what do? Sending a detective to Spain."

"I don't know. You'd have to ask him that—the detective."

Of course, Paul was right—it was mad, all of it, she did see that. Yet she would not give in.

Paul ate the last square of ham, pushed his plate aside, wiped his mouth on a paper napkin and lit a cigarette.

"This detective," he said, "who is he?"

"His name is Strafford."

"What age is he?"

She shrugged.

"Ancient. Thin as a rake, in a three-piece tweed suit. Oh, and he wears a fob watch."

"What? What is this, a fob watch?"

"You know, on a chain." She traced a loop across her midriff. "And he's a Protestant, I think. He has that accent."

Still he fixed her with his mesmerist's unblinking stare.

"And when will he travel to Spain?"

"Same day as me."

"What? And on the same flight?"

"I imagine so."

She rose from the table and gathered up their plates and turned with them to the sink.

"I really do not like the sound of any of this," Paul said.

"It's just for a few days," she answered, annoyed at herself for seeming to apologize. What had she to apologize for?

She turned on the hot tap. Despite herself, she was excited. It was as if she had suddenly come smack up against a large, intricate and perilously delicate object, something like a grandfather clock, or that thing people keep on the wall that predicts the weather, which the slightest move on her part would bring

crashing down in a glorious jangle of springs and broken sprock-
ets and splintering glass.

"Let me understand this correctly," Paul said behind her, in
that ominously calm tone he adopted when he was trying not
to be angry. "You and this Stafford—"

"Strafford. With an *r*."

"—you and this person are flying off to Spain together, you
to identify a woman who may or may not be your dead friend,
while he is to investigate what, exactly?"

She bit her lip. She was in the grip of a kind of mad hilarity.
She must not laugh, really she mustn't—and what was there to
laugh at, anyway?—for if she did, everything, somehow, really
would fall asunder, beyond fixing.

"I don't know what he's going to investigate, *exactly*," she said.

She turned to face him, bracing her hands on the edge of the
sink behind her. He expelled a stream of cigarette smoke and
smiled thinly.

"Perhaps you can be his assistant," he said, "his—what do
you call that character?—his Dr. Watson."

"Very humorous."

A wrinkle developed above his left eyebrow. She could see
that humor was the last thing he had intended. Paul doled out
his jokes like banknotes.

"Perhaps I should go also," he said. "To Spain, that is. I have
some leave that I haven't taken."

"I don't think that would be a good idea," she said, too
quickly. Oh, God, what she had feared would happen had happened.

"May I ask why not?"

"You know very well."

"No, I don't. Tell me, please. Explain to me the reasons why
I shouldn't go to Spain with you and your detective."

"He's not my detective." Something tightened in the air between them, as if a wooden peg had been given a sharp twist,

making a stretched string quiver. She gave a sigh of exasperation. "Look, we both know how much you disapprove of my father."

"It is not your father I disapprove of."

"Then what is it?"

"Sometimes," he said, "you are too much like him. For your own good. For our good."

They looked at each other steadily, then Phoebe turned and walked out of the room. In the little hallway outside the kitchen she took down her coat from its hook and struggled into it and opened the door onto the landing. Paul appeared behind her. She noticed he had taken the time to light a fresh cigarette.

"Where are you going, may I ask?"

"Out."

"Out where?"

She turned from him and hurried down the stairs. On the return, she paused and glanced back up. Paul was still standing in the doorway, the fingers of one hand holding his cigarette and the other thrust into the side pocket of his buttoned-up suit jacket.

"When will you be back?" he asked.

She didn't answer, but went on down, seeming to feel that big poised mechanism, that clock or weather thing or whatever it was, rock from side to side, its innards making an ominous cacophony of clicks and rattles and chimes.

31

Terry Tice stopped in a pub for a drink. After all, he was on his holidays, or sort of. He sat on a high stool at the bar, turning a cork beer mat over and over on its edges, like a square wheel. He was thinking of nothing much. It was pleasant, being adrift like this. He wondered if Percy Antrobus's body had stayed down in the water or if it had bobbed up again, buoyant with corpse gas. He didn't care, really. Sooner or later someone would raise the alarm. Percy was a popular chap, knew a lot of people, frequented a lot of places. He would be missed. Someone would take it into his head to alert the rozzers.

"Another half of Smithwick's, here."

It still tasted of soap, but he hadn't found anything more palatable. Bass he had never liked, and the new Scandinavian stuff that was all over the place these days, advertised on every bill-board, that was pure piss.

"A glass, we say here," the barman said, setting down the drink in front of him.

"What's that?" Terry asked.

He didn't approve of talking barmen. They were there to serve up drinks and keep their traps shut. This one was a big slow fellow with a sloping forehead and a keg-sized belly. He meant no harm.

"We say a glass, not a half," he said. "A glass of stout, a glass of Smithwick's. See? It's just a difference." He leaned a chubby elbow on the bar. "English, yourself, are you?"

"That's right. London. Cockney to the core. Bow bells, all that."

It amused him to tell these little lies. It was like firing an air rifle. Harmless practice. Anyway, he might be a Londoner, for all he knew. No one had ever told him what he was, or how he had come to be in an orphanage, in Ireland.

"A cousin of mine is over there. Works at the building—McAlpine's Fusiliers."

"What's that?"

"It's a sort of a nickname they give themselves, the lads on the building. Roads. Skyscrapers. The Irish will have rebuilt London by the time they're finished."

Percy Antrobus had known a McAlpine, Terry recalled. Jimmie McAlpine? Jamie? Quite the boy. Collected cars, Rolls-Royces, Alvises and the one with the Spanish-sounding name, Hispano-something. Never out of the clubs, roistering till dawn. Decent chap, though, Percy said, and free with his dosh. Terry thought now of Oxford Street at night, lights gleaming on the wet pavement and music coming up from the Soho dives. He felt a twinge of homesickness, then laughed at himself. Barely a day away from the Smoke and already he was crying into his beer.

"One and six, that'll be," the barman said. "You should have come over sooner, they put tuppence on in the last Budget."

Terry counted the coins onto the prickles of a rubber mat. An elderly type at the far end of the bar, in a brown overcoat with a fur collar, was giving him the look. He wondered, not for the first time, what it was about him that attracted the old buggers in particular, the ones with dentures and dandruff and gummy eyes.

Reaching into the inside pocket of his jacket he brought out Percy's wallet, which he had taken off him before rolling him into the arms of Father Thames. The leather was soft and warm and oily to the touch—it could have been a slice of Percy's hide, preserved and polished. There wasn't much in it—a few taxi receipts, a laundry slip, a bill from Berry Bros. & Rudd for a case of Gevrey-Chambertin 1943. Liked a decent drop of plonk, did Percy. The Messrs. Berry and Rudd could sing for their money, now. He turned up the wallet's leather flaps and peered into its musty-smelling pockets. No personal things at all, not even a wrinkled photo of Mummy and Daddy Antrobus. Poor Percy and his lonesome life. Terry sighed. He had to admit he missed the old poofter, bad breath and all.

He finished his drink, nodded to the barman and went out into the meager April sunshine. The ale sat sourly on his stomach. He should eat something, but the thought of food made his gorge rise. The crossing from Holyhead had been rough, and a couple of times he thought he was going to puke. Reminded him of his navy days.

A bus honked at him as he was crossing the street, and a delivery boy on a bike, who had to swerve to avoid running into him, called him a bollocks and rode on, standing on the pedals and laughing.

Here was the bookshop again. He hesitated, then slipped inside.

So many books—so many words. Why did they do it, he

wondered, why did they keep at it, hundreds of them, thousands, all hunched over with pen and paper, scribbling away, stopping now and then to stare into space, picking their noses or scratching their balls. Strange business, making up stories and expecting people to pay to read them.

The woman at the cash register was watching him, her spectacles glinting. She would know by the look of him he didn't belong here, he thought bitterly.

He picked up a paperback, flicked through it. He had never heard of Brighton Rock. Then it came to him—it wasn't a place that was meant, but rock, the sugar-stick kind. *Brighton Rock.* Clever, that.

A name jumped out at him. Pinkie. That was what Percy Antrobus used to call him sometimes, when he had booze taken. "Hello there, Pinkie," he would say, his glistening purple lower lip hanging slack and his rheumy eyes full of merriment and malice. This must be where he got the name, from this book. Terry felt a surge of indignation. Being called Pinkie was bad enough—what kind of a name was it, anyway?—but to think Percy had lifted it out of a bleeding storybook, that was the limit.

He ran his eye down the page, stopped. "...a shabby smart suit, the cloth too thin for much wear, a face of starved intensity, a kind of hideous and unnatural pride."

Hideous pride? What was that supposed to mean?

The shop woman approached. She was smiling, but still suspicious. She asked if she could help, in that prissy way they all did. Genteel, that was the word. He would have liked to smash her face in, see how genteel that would leave her.

"This book," he said, holding it carelessly in his left hand, "how much is it?"

"One and six," the woman said.

Same as the glass of dishwater he'd drunk in the pub. This amused him, he wasn't sure why, and he smiled back in the bitch's face. He fetched out a florin. The drawer of the cash register sprang open with a crash and the sound of a bell. She handed him back a sixpence, and his receipt. He gave her a last, disparaging half-grin, and walked to the door. When he opened it, there was the *ping!* of another bell, over his head this time, and a waft of dampish air came in from outside. He dropped the receipt on the mat, and stepped over the threshold. The woman had put the book into a bag. He lifted it briefly to his nose. He had always liked the flat, dry smell of brown paper.

Pinkie, eh?

Back there in the pub he had almost begun to regret what he had done to Percy, but now he was glad.

Turning into Merrion Street, Phoebe spotted April's uncle, Bill Latimer, in his big black coat, coming out of the Office of the Taoiseach. He didn't see her, and turned left and strode down a little way and entered Leinster Lawn by way of a narrow black metal gate. The Garda on duty saluted him, and was ignored.

Phoebe walked on. She had fairly flung herself out of the house, furious at Paul, but by now she was calmer. She had harbored doubts about Spain, but the row with Paul had banished them. The thing was done, and she would go. Her airline ticket was in the drawer of the cabinet beside her bed. There were also some Spanish pesetas she had got at the foreign exchange counter of the Bank of Ireland, and a satisfyingly solid little block of traveler's checks from American Express. She had even laid out a summer frock, black, of course—she never wore anything else—but lightweight, and fetched up a pair of espadrilles she had bought in France when she was there on holiday. Some grains of sand still clung to the rope soles. French sand, from two years ago. She smiled wistfully. Quirke had taken her to Paris, and then on to Deauville. He had been nice, and had stayed mostly sober.

She came level with the gates of the National Gallery. Suddenly she faltered, thinking, *What have I done?* Spain, April Latimer, the scene with Paul—the whole thing overwhelmed her.

She and Paul had exchanged hardly a cross word in the years they were together. Maybe they should have. Maybe a few small fights would have helped them cope better with the big one they'd just had. She shouldn't have walked out like that, out of the flat. It would have been different if it was Paul's home, too, but it wasn't—it was hers. She should have stayed, she should have stood her ground and fought him to a standstill. She hated when things ended inconclusively, hated the untidiness. Paul would come around that evening and they would both pretend nothing had happened. She despised that kind of polite dissembling. Words spoken could not be unspoken, things done could not be undone. To pretend otherwise was self-betrayal.

She could abandon the trip to Spain and peace would be restored. She could do that. But if she did, a trace of her capitulation would linger, like the phantom pain of a severed limb.

She walked on, and turned left into Clare Street.

It was over between her and Paul. She saw that clearly. Oh, there would be no dramatic parting, no tears and shouted recriminations and the furious slamming of doors. Paul simply wouldn't have that kind of thing. Everything would resume, and seem the same, except that they would both know it wasn't. And in the weeks and months that followed the strain between them would slowly intensify, until one day they would separate, like an iceberg breaking in two in the silence of a frozen sea.

Was that what she wanted? Was that the chance she had grabbed without hesitation when her father called her in the night and asked her to come to Spain? Was that the open doorway she had stepped through, no, had leaped through, when Superintendent Hackett summoned Strafford, Strafford the Protestant, the son of the Ascendancy, and she had tacitly accepted him as her traveling companion, fob watch and all?

It wasn't often that she actively disliked herself, but just now she did. All the same, she wasn't prepared to go back on what had been done.

On Nassau Street, she spied again the young man in the fawn overcoat whom she had seen earlier looking into the window of the bookshop. He really was a sorry runt of a thing. He was going along at a rapid sort of strut, shoulders back and pelvis thrust forward, his hands in his coat pockets and his elbows pressed tight against his ribs. It was as if he were bearing himself along, clasped in his own arms, like a not quite life-sized and in some way damaged mannequin.

She wondered who he might be. Not a tourist, she was sure of that, but not a Dubliner, either. He had the air of one who had come from nowhere, and of not being on the way to anywhere, despite that quick, stiff-legged strut. Someone really should tell him about those fawn trousers, they gave him the look of a prematurely aged and ravaged boy. He passed her by without a glance. He was carrying a paper bag containing what must be a book. He didn't strike her as the bookish type. In fact, he didn't look like any type at all. He would be, she thought, with a faint shiver, one of a kind.

32

Ned Gallagher regarded politicians of every stripe with what he considered to be a healthy contempt, which he found hard to hide. He had never known a straight one yet. Also, the majority of them were as thick as planks. Thank God for the civil service, the backbone of government. Without people like himself, the whole intricate business of running the country would come to an ignominious halt. This was rarely admitted but known to all, except the jumped-up gombeen men, a new one of which, proud as Punch in his ministerial colors, was foisted on him in the wake of each cabinet reshuffle or general election.

His colleagues in the service were not all geniuses, either—that went without saying. But certain qualities and skills were universal among them. They knew their place, or at any rate made a good fist of pretending that they did. Even the worst dolts among them kept their mouths shut when that was what was required of them, and would offer advice or venture an opinion only when it was absolutely unavoidable. It took the rawest recruit up from the country no more than a month or two to learn how to bury a file beyond finding, or, at the other extreme, how to bamboozle a minister with an avalanche of documentation, preferably handwritten.

And when there was a cock-up, all of them, the old hands and the new, were masters at passing on to someone below them the blame that should rightly attach to themselves. This was only as it should be, in Ned's view.

In his school days, Ned had always been top of the class in Latin, and it was he who had come up with a motto that everyone in the service could quote from memory, even if they didn't know where it had originated: *Nunquam licentia revelat operimentum tuum in ano est*—never leave your arse uncovered.

Today's visit by the Minister had rattled him, he had to admit it. In his time, he had been required to carry out some questionable tasks, but this one took the biscuit. The thought of the possible repercussions from what Bill Latimer had asked him to do—and there was no mistaking what it was—made the collar of his shirt seem all of a sudden two or three sizes too small for him. Even now, a good hour after the Minister had left, his mouth was still so dry he found it hard to swallow.

It was true that the thing in need of solving was partly his problem, too. He had always feared that the nationalist zeal of his early years would someday come back to haunt him. But there was nothing ghostly about the peril he suddenly found himself facing.

He rose heavily from his desk and walked to the window and stood with his fists thrust deep in the pockets of his suit jacket. The sharp-edged brightness of the April day was beginning to fade. He gazed gloomily at the row of redbrick eighteenth-century houses on the far side of the road. In one of them the

Duke of Wellington had been born. He paced back slowly to his desk. How many Brits were aware that Wellington was an Irishman? He was their hero, one of the class that had sought over the centuries to crush the spirit of this country. That project had failed, and Ned Gallagher was proud to have made his contribution to the fight that had ensured that failure.

All the same, the war wasn't over, only suspended. The forfeiture of the Six Counties was an open wound in the body politic. Until they were got back, and the British driven out of Northern Ireland for good, people like himself, the *fíor-Gaels*, the true Irish, would never sheathe the *Claíomh Solais*, the shining sword of freedom, nor would they—

Stop right there, Ned, he told himself, stop right there. This was no time to be indulging in the rebel sentiments of the old days. He was the Secretary General of the government, the head of the civil service and one of the most powerful men in the country—indeed, *the* most powerful, according to some, himself included, though he'd never dream of letting on that he thought so.

What Bill Latimer was asking him to do could land him before the courts. Jesus, it could put him behind bars. Latimer had said nothing outright, had given no specific directive—he was far too much of a cute hoor for that—but all the same he had no doubt as to what he wanted done. And what choice had Gallagher but to do it? If that bloody niece of Latimer's were to come back from the dead and spill the beans—well, both himself and Latimer would be in the soup, and the soup would be very, very hot.

He dropped his face into his hands. The years of labor he had put in, the conniving and scheming, the groveling at the feet of talentless bastards who weren't fit to tie the laces of his shoes, all, all of it could go for naught. And why? Because the Latimers, those pillars of nationalist rectitude, those guardians of the sanctity of the Cause, were in serious danger of having their dirty secrets hauled out into the light of day for the country to see and rub its hands and gloat over.

Wearily he lifted his head and gazed toward the window and the Iron Duke's birthplace beyond. Don't think about it, he told himself, don't brood on it. Just get it done. He hadn't risen to the heights he commanded today by wringing his hands and worrying. Be a man, he told himself. Act.

From the rack behind his desk he took down his black wool overcoat, and was halfway into it when he paused and took it off and hung it up again, and chose instead the wrinkled old mackintosh he hadn't worn in years. It wouldn't do to look too respectable, not this evening.

33

Detective Inspector Strafford stepped into the hallway and stopped, still with the front-door key in his hand. The empty house seemed to stop, too, as it always did nowadays when he walked in, especially at an unusual hour. Everything wore a slightly affronted air—what did he mean, coming home at this hour of the day? He sympathized. He was himself a stickler for the proper observances. Routine was the engine by which his life was run, especially in the absence of his wife. He contemplated going out again and spending a couple of hours in the National Library and returning home at the usual, proper hour.

The fact was, he had never felt entirely at home in this house, even when Marguerite was still here and life had at least the semblance of normality. But then, where would he feel at home?

The living room was chilly and he turned on the gas fire. It

had fake logs, around which the pale flames flickered and sput-
tered. It didn't look anything like a real fire. Marguerite had
installed it, to "cheer up the room," as she said, giving him a
look that dared him to dissent. He was depressed by the thing,
by its kitschiness, its commonness. His wife had a bourgeois
streak that, when she let it show, always took him by surprise.
She went in for plastic flowers and lace doilies and painted fire
screens. There was even a fake-fur cover on the lavatory lid.

My God, what a snob I am, he thought.

Yet Marguerite's family was rather grand, in a down-at-heel
sort of way, like his own. The ancestral home was an early
eighteenth-century manor house just across the county border
from Lismore. It was to there that she had taken herself off at
the beginning of the previous summer, which meant that he had
been on his own for the best part of a year. Supposedly she had
gone to look after her ailing mother, but the weeks had passed,
and then months, her mother hadn't died, and still there was no
talk of her returning.

He was not as put out by her absence as he should have been,
which made him feel something of a scoundrel. At first, Marguerite had written regularly, three or four letters a week, but
gradually the correspondence had fallen away and at last she
had gone silent. She had telephoned once, but only to ask after
some knickknack she wished him to send on to her, as she was
missing it.

If he were a gentleman he would plead with her to come
home, but every time he thought of it he was overcome by a
disabling apathy. Anyway, what good would pleading do? Marguerite was a willful woman, one not to be swayed by gentle
words. What he should do was descend on Perrott House bran-
dishing a horsewhip, like a squire out of *Castle Rackrent*, and
drag her home by the hair, if necessary—that was what was expected of true gentlemen, at least in the old days. He thought
that might be what she was waiting for him to do. Well, she

could wait. On one of her early return visits she had said something that irritated him, he couldn't remember what, and it had driven him to inquire, in his usual diffident fashion, if she didn't think it rather, well, rather middle class of her to have done something so banal as "going home to mother." She had made no reply, had only gone very red in the face and flounced out of the room. At least she hadn't thrown something, as she would have done in the past.

He was fond of her, and missed her quite a bit, at night especially, though not for the obvious reason. It was just that the nights were very long, and he was a bad sleeper, and craved company. He supposed she would come back, sooner or later. Meanwhile, he must get on as best he could with the doilies and the coasters—though he did remove the pink cover from the lavatory lid. Things could have been worse. He had been spared a set of flying china ducks on the wall above the fireplace. That would have exceeded the limits of even his tolerance.

He fetched a glass from the kitchen and poured himself a whiskey from one of the dusty bottles on the sideboard. The room and its furniture seemed to draw back in shock. Drinking, him, at half past four on a Thursday afternoon? He almost never drank alcohol, and certainly not in the daytime. But today he was in something of a dither. What was Hackett thinking of, to send him off to Spain on a harebrained search for a young woman who was supposed to be dead but who seemingly wasn't? And all on the word of State Pathologist Quirke, a notorious drunkard.

Still, he had never been to Spain, and he had to admit he was quite looking forward to seeing it, or at least the small part of it that he would see. He wondered what the weather would be like in San Sebastián. He was not a man given to excitements, but just the name, San Sebastián, stirred something in him that he had not experienced since childhood. He pictured coral-blue waters and a tawny shore, and a barquentine sailing straight out of the pages of Robert Louis Stevenson. He laughed at himself. It was Spain that was in question, not the Spanish Main. Not that he knew where or what the Spanish Main might be, or even if it was a real place.

What had come over him, to be entertaining such frivolous fancies? It must be the whiskey, he decided.

He drank the last of it and, to his surprise, found himself pouring another, albeit a very small one. He lifted the glass in an ironic salute to the window and the view in it of the little garden outside, damp and sparkling in the still vigorous light of the latening April afternoon. How did one say *cheers* in Spanish? Whatever the word, he supposed it would have an upside-down exclamation mark in front of it. He racked his brain, but all he could come up with was *¡Viva España!* When he spoke the words, he was taken aback by the loudness of his voice, booming in the silence of the empty house.

Phoebe Griffin. He had been putting off thinking about her. He knew there had been some trouble about her being Quirke's daughter. Hadn't he handed her over as a baby to his adoptive brother and his wife, to rear her as their own? Which was why her name was Griffin and not Quirke. She was an oddly self-possessed young woman, yet at the same time there was something about her that was tentative and remote. He found her slightly unnerving, in her black dress with the bit of lace at the collar, with her thin pale hands resting in her lap. She wore no makeup, except for a touch of unemphatic lipstick. She was interesting, there was no denying that, though for his part he wasn't sure he would care to be the subject of *her* interest. He suspected it would sooner or later involve a mauling, though if she did sink her claws into him she would do so absentmindedly, as cats sometimes do, unintentionally, when they're thinking of something else.

He took his drink with him upstairs, and went into the bedroom where he now slept alone. He should think about packing a bag. He had no clothes suitable for a sunny climate—he was a homebody and didn't care much for abroad, and avoided hot countries especially. Having gone through his wardrobe, all he could come up with were a baggy pair of khaki trousers he hadn't worn for years, and a lightweight pale-gray suit smelling of mildew. He would have to buy things, short-sleeved shirts, slacks, suchlike. But not sandals. He drew the line at sandals. There was little to choose between sandals and a flock of china ducks flying up the wallpaper over the mantelpiece.

He went back downstairs. He was tempted to have another whiskey, but didn't. The two small tots of Jameson he had drunk had started up a buzzing in his head. He stood in the middle of the living room, looking out again at the garden. A shower of rain fell; it lasted only a matter of seconds, then the sun came out again, making the lawn sparkle. A cobweb in an upper corner of the window outside was laced with tiny, jewellike droplets. He liked the Irish climate. His skin was pale, the Spanish sun would turn it pink in a matter of minutes. The hot, slightly tacky feel of sunburned skin gave him the shivers.

Sunglasses. He couldn't remember if he had a pair. Well, he could buy them down there, in San Sebastián. That name again. He wondered where the emphases fell. That accent on the final *a* worried him. Sebasti*aan*?

There was something, other than the thought of Phoebe Griffin, that he had been circling around in nervous anticipation since he had come home an hour ago. Now he sat down on the sofa and opened his briefcase and took out a small, plain rectangular cardboard box and set it on the kidney-shaped coffee table in front of him—Scandinavian furniture was another of Marguerite's enthusiasms. As he lifted the lid of the box and folded back the tissue paper inside, he savored also the almost fleshy fragrance of fresh machine oil. He laid the tissue paper aside and lifted out of the box, with the fingers of both hands, the short, shiny, deadly little weapon.

It was a snub-nosed Smith & Wesson police special, very compact and neat. It sat snugly in his hand, a sort of lethal toy. He had got it from a chap in the Pearse Street firearms department, whose name was Balfe. The thing had been done on a semiofficial basis. Strafford had signed for it, as he was required to do, but Balfe had put the chit away at the bottom of a drawer under a pile of outdated documentation.

The gun came with a shoulder holster, which was the next thing he took out of his briefcase. He removed his jacket and put his arm through the complicated leather strap, and did up the buckle at the back. Then he put on his jacket again, and fitted the gun into the holster, and went into the downstairs bathroom and looked at himself in the full-length mirror on the back of the door. There was only a slight bulge beside his heart, barely noticeable. He drew back his shoulders to stretch the cloth over the holster, but still it hardly showed.

He took out the gun again, and again let it rest in the palm of his hand. He was unashamedly delighted with it, which should have made him feel foolish, but did not.

The gun wasn't new. In fact, it was quite old. Balfe had said it had been taken off the corpse of a member of the Cairo Gang, the British Army intelligence team sent over from Britain to deal with the IRA in the War of Independence. Strafford didn't know whether to believe this. Could a weapon that old still be in working order, as Balfe had assured him this one was? Had it been used to shoot men dead? He found the notion darkly stirring. He had killed a man, mostly by accident, years ago, when he was starting out on the Force. He had hardly been aware of pulling the trigger, and the thing had been over in an instant. Sometimes in dreams he revisited the scene, the cars stopped on the country road, and the bodies lying on the ground in the glare of the headlights, grotesquely asprawl, like life-sized mannequins. But it didn't trouble him. He felt no remorse. The man who died would have shot him if he had fired first.

Now he walked to the window again, with the revolver dangling loosely at his side. One was never too old to learn new aspects of oneself, he reflected. He didn't know which was stronger, the thrill of being in possession of this murderous object, or the absurdity of the notion of himself as an armed man. He was glad Marguerite wasn't there to see him so shamingly pleased with himself. He felt like a schoolboy who had got hold of a cache of dirty pictures. He recalled roaming the fields around Roslea as a boy, armed with a toy wooden rifle carved for him from a hurley stick by the family blacksmith. Bang bang, you're dead.

What impressed him most strongly was how serious a thing the weapon was. Most of the objects that passed through one's hands were trivial, so that one hardly registered them. The little gun was weighty far beyond what it weighed. It was a thing of dark intent, secret and essential.

He sighed, and closed his eyes and pressed a thumb and the knuckle of an index finger hard against the bridge of his nose. What did he think he was about, exulting like this in the possession merely of a gun? It was the whiskey, he told himself again, but this time he didn't believe it.

Possession. That was the word. But which was the possessor, and which the possessed? He slipped the revolver into its holster, and went upstairs to finish packing. He stumbled on the top step and very nearly fell backward down the steps. That would be a fine thing, to be discovered at the foot of the stairs with a broken neck, smelling of whiskey and with a slightly illicit gun tucked neatly under his armpit.

34

Ned Gallagher told the taxi man to drop him off at the King's Bridge, on the left-hand side of the road, by the railway station. He waited until the taxi was out of sight before crossing the river. Taxi drivers had remarkable memories, and liked nothing better than to be called as court witnesses.

He walked along the north side of a small, deserted square, and entered a cobbled street with a crooked church at the far end of it. Halfway along he stopped in front of a pub. O'Driscoll's, it was called, but everyone knew it as the Hangman. There was a garage on one side, and, on the other, an extensive patch of waste ground where there had been a mattress warehouse the last time he was here. The look of this empty space gave him a feeling of unease. How could so substantial a building just vanish, leaving hardly a trace of itself? All that was there now was

ragged grass and a few low mounds of rubble and a sign warning that trespassers would be prosecuted. He had an urge to turn
on his heel and walk away as fast as his legs would carry him.

When had he been here last? Three, four years ago? More? He
wished he wasn't here now. He craned his neck and scanned the
frontage of the pub. It was a dingy-looking establishment, dour
and uninviting. The lowering sun shone on the upper windows,
blinding them. Inside, they were hung with cretonne curtains.
Why curtains? Why cretonne? They made a ghostly impression, hanging lankly there behind the soot-grimed glass. Those
rooms must have been empty since the house was turned into
a pub, before the war. He thought of the people who had lived
there once and were dead now.

In the saloon bar a single paraffin lamp glimmered; he smelled
its sweetish, oozy smoke. He took off his hat and peered about.
Nothing had changed. There was even the same skinny barman, with sloped shoulders and a purplish tip to his long, thin
nose. He, too, looked the same. Only his long black apron was
a bit older, a bit shabbier.

"A ball of malt."

"Will you take a drop of water in it?" the barman asked, in
his nasal voice, with weary indifference.

"It'll do by itself."

Ned Gallagher leaned on his elbows on the bar and drew his
head as far down between his shoulders as it would go. Though
it was unlikely anyone would recognize him from the old days.
The type he used to come here in search of tended to die young,
or end up in jail, or just wither away, like the leaves of autumn.

All the same, you never knew when the past was going to
come up behind you and bite you on the backside. The circumstances of his last visit here were branded deep in his memory,
and the brand-mark smarted even yet. It was Hackett who had
summoned him. Hackett had the goods on him, after that mis-
fortunate incident in the gents' on Burgh Quay, and intended

never to let him forget it. The crafty bastard had let him off that time, but there was a catch. The detective had called on him on a number of occasions when he was after this or that bit of inside information, or when he needed something done on the quiet. Nothing serious, nothing heavy—not anywhere near as heavy or as serious, certainly, as the business Ned Gallagher was about this evening.

It made him break out in a sweat to think of the trouble he could be letting himself in for, just by being here. But when Bill Latimer asked you to do a thing, you didn't say no. He was one of the very few members of the House who had made it his business to familiarize himself with the inner workings of the civil service, and there was nobody more expertly placed to drop a banana skin square in your path. Besides, it could be that he knew about the Burgh Quay thing. He had never mentioned it, had never dropped the slightest hint, but all the same, there was something in the way the man looked at him sometimes, with what seemed a glint of mockery and sly contempt, that froze Gallagher's blood.

So here he was, in the Hangman again, waiting for that vicious little bugger Lenny Marks to come strolling in, with his hands in his pockets and a fag in his mouth, grinning all over and cracking jokes and cadging drinks. How was it people fell for his poor-mouthing, considering the money he made in what it amused him to refer to as the "hardware trade"? Maybe he had the goods on the lot of them, the way Hackett had the goods on him. Or the bads, more like.

Gallagher was ordering a second whiskey when Lenny arrived, cocky as ever.

He was a skimpy little fellow with a thin face and a crooked little pointed nose. A comma of slick black hair was stuck to his forehead, like an unruly curl still there from years before when his mother had plastered it down with a spat-on finger before sending him out into the world. He had a peculiar, corkscrew walk, sort of hugging himself as he went along and setting one foot directly in front of the other, like a ballet dancer. He was wearing one of the limp, grayish-white linen suits that he had tailored for him in some sweatshop out East. They were a bad fit, and he never stopped wriggling around inside them, as if they were infested with ants. He carried his head at a permanent tilt, his right jaw tucked in against his shoulder. This was due to a congenital defect—the pub wits said that when he was being born the doctor took one look at him and tried to push him back in again. Also, he had a permanent twitch at the side of his mouth. He was called by various nicknames, the Jew boy, or the Suit, but most people just knew him as Little Lenny. He had started out as a deep-sea sailor, and claimed to be able to speak half a dozen languages, which must be useful in the hardware trade.

"Neddy, my boy!" he said, punching the big man lightly on the upper arm with the point of a miniature fist. "Have this one on me. What? Sure? All right, then." He spoke to the barman. "I'll take a gin and water, Mikey."

He turned about and leaned his elbows on the bar and surveyed the dim, shabby room with his thin-lipped, twitchy smile. He lit a cigarette.

"How's it going, Lenny?" Ned Gallagher said, regarding him sideways with a look of distaste.

"Never better," Lenny replied jauntily, "never better." He brought out a coin from his trouser pocket and rolled it along his knuckles with flicks of his thumb. It was one of his tricks, and he was proud of it. "Haven't seen you in a while," he said. "What are you after?" He grinned. "The usual, I suppose?" He glanced about the bar again. "No likely lads in tonight, though, or not yet, anyway."

"Come on," Gallagher said, taking up his drink and turning aside, "we'll sit down over there."

He led the way to a low circular table in a corner. Lenny, still showing off his skill with the glittering shilling, detached himself from the bar and ambled after him.

They sat on rickety spindle-backed chairs. The barman brought Lenny's gin.

"Here's spit in your eye," Lenny said, lifting his glass.

For a time they sat in silence, Gallagher hunched over the table with his shoulders lifted, while Lenny turned and again considered the room. "Right fucking kip, isn't it," he said fondly.

Lenny's father, long dead, had been a rag-and-bone man around the Liberties and the Coombe. His mother still ran a shylock business, in a small way, from a sweetshop in Clanbrassil Street. She was immune from prosecution thanks to Lenny, and Lenny's contacts. He visited her sometimes, and brought her back little gifts from his frequent travels around the world.

Lenny was always busy, taking the ferry to Holland or the train to Marseilles, sailing to the Channel Islands with a briefcase chained to his wrist or flying to mysterious places on the shores of Asia, to talk to shady people about dodgy deals, or, as he would have said, hobnobbing with bigwigs and clinching lucrative contracts. Guns, it was always guns, that was his trade. No one knew how it was he hadn't been nabbed long ago and locked up—no one, except the knowing few, including Ned Gallagher and the Minister of Defense, Dr. William Latimer. Lenny had a lot of friends, whether they liked it or not.

"You going to tell me why you've summoned me up here to the Ritz, Neddy?" he said.

He always called Gallagher by this pet name, which he had invented and which no one else used, and which annoyed Gallagher intensely.

"There's a bit of business that needs seeing to," Gallagher said, lowering his voice. "I thought you'd be the man to suggest someone who might take it on."

"What sort of business?"

"Delicate."

"And what sort of someone?"

"Someone reliable. And experienced."

Lenny always seemed to have something in his mouth to work on, something like a seed, or a small, hard nut. It was a variant of the twitch at the side of his mouth.

"Are we talking about the kind of someone who might be a customer of mine?" he asked.

Lenny, some years before, had facilitated the movement of certain materials from somewhere abroad into and through the port of Belfast. It wasn't one of his own jobs, but a thing he had been asked to do—the kind of immunity from the penalties of the law that he enjoyed came at a price. Ned Gallagher hadn't been directly involved in the enterprise—God forbid!—but he had been apprised of it, on the quiet, through cross-border channels. The lads up north were always in need of hardware, even though when they got it they did precious little with it. It was said by some that they sold the stuff on to more determined organizations abroad, in the Caribbean, or certain South American banana republics. It was no concern of Lenny's where the goods he supplied ended up.

"We're talking here," Ned Gallagher said, more quietly still, "of somebody of a professional nature, an experienced operator with a clean record. International, not one of your usual eejits who could be depended on to shoot his own foot off."

Lenny pondered this, stroking his sharp little chin. Gallagher watched him. He didn't like Jews—the Germans, now, they'd had the right idea on what to do with Christ's crucifiers. He kept his views on the matter quiet, of course, but there were influential people who shared them, as he had cause to know. Some of them were in parliament, and were even hotter on the subject than he was.

Little Lenny was shaking his head slowly from side to side.

"I've got to tell you, Neddy," he said, "I don't much like the sound of this."

Gallagher smiled, showing his dentures.

"And I've got to tell you, Jew boy," he said softly, "that I don't give a fuck whether you like it or not."

Lenny swallowed, his Adam's apple bobbing. He didn't mind being insulted, he was used to it, but Gallagher was frightening, when he chose to be.

"All right, all right," he said, grinning uneasily in the big man's face. "Keep your hair on."

Gallagher shifted on the chair and settled into the wings of his overcoat.

"It's a foreign job," he said. "That's why we need someone international, who knows his way around."

"Foreign where?"

"Foreign none of your bloody business where." Lenny nodded. He was impervious to such rebuffs. "All I need is for you to find me someone," Gallagher went on grindingly, "a name, a phone number, some kind of contact."

Lenny nodded again, nibbling on whatever there was or wasn't in his mouth.

"Is this a terminal job we're talking about?" he asked.

"There's a person who disappeared who has turned up again, and who needs to be gone for good."

Lenny puffed out his cheeks and let them deflate with a pop.

"Right, then," he said. "Right."

He had finished his drink and was toying pointedly with his glass. Gallagher chose not to take the hint. Lenny sighed, then remembered to refresh his grin. He wore this grin all day. At night, Gallagher thought, he must crawl off to whatever hole it was he lived in and take it off in front of the mirror, peel it off like a rubber mask, and put it away for use again the next day.

"Funny thing," Lenny said, still jogging his empty glass.

"What?" Gallagher said, suspicious.

"A coincidence. I spoke to a fellow today, in here, in this very place, who might be just the operator you're looking for."

"What sort of fellow?"

"Irish, or used to be, based in England."

"I suppose that's international enough. Name?"

Lenny grinned.

"Whoa up there, big boy," he said. "First there's the fee to be discussed."

"The fee?" Gallagher said, giving him a large, incredulous look. "What do you think you are, a consultant, or something?" He put his mouth close to Lenny's ear. "A name, Lenny. A phone number. Your fee will be the joy of knowing you've added a drop of oil to the machinery of state."

Lenny shrugged. His grin had become strained. The state machine was one in the works of which he couldn't afford to become entangled. Gallagher produced a clipped bus ticket from his coat pocket, and Lenny wrote down Terry Tice's name on the back of it, and the name of the place where he was staying on Gardiner Street. Gallagher scanned the information, and stowed the ticket in his wallet. He picked up Lenny's empty glass.

"I'll get you another one," he said. "But you can drink it by yourself."

35

Terry Tice lay on the lumpy mattress in his room at the Gardiner Arms, reading the book he had bought. The knob on the radiator was broken and the room was too hot—he had complained to the geezer at the front desk but of course nothing was done—and he had stripped down to his undershirt and drawers. He was wearing his shoes and socks, though, since he didn't fancy walking barefoot on the carpet. He had always been particular about where he put his feet. Very clean and neat, he was always that, even in his orphanage days. He was known for it.

The book wasn't bad, though he hadn't read many books so he couldn't really judge. The people in it were the sort he knew, though they were described in an exaggerated way. They were loud and brightly painted, like the characters in a pantomime. Cubitt and the rest of the gang he recognized, but he couldn't believe they'd let themselves be led by a seventeen-year-old kid, even if he had proved himself as a fearless killer. The writer referred to him only as "the Boy," though everyone else called him Pinkie, which couldn't have been his real name in the first place, surely. Pinkie had a chip on his shoulder the size of a telegraph pole. And he kept going on about God, and Hell and damnation, and all that stuff. Terry knew after a few pages what Pinkie's real problem was—queer, without admitting it, not only to others but to himself as well. Funny, but the writer who had invented him didn't seem to spot it, either. Too busy brooding about death and the hereafter. The Brothers in the orphanage were always banging on about that kind of thing, when they weren't busy banging Terry and half the other lads in their care.

The girl in the book, she didn't work at all. A real-life Pinkie wouldn't have touched her wearing welder's gloves. He might have given her the odd poke, but that would be the limit of it.

He was quite the lad, was Pinkie. What had Percy seen in him that made him think Terry was like him? Because he wasn't like him, was he? For a start, Pinkie was more a knife man than your regular gunsel. "Gunsel" was a word Terry had picked up from some old movie, he couldn't remember which one. He liked it. Terry the gunsel. Gerry the tunsel. Heh.

The phone rang, giving him a jolt. He had drifted into a doze, the book fallen forward on his chest. He struggled upright on the bed, his heart racing. His nerves must be bad. That's what being away from home did to you. Not that he'd ever had a home, not to speak of.

"What?" he said into the receiver, and straight off fell into a fit of coughing. "Who's that?" His voice had become a croak. "Lenny?" Lenny Marks. The Jew boy. He had an irritating way of whispering into the phone, as if he thought everyone around him must be listening. "What you want, Lenny?"

A job. Abroad.

"Nice trip down south," Lenny whispered coaxingly, "sun and sand and all the quim you could ask for. What do you say?"

"I dunno," Terry said, trying to sound like a jaunt to Spain was the last thing he wanted, which wasn't the case. The fact was, he had been getting a bit concerned about what his next move was to be. This would give him time to relax and ruminate. That was another word he liked, "ruminate." It meant thinking, but in a slow, deep way.

"All expenses paid," Lenny cooed. "And a handy three hundred quid, one-fifty into your mitt now, in crisp new notes, the other half on completion." He paused. They listened to each other breathing. "Come on, Terence, say yes." Lenny did a nasty little laugh. "It's a government-sponsored job—legit lolly."

Terry was humming a tune in his head.

Oh, I do like to be beside the seaside…

A stick of Brighton Rock would do very nicely, right now.

DONOSTIA

36

The first thing she noticed was his clothes. His cricketer's jacket, once white but now gray, had seen better days, and so had his baggy, khaki-colored trousers. He wore a pair of stout brogues, of a remarkable shade of yellowish-brown, with cracked uppers and strips of metal reinforcement on the toecaps. All he lacked was a solar topee. In his hand was a well-thumbed volume bound in faded green cloth. He held it close in front of his face. He should wear reading glasses.

He jumped when she spoke to him, and scrambled to his feet, closing the book but keeping a finger between the pages to mark his place. His raincoat began to slip to the floor, and they both bent forward to make a grab for it, and almost bumped foreheads.

They walked together toward the departures area.

"What are you reading?" Phoebe asked.

He looked at the book he was holding as if he had never seen it before.

"Tacitus," he answered. "The *Annals*."

"Is it good?"

"Good? Yes, I suppose it is. A bit dry. Although there is Tiberius." He indicated the page he had marked with his finger. "I'm still on him."

"Ah," Phoebe said. "Tiberius. Yes."

He wore no wedding ring. Might he be, as her friend Isabel Galloway would nudgingly put it, inclined to the leeward side of Cape Perineum?—it had taken Phoebe a moment or two to work that one out. Isabel was an actress, and knew about such things. She hoped he wasn't one of "those." She had nothing against them, but she didn't want him to be one.

She thought the flight would never end. There was turbulence over the Bay of Biscay, and she was afraid she would have to use the paper sick bag. All she could think of, as the plane bucked and yawed, was the soft-boiled egg she had eaten for breakfast, and the wrinkled scum of milk on the surface of the cup of coffee she had paid for in the airport bar and hadn't drunk. Just as they reached the coast of Spain—how far down the earth was!—the plane banked sharply and her innards banked with it. Strafford was engrossed in the horrors of the reign of Tiberius.

The train was better, though noisier. It rattled along at a tremendous rate, curving across parched hillsides and plunging into deep, verdant valleys. She watched from the window hour after hour, enthralled by the familiar foreignness of the landscape. The carriage smelled strongly of garlic and sweat and something that she couldn't identify. It was simply, she supposed, the smell of Abroad.

They arrived at their destination in the early hours of the morning. She was surprised by the softness of the night air. The city was quiet under a dome of stars. She could smell the sea. It didn't smell like the sea at home.

Quirke was at the station, waiting for them with a taxi. He came forward and kissed her. She caught only the faintest smell of drink. Maybe he was behaving himself. Evelyn had so far been a sobering influence on his life, but that was at home. She hoped he wasn't using Abroad as an excuse to relapse into his old ways.

He was wearing, of all things, a panama hat. Evelyn must have made him buy it. Phoebe told herself she must not laugh.

"It's wonderful!" she exclaimed.

He shrugged.

"It's just a hat," he said.

"But you look so handsome in it." He didn't. Now she noticed his bandaged hand. "What happened to you?"

"I got bitten by an oyster."

Strafford had hung back, and now Phoebe turned and put out a hand to draw him forward, and in doing so she was, for a moment, for Quirke, the reincarnation of her dead mother.

"This is Inspector Strafford," she said brightly, as if he was for sale and she was offering him as a bargain. "We were on the airplane together, and then the train. He's reading Tacitus."

The two men shook hands warily. Quirke regarded the detective with a cold eye. They had dealt with each other on a number of occasions, distantly, in their professional capacities.

"Hello, Strafford. Fancy meeting you here."

The tone was dryly ironic. Strafford said nothing, only nodded, smiled. The antipathy was mutual.

"Did you have to wait long?" Phoebe asked.

"They told me you'd be late," Quirke said. "I kept the taxi."

He looked cross. There were moments, not many, when Phoebe was a little afraid of her father. Something lay coiled in him that at the slightest pretext might rise up and strike. His past was the serpent, and it never slept.

"Come on," he said shortly, turning away.

The taxi driver, who was swarthy and fat and somewhat smelly, took Phoebe's and Strafford's bags and heaved them into the trunk. Strafford held open the rear door, and Phoebe, flashing a small smile of thanks, dipped past him and seated herself. He shut the door and walked around to the other side. Quirke was in the front, beside the driver, his hat on his knees. Seen from the back he was a monolith, large, square, silent. The driver started the engine, and the taxi, its tires squealing, shot away into the night.

Phoebe was sorry she had come. She was angry at Quirke. He had urged her to come down here, and now he was in one of his moods and hadn't a civil word to say to her. Strafford's leg was touching hers. She was not sure if he was aware of it. She moved to her own side, and looked out of the window. They drove for some way beside a river, very fast, then turned abruptly and crossed a bridge and entered a narrow cobbled street.

"This is the Old Town," Quirke said, without turning. "The seafront is over there."

Bars were still open, and there were colored lights, and, faintly, the sound of guitar music.

Oh, why did I let myself be persuaded to come? Phoebe thought, with an inward wail.

37

The hotel was a happy surprise. She had expected something dingy and faded, certainly not this smoothly elegant establishment. Quirke said yes, it was nice enough. He managed a grudging smile.

As they entered the lobby Phoebe looked about for Evelyn, but Quirke said she had probably got tired of waiting so long and gone to bed. Phoebe thought of pointing out that it wasn't her fault the train had been late.

"Oh, I was so looking forward to seeing her," she said.

In anyone else it would have been rude not to have waited up, she reflected, but Evelyn was not anyone else. All the same, it was a pity she wasn't here. She had a moderating effect on her husband, who was, Phoebe suspected, a little afraid of her.

Strafford hung back, wary of coming between father and daughter. Quirke's violent temper was legendary.

"What about a nightcap," Quirke said. It wasn't a question.

A porter had gone off with the suitcases. The receptionist, absurdly handsome, was tall and thin with oiled black hair combed smoothly back and a neat black mustache. His expression was one of polite disdain.

Phoebe and Strafford signed the register and handed over their passports, and Quirke led the way into the bar. They were the only ones there. A big, exquisitely detailed model of a sailing ship stood on a shelf behind glass. They sat at a low table. Phoebe could hear faintly from outside the sound of a wave softly collapsing. She had the sense of moonlight, too, though she hadn't noticed a moon when they arrived. The foreignness of everything made her feel a little dazed, yet at the same time there was nothing she didn't recognize—the ashtray on the table, the feel of the carpet underfoot, the glossy darkness in the windows.

An elderly waiter appeared out of the shadows, bowing and smiling. Phoebe asked for a glass of wine.

"There's a local white that you'll like," Quirke said. He spoke a word to the waiter that she didn't catch. Strafford would take only mineral water, and Quirke couldn't mask his look of scorn. For himself he ordered a Jameson.

Strafford drummed his fingers on the arm of his chair and looked about incuriously. Phoebe thought she had never known anyone so lacking in affect. That would be the Protestant in him, she said to herself, and immediately felt guilty.

The waiter came with the drinks, and little glass bowls of crackers and olives, and rolled pieces of raw ham stuck through with toothpicks.

Phoebe took a sip of wine. There were tiny bubbles in it. They went up her nose, and she had to suppress a sneeze.

She turned to Quirke. "So—April is alive, and you've met her."

It was the first mention she had made of her friend. Quirke bridled.

"I believe it's her," he said defensively. "That's why you're here, to prove me right, or wrong."

"Did you say you had dinner with her, you and Evelyn? Did you tell her you knew who she was?"

Quirke didn't reply, only tightened his mouth and looked away. It was as if she had accused him of some childish dereliction.

She had taken only a few sips of wine yet suddenly she felt dizzy. She put down her glass and rose, somewhat unsteadily, to her feet.

"I don't feel well," she said. Quirke frowned, in disapproval, it seemed. Now it was she who might be the undutiful child. "It's all that travel," she said. "I think I should go to bed."

Strafford, well-mannered to the point of tiresomeness, stood up, too, unwinding himself from the chair's embrace as if he were uncoiling a length of particularly flexible rope. Phoebe stepped past him and went toward the lift.

The old waiter again appeared, seemingly out of nowhere. He went ahead of her and opened the door of the lift and smilingly ushered her inside and stepped in after her. There was hardly room for the two of them. The old man gave off a smell of dust and dishcloths. He stood canted toward her with a fixed smile, speaking rapidly in what she supposed must be Spanish—or did the Basques have a language of their own? His voice was a faint rustle, like the sound of dry leaves blowing along a pavement. As the ancient lift clanked its way upward they were given glimpses of the successive floors, each with its identical corridor, leading away. She felt dizzier still.

The waiter had her key, and he scuttled ahead of her and opened the door of her room. Once more he followed after her, almost crowding on her heels. She found her purse and gave him a coin—she didn't know how much it was worth—and to her relief he departed, bobbing his head and obsequiously murmuring. The last thing she saw of him was his smile, lingering like the Cheshire Cat's, as he slowly drew the door shut on himself.

She stood a moment in the middle of the floor with a hand to her forehead. She thought she might be developing a fever. The rhythm of the train's wheels was still beating in her head. She was not a good traveler. She wished again, almost passionately, that she hadn't come here.

She switched off the light and drew back the curtain. The lamps along the seafront glowed grayly, like dandelion heads. The sea beyond was a dark gleam, with here and there a flash of phosphorescence in the fold of a wave. On the surrounding hills, the windows of houses glowed yellowly. Strange to think of people behind each window, people she would never meet, would never know, hundreds, thousands of them, the countless ones. The enigma of other lives assailed her.

What she had taken to be the window was in fact a floor-length sheet of heavy glass in a heavy wooden frame. She opened it and stepped out on to the shallow balcony and set her hands on the wrought-iron rail. The night air was chilly, but pleasantly so. She drew the smell of the sea deep into her lungs.

If April wasn't dead, then she was alive somewhere, now, at this instant, doing something, living her life, being herself.

Suddenly, to her dismay, she began to weep.

Downstairs, Quirke had summoned the creaky waiter and ordered another whiskey. Strafford's heart sank. He was tired, at the close of this long and trying day. He thought of the room awaiting him upstairs, anonymous, undemanding, a space that knew nothing of him. He thought of the high broad bed and the smooth sheets and the pillow cool against his cheek.

"I'm not sure I know why you're here," Quirke said to him, lighting yet another cigarette. "Are you?"

"Chief Superintendent Hackett asked me to come."

Quirke made a cold little smirk.

"Asked? He's your boss, isn't he?"

He was flushed and sweaty, in his rumpled linen jacket and suede shoes, slumped in the chair with his glass of booze in one hand and cigarette in the other and his paunch straining at the buttons of his shirt. Strafford had once been trapped in a corner of a hay field by an angry bull. He had felt no fear then, either.

"You met Miss Latimer before, didn't you?" he said, for the sake of saying something.

Quirke studied the ashy tip of his cigarette.

"Once, in Dublin, years ago. She was with Phoebe. It was night, it was raining." He shrugged. "Maybe I'm wrong, maybe it's not her at all, and your journey is wasted. But at least"—a sour laugh—"you'll get a suntan."

Strafford smiled politely.

"Did you tell her you remembered her, that you knew who she was?"

Quirke shook his head.

"Hardly the kind of thing to come out with over dinner in a fancy restaurant. 'By the way, I know it's you and I can see you're not dead.'"

He took a swig of whiskey. Strafford smelled the alcohol, a waft of it came across the table, sharp and at the same time sickly sweet.

"Do you know why she ran away and came here?"

"Maybe she was bored."

Strafford brushed a lock of hair out of his eyes, then brought his hands together palm to palm and pressed them between his knees. Quirke watched him narrowly.

"You know about the Latimers, don't you?" he asked.

Of course he knew about the Latimers. The story of that scandal was routinely whispered up and down the corridors of every newspaper office, law court and Garda station in the land.

"Conor Latimer, the father, shot himself," Quirke went on.

"That was in '47. Big scandal, and of course it was hushed up—tragic accident, terrible loss, the usual. Conor, it turned out, had been interfering with his children for years, both of them, April and the brother. Which probably accounts for the two of them carrying on together the way they did after the father was gone." He held up his glass and gazed at the remaining quarter-inch of whiskey, in which a spike of amber light trembled. "April got pregnant by the brother—did you know that? Did a job on herself to terminate it, nearly bled to death in the process." He made a wry face. "Nice tale of family life, eh? And you wonder why the girl ran off."

Strafford was keenly aware of the vast dark space of the sleeping hotel all around him, and of the night outside, and the dark sea. He really was very tired. Quirke, he could see, was itching for a fight. He knew very well the source of his rancor. He was afraid he had made a fool of himself. Even if the woman he had met was April Latimer, would it not have been better to keep silent? He had probably been at least halfway drunk when he telephoned his daughter, and now he was stuck with the consequences. He said, "You don't like me, do you, Strafford."

Strafford sighed.

"I neither like nor dislike you. What does it matter?"

He wondered how much Quirke had drunk this evening before setting out for the station. His eyes were blurred, slow-moving, the lids swollen.

"What do you think of my daughter?" he asked.

Strafford made to speak, but paused. He envied people who drank. It must be like putting on a mask. With a mask to shield you, you could say anything you liked.

"Dr. Quirke, I was told—not asked, no—I was told to accompany your daughter on this trip. I'm not sure why, as I said. Chief Superintendent Hackett works in mysterious ways, as you know. But I'm here now."

There was silence, then Quirke drank off the last of the whiskey and stood up. Strafford was surprised to see how steady he was on his feet. Perhaps he wasn't drunk at all, perhaps he had only been pretending. That would be another kind of mask.

"I'm sorry," he said shortly, doing up the middle button of his summer jacket. "I didn't mean to provoke you."

Strafford smiled.

"I'm not provoked."

"Yes, well."

Quirke turned and walked away across the lobby. Strafford waited a second, then followed him. The lift door opened with a skeletal rattle. They stepped into the cage and stood side by side, hands clasped before them, like a pair of mourners on the way to a funeral. The lift jerked into motion.

"It is her," Quirke said, his gaze fixed straight ahead. "It is April Latimer."

"I'm sure you're right. Here's my floor. Good night, Dr. Quirke."

He stepped out into the corridor. He began to shut the gate, but Quirke put up a hand to stop him.

"Are you armed?"

"What?"

"Are you armed? Have you got a gun?"

"No," Strafford said. "Why?"

"I have a bad feeling. I wish I'd never spotted that bloody woman."

Strafford gave a smiling shrug.

"Yes, well."

And in the middle of the night he woke up and wondered why he had lied about the gun.

38

Terry Tice had never been up in an airplane before. It hadn't occurred to him to be scared, until he was strapped into his seat and the ground was speeding by in the little window beside him as they hurtled along the runway. Now, all of a sudden, he was in a blue funk. This thing, with propellers attached to its wings, this crazy machine made of tons and tons of metal, with scores of people sitting inside it, was actually going to climb into the air—into thin air.

It wasn't right. It wasn't natural.

The gun was in his suitcase in the hold. That was another reason to be uneasy. What if he had to open the suitcase at the customs desk when he got to Spain? He had slit the lining and hidden the weapon there, in its holster. It wouldn't be hard to find.

The wheels of the plane bumped over the joins in the runway, faster and faster, thump thump thump thump *thump*!

He wanted to unbuckle himself and leap up and call out for the plane to stop and let him get off. Instead, he sat dumbstruck, unable to open his mouth or lift a hand to summon help, not that there was any help on offer. This was what it would be like to find yourself in front of a firing squad, goggling at the line of soldiers facing you with their rifles to their shoulders, grappling with the amazing fact that in a moment they weren't going to throw aside their arms and break into laughter at the great joke they had been playing on you all along, but that on the contrary, at a shout from their commanding officer, in his puttees and his cap with the shiny peak, they were going to press the triggers and blow a dozen ragged holes in your chest. Or eleven holes, anyway—wasn't one of the bullets always a blank?

Then, with a jerk and a bump, the world tilted, and they were in the air.

He shut his eyes and heaved a sigh. He pressed his head back against the seat. He was still afraid, but the raw terror of the past few minutes had begun to ease. Maybe he would survive. Maybe this contraption would stay airborne, after all.

Later, when they had reached what the captain, in an announcement from the cockpit, described as their cruising altitude, the plane gently dipped its nose and then seemed to hang motionless. He was offered a drink. There was tea or coffee, wine or spirits. He would have preferred a beer. He asked for tea. He was given a tray, with sandwiches on a plastic plate, and a piece of cake and a miniature glass of water and a sweet wrapped in crinkly paper. These things, so homey and familiar, comforted him. They were a link with the ground, a lifeline to life.

He ate his cake, he drank his tea. He peered out of the window and saw a flat, unmoving sea that seemed to be a sheet made of countless tiny flakes of gleaming tin. None of it looked real, the coast inching away behind them, and a bank of fluffy white clouds motionless on the horizon, and the sun steadily shining somewhere unseen. The stillness, that was another comfort. At this height, everything became suspended, and there was hardly any sense of speed. He was afloat.

The air hostess had a snub nose and smelled of Evening in Paris. When she minced past him along the aisle, he admired her ankles and her neatly packed bum. The seam of one of her stockings was crooked, and at the sight of it something inside him, that for the past half hour had been paralyzed with fright, stirred itself and lifted its head and managed a tentative little cheep. Flesh, perfume, a girl's stockings. Life.

In a little while the hostess came back, offering him more tea. He thought of asking her if she would be staying in Madrid overnight. But what good if she was? When they landed he would have to go straight into the city, and to a railway station there—he had the name written down on a blank page at the back of the book he was still reading—and find the train that would take him north, to the coast, the very coast they would soon be flying over.

A sleeper train, it would be. He had booked a first-class compartment for himself. Spend the night with two or three dagos stacked on bunks above and below him, smelling of armpits and dirty socks? No thank you, *señor*. Terry valued his privacy.

After the long descent, the plane landed. He got through customs like a breeze, found a taxi, gave directions to the station. The air was dense with an unfamiliar mugginess. Everything smelled foreign. Well, it would, wouldn't it.

He didn't sleep much on the train. Too noisy, and too hot. He reached his destination as the dawn was coming up. The sun was shrouded in a blur of mist, dull as a sixpence, with no heat in it yet. He stood in the middle of the busy station with his suitcase in his hand, dazed and disoriented. He didn't feel at all well. For his dinner in the dining car the night before he had eaten some sort of fish mixed in with rice, and it hadn't agreed with him. Sometime in the small hours the rumblings in his stomach had woken him. He was in a sweat, and shivering. When he got to the lav at the end of the swaying corridor, there was someone in it. He stood outside the door, barefoot, with his trousers and jacket on over his pajamas, afraid that if he went back to the compartment someone else would come along and get in ahead of him. He was in a bad way by now. His guts were heaving, and he didn't like to think of the stuff inside him, and he wasn't at all sure which end of him it was going to come out of first.

At last he heard the lavatory flushing, and a fat old totty in a silk dressing gown emerged. She glared at him as he dived past her. He kicked the door shut behind him with his heel.

He sat down on the still-warm seat, breathing through his mouth so as not to smell the pong the old bitch had left behind her. She must have eaten the same thing he had.

His bowels opened. Oh, suffering Christ!

Now, here in the dawn light in the station, he tried to get himself sorted, trying not to think about fish and greasy rice and fat old women. He couldn't move, he was that distracted. He cursed himself for not having booked himself into a hotel beforehand. Where was he going to stay? He looked around to see if there might be a desk or a kiosk with someone behind it who could telephone some place and get him a room. But there was only a café and a newspaper stand and a bar that was open already, with a few old guys in shirtsleeves sitting on cane chairs at little round metal tables drinking little cups of coffee and some kind of spirit, it looked like, from tiny glasses. Maybe he should sit down, too, and order a shot of the same stuff. It might settle his stomach. But no, he couldn't face it.

He went out into the smoky light—the sun was burning strongly through the mist now, the glare of it dazzling his eyes—and made for the taxi rank. There was no queue, which was just as well, since there was only one taxi. The driver sat with

his arms folded, his head lolling on the back of the seat and his
mouth open, asleep. Terry rapped a knuckle on the window,
and the fellow woke up with a start—you'd think someone had
fired off a pistol beside his ear. He scrambled out, grinning, and
took Terry's case and put it in the back seat and got back behind the wheel.

"Okay, meester," he said, "where you want to go?"

It didn't take Terry long to make him understand that he
needed somewhere to stay.

"Sure, meester, sure. I find you, no problem."

They drove through the city in a suspiciously roundabout
route—Terry guessed the driver was going in circles, to up the
fare, but he hadn't the energy to protest—and at last came to a
shrieking stop in a narrow back street. There was a lot of noise,
with people shouting and cars honking, and music from a wireless set or a gramophone blaring out of an open window somewhere above. Laundry was draped on first-floor balconies. On
one of them a toddler in a dirty undershirt put his head over
the metal rail and grinned down at him.

The hotel, so-called, was tall and narrow, driven like a wedge
into the space between its neighbors on either side. In a dim and
smelly hallway, a fat fellow with a scar sat on a very low chair
behind a sort of counter. He needed a shave, and a big clump of
glittery black chest hair stuck out of the vee at the unbuttoned top
of his shirt. There were big round sweat stains under his armpits.
He named a sum in Spanish money, had Terry sign his name in
a ledger, handed over a key and a tiny, folded hand towel and
went back to the newspaper he had been reading.

Terry climbed the steep stairway, his suitcase bumping against
his knees. When he got to the first landing a door opened and
a couple appeared, a woman in her shift, and a fellow in a tight
suit who turned his face away and sidled off down the stairs,
while the woman leaned in the doorway, grinning after him.
As Terry went past, she gave him the eye.

Later he told himself what a chump he was not to have realized straight off that it wasn't a hotel he had checked himself in
to, but a knocking shop. How Percy would have laughed! But
Percy wouldn't be doing any more laughing.

In fact, the place turned out to be not bad at all. The girls were
friendly, and there was a boy, or he might have been a midget,
who for a few pesetas would run down to the restaurant next
door and bring back hot food wrapped up in newspaper. The
food was good, too, if a bit on the oily side. There were things
like miniature sandwiches held together with toothpicks that he
really got to like. He asked the little guy what they were called,
but the word was unpronounceable. Anyway, they tasted fine.
He wouldn't starve.

That evening, when he was lying on the bed smoking and
reading his book—Pinkie seemed to be in for it, with people
asking questions about the murder he and the gang had done
and the law sniffing after him—there came a soft tapping at his
door. He was in his underpants and shirt and socks.

Her name was Pepita, or so she said. She was tiny, way under
five foot by his estimate, but she was a looker, with a heavy
swatch of crow-black hair and shiny black eyes and little brown
hands that made him think of some small furry creature, a squir-
rel, maybe, or one of those prairie dogs he'd seen in a magazine
in a dentist's waiting room.

On the first attempt, he wasn't able to do anything. The Girl
didn't mind, and snuggled up against him contentedly and played
with the short fair hairs at the nape of his neck. He was already
thinking of her not as Pepita but as "the Girl," the same way that
in the book Pinkie was "the Boy." Only she was no Pinkie, that
poor loser. She was bright and quick, with a big wide smile, and
smart, too, in her way. She had a lovely smell, musky and hot, as
if she had been spiced, like food is spiced. Terry was very sensi-
tive to smells.

The light in the window above them thickened and turned to

a deep blue—or no, not deep, but thick, rather, a thick, torrid blue. He brushed his fingers up and down the Girl's back until she made him stop, because it tickled. He listened to the sounds in the street, and after a while he fell into a doze.

When he woke up, the Girl was asleep with her head on his chest. A trickle of spit had come out of her mouth at the corner and fallen onto his skin and gone dry. That wireless or gramophone, or whatever it was, in the room above, was playing again. He thought he recognized the tune, though so far all the music here sounded the same to him.

He woke the Girl up, and this time it was fine. She had let him know, with gestures more than words, that she wouldn't be charging him. He pressed some money into her dry little fist, anyway. She was all right, for a tart. She called him Tirry, and said she liked his eyes. His eyes? As far as he knew they were the same as everyone else's. Women were strange, he told himself, not for the first time. He got up and peered at his reflection in the bit of speckled mirror that hung on a hook beside the window. Percy, one night when he was half seas over and in an ugly mood, had told him he had the eyes of a ferret. He didn't know how he had stopped himself from giving the fat old sot a good going over, which he richly deserved.

They stayed in that night, he and the Girl, and ate food that Terry had paid the kid to bring up. The Girl had a shift to work, but knocked off early and came back to the room. He was ready to do it again, but she smiled and said she was tired, and touched her fingers lightly to his cheek.

In the morning he walked around the city for a while. The area he was staying in was rough, but there were some nice places, especially on the seafront and along by the river. At noon he came to a square on one side of which was a building with cannons on it and a harmless-looking stone lion. He stopped at a bar and sat down at a table under a stone archway and ordered a beer. The sun was shining and the air felt just right, warm but not too warm. Springtime.

He had almost forgotten what it was he had been paid to come down here and do.

He finished his beer, threw some coins onto the table and headed back to the *lupanar*—that was the Spanish word for a whorehouse, the Girl had taught it to him, giggling and blushing. In the room, he changed into his fawn slacks and slip ons with the gold buckles. He had bought a new shirt especially for the trip, with red and blue stripes in it, and floppy sleeves. He wasn't sure about it, especially the stripes. He was worried it might make him look like a Spanish dancer or, worse, a queer. He took it off, then changed his mind and put it on again. What did it matter?—Spanish men all looked a bit iffy, with their tight trousers and built-up heels and penciled-on mustaches.

Today the street was even noisier than it had been last evening. Everybody seemed to be outside. They never stopped, these people, swarming all over the place and jabbering at each other like parakeets. Moving among them, he felt he was being swept down a fast-flowing river between sheer, high cliffs.

Suddenly, to his relief, he came out at the river. His street map told him it was called the Urumea, unless that was just the Spanish or Basque word for "river." It meandered all over the place, up and down and around, like the city's gut.

He had to walk for a long time before he found a taxi rank. He showed the driver a crumpled betting slip on the back of which he had written down the name of the hospital in block letters. The taxi shot off from the curb so suddenly that he was thrown right back against the seat. He swore. The driver must have understood the word, for he looked at him merrily in the driving mirror and laughed.

The hospital was on the side of a low hill. It had a black roof made in a series of domes, and terra-cotta walls, and, on the

front wall, white pillars and white balconies. He walked up and
down outside the gate for a while. He had thought he'd surely
find a bar somewhere around here, but there didn't seem to be
any. There was a hotel, higher up the road, but it looked too
posh. Places like that made him nervous.

He had no plan. He didn't go in for plans. He was superstitious that way. Things always worked themselves out, somehow, or maybe it was that he had a golden touch. Yet he knew
enough to know there was no luck, that it was just a word. If
you believed in luck you would have to believe in all the things
Pinkie believed in, God and the Virgin Mary and the saints and
Hell and damnation and the rest of it. No, there was no such
thing as luck, no coincidences, no golden touch, only willpower
and determination. And you had to keep cool. Always you had
to keep a cool head, and not get fussed. He had got fussed that
night on the dockside with Percy, and look what had happened.

At a bend in a slope of the road he spied an old-fashioned
wrought-iron bench, and sat down. The heat was making him
tired. From here he had a clear view of the hospital gate. He
didn't really expect her to come walking out, just like that. And
even if she did appear, he probably wouldn't know it was her,
at this distance.

In fact, he wasn't sure he'd recognize her even if he met her
face-to-face. He only had a photograph of her, passed on to him,
along with a wad of money, by that kike he'd bought the gun
from in Dublin. It was a studio job, taken by a professional. She
was standing in a fake sort of bower, beside a fake pillar and in
front of a painted backdrop. She was thin, with a thin face and
a small mouth and bony shoulders pressing against the stuff of
her expensive-looking frock. The photo must have been taken
on her birthday, or some other occasion. It was from six or seven
years ago, at least, and she would have changed in the meantime.
A woman only had to get a new hairstyle and slap on different
makeup to look like someone else.

The thing to do, he decided, was to phone the hospital and ask for her. He could say he was here on a holiday and that someone had told him to look her up. He grinned to himself. *Hello, Miss Latimer, you don't know me, but a bloke in Dublin asked me to give you this—*

It was a beautiful day, the sun warm on his face and on the back of his hands. The sky had lightened, and was a delicate shade of blue, like the shell of a bird's egg, and there was the scent of some flower or shrub in the air that reminded him of the Girl's hot dark buttery smell.

Yes, there was a lot to be said for Spain. He wouldn't mind hanging around here for a few months. Maybe he could meet up with somebody, a fixer with a bit of money, like Percy Antrobus. A lot of English lived down here, so he'd heard. It was a place you went to when things got too hot at home. There was a fellow, another Jew, who had masterminded a job at a jewelry place in Hatton Garden. Someone squealed on him and he had to scarper, and chose Spain to hide out in. Solomons was his name, everybody called him Solly. Reggie Kray used to have a joke about that, something about the Costa del Solly. Plenty of blokes like him around. Yes, maybe. Just maybe.

A bus came along and he flagged it down and got on. There was a to-do about his not having the exact fare, and in the end, he just dropped a handful of coins in the driver's lap and gave him a look that shut him up. The tires hummed on the winding road. Luckily the bus was bound for the city center, and soon he recognized the square with the building with the twin cannons where he had stopped earlier for a beer. He might go to the same place again, and have another glass. There was no hurry. His time was his own. The kind of job he was on shouldn't be rushed. Rushing things could prove fatal.

Fatal! That was a good one. He'd be proving fatal himself, any day now. He chuckled, and sauntered off across the square in the morning sunshine.

39

Breakfast next morning at the Londres was, for Phoebe, a travesty of normal life, although the farcical aspects of the occasion would, in other circumstances, have pleased her. They sat at a table by a window in the dining room, the four of them—Quirke and Evelyn, Strafford and herself—like actors in a brittle little comedy about a well-to-do middle-class family on holiday abroad. Even the light in the window was unreally effulgent, as if its source were not the sun but a battery of carefully arranged arc lamps up in the flies. When they had first come in and the waiter was seating them, she had caught a number of the other guests looking up with warm and seemingly appreciative smiles, as if in acknowledgment of the cut of the quartet's stage costumes and the persuasive manner in which they carried themselves. She and Strafford would be taken for a recently married couple, she still with something of the young bride about her, he the doting older husband, while Quirke and Evelyn would be the parents of one or other of them, her, most likely.

She had already seen, the night before, that there was no love lost between Strafford and her father. Quirke this morning was subdued, keeping his head lowered over his plate and saying little. As if to compensate, Evelyn was all talk.

"My dear," she said to Phoebe, "we must go out immediately after breakfast and find you a dress."

"Oh, yes?" Phoebe responded, smiling. "And what's wrong with this one, may I ask?"

"Down here you cannot wear your 'black habit.'" She glanced at Quirke and smiled, and, getting no response from him, turned back to her stepdaughter. "You will be taken either for a young widow or a *duenna*. You must have something sunny and bright. There's a shop nearby that I have seen; we shall find something for you that will be perfect."

Strafford appeared not to be listening. He was drinking his coffee and looking out distractedly at the seafront and the people passing by. It was a fresh, clear morning, the night's fall of dew drying off the ground in big shapeless patches. The air had a rinsed look, and the houses on Santa Klara off at the mouth of the bay seemed much nearer than in fact they were, their details showing in sharp relief.

He, too, was conscious of the absurd predicament into which he had landed, through no fault of his own. Quirke, he saw, was either suffering from a hangover or was working himself into a fresh bout of rage—or both. How did that wife of his put up with him? She was so calm, so pleasant, so amusedly ironic. He had caught her eye as they were entering the dining room and he was convinced she had given him the ghost of a wink.

He supposed he would have to meet the young woman Quirke believed was April Latimer. What would he say to her? How was he supposed to behave? Good behavior, of which his father had been the very model, was important to Strafford. To carry oneself well was one of the marks of a gentleman, and he was nothing if not that, by design as well as by nature. He knew the world took him for a prig. Well, let it.

His coffee had gone cold. He looked out again at the morning—it might be a watercolor scene by Raoul Dufy. Who but the likes of Quirke would allow himself to be glum in this paradisal place of beige and white and pellucid blue?

He was sharply conscious of Phoebe where she sat next to him. He breathed deep and caught the scent of her well-scrubbed skin. All high-strung girls smelled the same, in his experience, which, as he would have been the first to admit, wasn't wide. It was clear that she, for her part, didn't think much of him.

Now she put down her napkin and stood up.

"I'm going to telephone the hospital," she announced.

Quirke lifted his head and stared at her. She stared back. What was she here for if not to meet the woman he believed was April Latimer?

"Ah, but what about our shopping expedition?" Evelyn exclaimed.

Phoebe had a small but seemingly insoluble problem, which was that she didn't know how to address her father's wife. She had worked for Evelyn as her receptionist—this was how Quirke had encountered Evelyn in the first place—and then she had been, simply, "Dr. Blake." But Dr. Blake was now her step-mother. Somehow, she couldn't bring herself to call this self-contained, slightly intimidating, complacently middle-aged woman by her first name, even if she was married to her father. It was a conundrum.

Strafford, too, rose to his feet. Phoebe gave him a questioning look. Did he intend to accompany her to the telephone and stand by while she placed her call? She wondered yet again why Chief Superintendent Hackett had insisted on sending him with her. She was hardly in need of a bodyguard, and anyway, Straf-ford hardly fitted the description.

"I'll call from my room," she said, and turned to go.

"Wait," Quirke said. "What are you going to do?"

"I told you—I'm going to phone the hospital, and ask to speak to Dr.—what did you say was the name she's going by?"

"Lawless. Dr. Angela Lawless. What are you going to say to her?"

"I don't know. I'll let her do the talking."

Quirke's eyes slid away from hers. He had, she saw, the queasy look of a man who in an unthinking moment had arranged an elaborate practical joke, only to find that he was himself the butt of it.

Phoebe walked away.

"I wonder, my dear," Evelyn said mildly to her husband, "if you ever listen to the way you speak to people."

Strafford cleared his throat.

"I think perhaps I'll take a walk."

He disentangled himself from the chair and rose and drifted in the direction of the sunlit front door. Quirke looked after him, noting his curiously sinuous, meandering gait, and scowled. He could have done with a drink, but even for him it was still too early.

Evelyn, too, was watching Strafford, who stopped now and turned to glance up at Phoebe ascending in the lift.

"Oh, dear, they are so lonely," she said. "And so careful to avoid seeing what is plain to see."

"Oh, yes?" Quirke said suspiciously. "And what's that?"

Ash from his cigarette dropped into his lap and he brushed at it vexedly.

"Oh, Quirke, my dear. For such a clever man, you know so little. They are like—"

"Chalk and cheese, that's what they're like."

"No, no. They're like those things, what do you call them, the things that attract metal."

"Magnets."

"Yes, that's it. They are two magnets, turned the wrong way and pulling against each other." She demonstrated with her hands. "Just one little twist and—" She smacked her hands together, and laughed.

Quirke's frown deepened. He didn't like the sound of this at all. Phoebe, and that chinless wonder?

"What about your nephew?" he said. "Aren't he and Phoebe—?"

"Not really. Paul is a good young man, very bright and ambitious. He may do something notable in the world. But Phoebe is not for him, and he is not for Phoebe."

"Christ," Quirke said, and slumped back on his chair. Not the least part of his dismay was due to the fact that it was by his agency that his daughter and Detective Inspector bloody Strafford had been brought together in the first bloody place.

In the corridor on the way to her room, Phoebe had a sensation of weightlessness, as if gravity had let go its hold on her. It lasted only a second or two, then she seemed to pass effortlessly through some glair-like substance, and was her solidly grounded self again. Yet even when she reached the door to her room and was inserting the key in the lock, something of that peculiar buoyant feeling remained. It was at once unsettling and faintly thrilling. She felt as one feels when the vase slips from one's hands and seems to hang suspended for an instant before plummeting to the floor and exploding into a thousand pieces.

In her room, she stood motionless in the middle of the floor, trying to regain her equilibrium. The window was open on to the pale-blue day. The gauze curtain stirred, the hem of it making a faint scraping sound as it brushed back and forth over the carpet.

The telephone stood on a cabinet beside the bed. A squat, smug black thing, it seemed to dare her to approach it. She felt the same antipathy to phones as she did to hotels. There was so much she had in common with her father, she thought ruefully. She lifted the receiver. The male operator, bright and brisk, spoke to her in fluent English, which for some reason she resented. He requested her to hang up, saying he would call her back. She put down the receiver. The feel of the Bakelite, heavy, smooth and chill, made her shiver.

It had occurred to her on the way down here that all this business of "Dr. Angela Lawless," and who she really was or wasn't, might be an elaborate ploy by her father to get her away from Paul Viertel. She wouldn't put it past him, for he was devious when he set his mind to something. He had never approved of Paul, even though—or because?—he was his wife's nephew. It had nothing to do with the fact that Paul was a Jew, she knew that. No, with Quirke, it was always personal.

She sat back on the bed with her hands pressed hard against the mattress on either side of her, thinking. Then she snatched up the phone again, intending to cancel the call to the hospital. But she got a different operator this time, whose English was poor, and she couldn't make herself understood, and in the end she hung up. She was flustered. She had an image of a bird floundering in a net as colorless as air.

The phone rang, making her jump, and the mattress springs jangled under her. She picked up the receiver. It was the first operator, informing her that he was putting her through to the hospital. Then a female voice spoke to her in Spanish. Stammering, she replied in English.

"Please, I wish to speak to Dr. Angela Lawless."

She waited, biting her lip. She could feel the beating of her heart.

There was a sort of hissing on the line, and the sound of people speaking in the background. An electric bell was ringing somewhere far off. Then she heard footsteps approaching. Rubber soles on rubber floor tiles.

"*Sí?*" It was a woman's voice. "*Quién es este, por favor?*"

"Forgive me," she said, "I don't speak Spanish. My name is Phoebe Griffin. I want—"

The line went dead.

40

Down on the beach, not far from the Londres, Terry Tice was lighting a cigarette. He held the match in his cupped fists, for there was a breeze coming in from the sea. He was sitting on a big striped towel, with his elbows resting on his knees. He gazed idly out over the bay. He was wearing his fawn slacks and the striped shirt with the big sleeves, which he still wasn't sure about. He didn't see the point of beaches, and hadn't even taken off his shoes, never mind his socks.

He felt conspicuous, with his white arms and whiter shins. Even as a kid he used to avoid the seaside, and when he was there, about the only pleasure he found was in kicking over the sandcastles the other kids had made.

People looked so stupid here, the tourists especially, the fat women as pale as suet, the men with the cuffs of their trousers rolled up and knotted handkerchiefs on their heads to ward off the sun. Then there were the he-men, flexing their muscles, as if they all thought they were Johnny Weissmuller. As for swimming, that really was for chumps. Imagine floundering around up to your neck out there, with them all screaming around you, and throwing water in each other's faces, or standing with their hands on their hips and that faraway look on their faces that told you they were taking a piss.

The Girl was stretched out beside him, wearing a shiny black swimsuit that made her look a bit like a baby seal. She was lying on her front, her face turned to one side and her cheek resting on the backs of her hands. She was asleep, or at least she had her eyes closed.

She was a little beauty, he had to admit it. Her skin was a shade of dark gold, and warm and slightly rough to the touch. Her hair fascinated him, it was so black and darkly shiny. He had never seen hair like it, except on certain tinker women in the west of Ireland, when he was over there, at Carricklea. They used to come around every September, selling handmade tin cans for collecting blackberries in.

One of them had spoken to him once, a big raw-boned woman with a shawl wrapped around her. He could hardly understand what she was saying, her accent was so strong—*Wisha Gawd bless ye son that ye may have a laang life and heppiness.* Then one of the Brothers had popped up out of nowhere and told her to get off with herself before he called the Guards. He'd given Terry a wallop on the back of the head, too, just for listening to her. Terry had looked back at the woman straggling off down the boreen, in her bare feet, the brightly shining tin cans strung on her arm and rattling, and something in him had yearned after her, as if somehow she had tied a bit of elastic to him and it was stretching out and getting thinner and thinner, until she rounded a bend and was gone, and the elastic went slack.

Maybe he had tinker blood, himself? He wouldn't mind it if

he had. They were hard people, tough and hard, you didn't give them any lip. One day a gang of them came to Carricklea and took away a young fellow, one of their own, that Brother Harkness had been giving a hard time to. They shouted for Harkness to come out and take off his holy collar and face them, but Harkness wisely kept indoors. Eventually the Guards were called and the tinkers scattered, dragging their young fellow along with them. The whole school had let out a cheer, and next day at breakfast, dinner and tea there was nothing on the refectory tables, only stale bread and rusty water. It was to teach them all a lesson. It didn't matter. They had already learned a bigger lesson, which was that you could be rescued.

The Girl, too, she had a bit of the look of a gypsy, especially in the bluish shadows under her eyes, and in the stringy backs of her agile little hands.

She was from the countryside, somewhere in the middle, where he supposed the land was parched and colored yellowy-brown. That was why she so loved to be by the sea. Any chance she got she was down here, lying on her blanket, with her eyes closed and her lips curled at the corners in a little secret smile. He had never known anyone so happy, so contented. She never complained, even when one of her johns cut up rough, or one of the other girls in the house got into a fight with her and pulled her hair. She was a fearsome fighter herself, and everyone knew to avoid those sharp little fists of hers.

One thing about the seaside was that cigarettes tasted better there. Must be something to do with the ozone in the air. He wasn't sure what ozone was, but people talked about it all the time so it must be something good.

He was thinking. Terry liked to think, liked to have a problem to be solved, a plan to be worked out. The question right now was how to get into the hospital to find Dr. What's-her-name and have a good look at her. He would need to make sure he had the right one. Percy Antrobus had given him an inaccurate description of a target once, a blacky from Bermondsey, and he had ended up knifing the wrong guy. That was messy, and, worse, it was unprofessional. He should have given Percy a smack, but Percy, soft and all as he was, just wasn't smackable, somehow. Shootable, yes, but not smackable.

He turned his thoughts back to the main concern. It was true, he could walk into the hospital and ask for her at the reception desk. What was to stop him? But what reason would he give for wanting to see her? And the receptionist would remember him, afterward. That wouldn't matter much, as he'd be long gone by the time they started looking for him. All the same, it was too risky. Not to mention untidy. He took pride in never leaving a trace of himself, when he did a job. *Mystery Killer Strikes Again.* That was him.

Once more the image came to him of Percy's bloated corpse wallowing in the oily waters of the Pool of London. It was bound to have bobbed up by now. He knew he shouldn't have done him in. He had let his temper get the better of him, which always meant trouble.

He stubbed out his cigarette in the sand. Down at the water's edge a little brown kid was squealing about something and kicking up water in a fury. His mother, at least Terry guessed it was his mother, grabbed him by his arm and gave him a shake, which only made him squeal all the louder.

There should be a law saying people had to get a license to have kids. Why did they want them, anyway? Millions of the little beggars, all over the place, wherever you went there they were, pissing themselves and bawling their heads off and getting walloped by their ma's and da's, who hadn't wanted them in the first place, or at least didn't want them when they had them, and it was too late. There were a lot of changes Terry would make, if he was given the chance. Yes, a lot of things would be different, if he was in charge.

A girl was walking down to the sea in a swimsuit with stripes on it. She had a nice backside, high and rounded. She dived into the waves, smooth and sure as—yes, as a seal. If there weren't kids there wouldn't be sweet girls like her, that was a thought. He watched her as she swam straight out, making hardly a ripple on the sea's smooth surface.

He had never learned to swim, himself. Never had the chance. Like with so many other things. That was one of the troubles with being an orphan, you had no one to teach you stuff. You had to do it all for yourself. Well, he hadn't managed too badly. He had got himself a profession, hadn't he? Someone had once asked him what he did for a living and he answered: garbage disposal. He grinned now, remembering. A girl it was who had asked him, in a club in Greek Street. When he answered her she gave him a funny look, and after a minute moved away from him. He supposed she thought he was a dustbin man.

He had brought his book with him. He was nearly at the end of it. Pinkie was planning to bump off the Girl, but it wasn't going to happen, that was plain to see. Even in books like this one the Girl didn't get done in—writers were too squeamish. Most likely it was Pinkie himself who was for it. He still had the bottle of acid in his pocket. That detail didn't ring true. Acid was bound to spill, if you carried it around with you.

The men in the book had these two words for women: "buer" and "polony." Terry had been around a lot, but he had never heard anyone referring to a woman by either of those words. Maybe the writer had made them up. A posh bloke trying to sound common. It didn't work, mate.

The light was too strong for reading, the page glared in the sun like a sheet of white metal with ants crawling over it. He looked out to sea again. The girl in the striped swimsuit was gone. Did she turn back and come out of the water without his noticing, or had she swum out so far she couldn't be seen? On the beach, everything looked as if it had been squeezed flat. Sounds, too, were different, either they were really sharp or really dull. Down to the left a little way, a dog was barking at the waves. The barks came to him as flat whacks on the air, like pistol shots.

Which brought him back to his problem, which was how to get into the hospital and make sure what-you-call-her was who she was supposed to be. What was her name? Something beginning with *L*. He had it written down in his notebook, but he had left it at the hotel. He took up his book and turned to the inside of the back cover, where he had stuck her photograph with bits of sticky tape. He studied her, where she leaned on the fake pillar in her lacy frock.

Lawless, that was it, that was her name. Angela Lawless. Or that at least was the name she was going under.

He leaned his chin on his hands and gazed out vacantly over the bay. Nice colors on the sea today, blue, and a kind of blueygreen, and a shiny, scaly silver that looked like the sheen on the flank of a fish. The Girl, beside him, hadn't stirred for the past ten minutes. He looked at her. She was definitely asleep. Sleeping was what she did a lot of. She worked hard, she was popular with the johns. Strange, that he didn't mind her doing it with all those other blokes. He despised them, and pitied them, too, in a funny sort of way. The truth was, he didn't get much out of doing it with her himself. Something mechanical about it. She had been at it since she was twelve, and there was no fight left in her. She was—what was the word?—passive. Whereas he liked a bit of resistance. He was fond of her, though. She was as tough as a terrier. Raised rough, like him. Terry and his Girl terrier.

He wondered what age she was. She had told him she was twenty-one, but they always lied. He put her at sixteen, seventeen tops. Not that it mattered. He didn't know his own age. At the orphanage one day they showed him some bit of paper, his birth cert, they claimed it was, but it wasn't his, the name on it was different. If anyone asked, he would say he was born on December 12, same day as Frankie Sinatra, Ol' Blue Eyes himself.

He was ashamed not to know the real date. It sort of summed up all he had been denied in life, all that had been taken from him. If ever he found out who his parents were, he would know what to do. *Hello, Mum, hello, Dad.* Then *blam! blam!*

He sighed. He was bored and yet he didn't mind. This beach wasn't like the ones at home. You could sit out here for hours doing nothing and not get the heebie-jeebies.

The simplest way to get into a hospital was to be sick. He hadn't been sick a day in his life. He could pretend, sure, but the doctors wouldn't be fooled. They had tests that they did. He would have to be running a temperature, or have splotches on his skin, or something broken. So that was out. The other way was to have someone in there that he could visit. No one would take any notice of him, walking along the corridors with a bunch of flowers in one hand and a box of chocs in the other. *How are you feeling today, sweetheart? How's the pain?*

He eyed the Girl again, her thin brown arms, her frail, breakable wrists.

41

Quirke told Phoebe he would go with her to the hospital, but she said no, that it would be better if she went alone. Then he suggested she let Evelyn accompany her. This offer, too, she turned down.

"At least phone ahead and tell her you're coming," Quirke said.

"I phoned once, and she hung up on me. Why would she do anything different if I call her again?"

They were in the hotel bar, which already she had come to think of as central headquarters of the Quest for April. Quirke had ordered a drink, though it was still only midmorning. At least it was wine he was drinking, not spirits—he didn't even consider white wine a real drink, only a sort of refresher, a post-breakfast pick-me-up.

"But what did you think, from the sound of her voice?" he asked. "Did you think it was her?—April, I mean."

She couldn't help but feel sorry for him. He had the anxious, pleading look of a little boy who had told a serious fib and was begging his big sister to cover up for him. The clumsy wad of bandage on his left hand made him more vulnerable still.

"I don't know whether it was her or not," she said, softening her tone. "She just spoke a few words in Spanish, asking me who I was, I suppose. I said my name, and the line went dead."

Evelyn was there, seated between them at the table and paying them no attention. She was knitting something shapeless in gray wool. Strafford had come down earlier and loitered for a while, before wandering outside and sitting at a table under an awning with his book. Phoebe felt sorry for him, too. He had no real reason to be here, and obviously was conscious of being embarrassingly superfluous.

She sighed. She was cross. She felt tricked and imposed upon. After the woman at the hospital had hung up on her she had sat for a long time on the side of the bed, staring at the infuriatingly incommunicative telephone. She still hadn't given up the idea that Quirke might have done all this in order to get her away from Paul, though the more she thought about it, the less likely it seemed. Quirke might be many things, but a jealous father he was surely not.

"So what will you do?" he was asking her now.

"I'll just walk into the hospital and demand to see her."

"What makes you think she'll agree to meet you, when she wouldn't even talk to you on the phone?"

"I'll say I won't leave until she comes. I'll say—I'll say your hand has got infected and I need to consult her."

"It wasn't her that treated me," Quirke said.

"Well, I'll think of something. I'll just sit there, for as long as it takes. Eventually they'll give in, and tell her she'll have to come and talk to me, if only so they can get rid of me."

Evelyn spoke then, startling them both—they had almost forgotten she was there.

"My dear, I should not have allowed your father to call you
in the first place, but it's so nice that you are here. Why don't
you and Mr. Strafford make a little walk, on the seafront? It's
such a lovely day. You can go to the hospital and search for this
young woman another time."

Phoebe didn't reply, and looked away vexedly. She had caught
the spark of hope that had lighted in Quirke's eye—plainly he,
too, would prefer her to "make a little walk" with that bean-
pole, whom she could see through the window, lounging outside in the shade with that book of his that seemed never out
of his hand.

"And there's that dress we must find for you," Evelyn went on,
continuing to knit. "We might go and look for it, you and I."

Evelyn's unshakable calm could be infuriating. It was as if she
lived inside an insulating capsule made of something transparent
but far finer than glass, and entirely impenetrable.

Phoebe rose to her feet, holding on to her handbag as if it
were a gauntlet.

"I'm going to the hospital," she said.

She crossed to the desk and handed in her key, and asked the
receptionist to call a taxi. Then she walked out into the sunlight,
lifting a hand to shade her eyes against the glare. Quirke came
out after her. He looked agitated. Serves him right, she thought.

"I'm sorry—" he began.

"What are you sorry for?" she said sharply. "I'm here, amn't
I—you got your way."

"Listen, I just—"

"Oh, leave it, will you, please?"

He was giving her a headache. He put out a hand to touch
her but she pretended not to notice, and stepped away from him.

Damn, she said to herself. Damn damn damn.

Where was that taxi?

She walked away from Quirke, and approached Strafford where he sat under the awning, poring over his book.

"You know, you really should go home," she said.

He looked up at her, pretending to be surprised. He was just like Paul when he brushed that limp wing of hair away from his forehead. She felt like kicking him on the shin.

"Why do you say that?" he asked.

"Well, you're not doing much good here, are you."

This he considered for a moment, looking past her to the sea. Then he turned his gaze on her again and smiled.

"Someone must watch, it is said. Someone must be there."

She blinked. This was not the response she had expected from him, or anything like it. To her consternation, she felt her face go red.

"Is that—is that a quotation?" she stammered.

"Yes. Kafka."

"Oh."

All at once she saw him in a new light, at once somber and bright. Shaken, in a way she didn't understand, she turned and walked away from him rapidly, seeming to herself to stumble.

Someone to be there. It was what she longed for.

Across the road, a young couple were coming up the steps from the beach. The girl, pretty, her mouth painted a garish shade of scarlet, wore a loose linen dress, and was barefoot. The young man following after her carried a beach towel and a straw basket. He also had a book, Phoebe noticed, a paperback with an orange cover. He wore fawn trousers and shoes with buckles. She frowned, watching him.

Quirke came and stood beside her.

"Do you know him?" he asked.

"It's strange, I think I've seen him before somewhere."

"He's not from these parts." He paused. "Orphanage boy."

She turned to him.

"What? How can you tell?"

He shrugged.

"We know our own."

Phoebe's taxi arrived at last. The doorman stepped forward smartly and opened the door for her. She got in. The taxi drove away.

Now Quirke walked over to where Strafford sat.

"You should go after her," he said.

Strafford looked up at him, feigning surprise.

"What?"

"Go after her," Quirke repeated. He gave a sort of laugh. "You'll get to say 'Follow that taxi,' like a real detective."

Strafford closed his book and stood up.

"What do you expect me to do, exactly?"

"I don't know. Keep an eye on her."

"Listen, Dr. Quirke, I really think—"

Quirke lifted a hand to silence him.

"Just watch out for her, will you, please? I told you, I have a bad feeling. There's a taxi, look—flag it down."

Strafford lifted his arm and the taxi pulled violently out of the line of traffic, veered across the road and drew to a smoking halt. Strafford hesitated—he felt as if his coat had caught in the cogs of a relentless and fast-moving machine. He climbed into the passenger seat. The window was down. Quirke laid a hand on the doorframe.

"Listen," he said in a low voice, "I'm counting on you."

Strafford nodded, though he didn't quite know what it was he was being depended on for.

Quirke stood back. The taxi driver spun the steering wheel.

The girl in the beach dress walked on, followed by the young man carrying the towel and the straw basket. They were going in the direction of the Old Town.

Quirke went back into the hotel. Evelyn, at the table, knitted on, uninterruptable. She smiled at Quirke. He sat down, and sighed. The wine that remained in his glass was tepid. His wife was watching him.

"I'll have another if I feel like it," he said.

She raised an eyebrow.

"Did I say anything?"

"You don't need to."

"Have whatever you want, my dear. I shall not try to stop you. Do I ever?"

He sat back in the chair and laid his wounded hand in his lap. The bandage gave him vaguely the look of a boxer at the end of an exhausting bout.

"You are worried," Evelyn said. "Are you afraid this young woman is not the one you think she is?"

"Of course it is," he snapped. Then he looked away, and sighed again. "I don't know. I was sure at first, but now—"

Evelyn freed a length of wool from the ball on the floor at her feet.

"It's good to have Phoebe here," she said, concentrating on the wool.

"You think I made the whole thing up just to get her down here, don't you," he said. "Maybe I did. As you like to tell me, I don't know anything about myself or what I do."

Evelyn clicked her tongue.

"No, no," she said, shaking her head, "I do not tell you such things. I do not like to tell anyone anything, since I know so little myself."

Quirke looked out at the bay. How innocent the sea seemed, out there, a sort of huge toy, to be paddled in and swum through and sailed on. He supposed there must be storms, in wintertime. Hard to believe, on a day like this. The people passing by outside were cut off at the waist by the window ledge. They reminded him of that Seurat painting of a Sunday crowd gravely disporting themselves on a grassy island in the Seine. There was something blandly uncanny in that scene, as there was here, too, with those doll–like half-figures gliding past the window. He felt unease stir in him, like a bubble in his gut.

"Why would she come here and hide herself away, this April Latimer?" Evelyn asked.

Quirke still had his eye on the window and the people passing by. They might be mounted on hobbyhorses, he thought.

"They're dangerous people, her family," he said.

"That poor young man, her brother, who killed himself. I would be glad to think he did not kill her, too." A ship, white with a blue stripe, had appeared on the horizon, beyond Santa Klara. "The mind has a mind of its own, you know. It does things of which we are not aware. It makes connections, invents fantasies. This is the secret world we move in when we dream."

"I'm not dreaming," Quirke said stubbornly.

He was looking around for the barman, his old pal.

"You are worried," Evelyn said again.

That trick of hers, to be able to read his thoughts. She had paused to count a row of stitches, speaking the numbers under her breath. She always counted in German. "...*siebzehn, achtzehn*..." Then she plied her needles again.

"There was an old Christian Brother, in the place where I was," Quirke said—he never spoke the name of Carricklea if he could avoid it. "His dentures were loose."

"Oh, yes?"

"They used to make a sound just like that, just like you knitting." The needles went still. She looked at him. He turned his eyes away from hers. "I think I shouldn't have made that phone call," he said. "I shouldn't have brought Phoebe here. I shouldn't have involved her."

"Why? Why do you think this?"

He was looking again to the window and the sea–bright day shining in it. A brass band was playing somewhere far off; the faint music came in billows, wavering.

"I don't know."

He spotted the waiter, gestured to him.

"The detective," Evelyn said, "what is his name, again? I've forgotten."

"Strafford."

"Strafford. He will protect Phoebe. I trust him." The waiter arrived, smiling and murmuring. It was Evelyn who spoke to him. "My husband will have a very large glass of white wine. And I shall take a tisane."

Quirke watched the old man shuffle away. He wore a red waistcoat, a white shirt, decidedly grubby at the collar, and dark trousers that sagged in the seat.

"I'm not much impressed by Inspector Strafford," he said.

Evelyn counted another row.

"He has a gun," she said, and severed a length of wool with her teeth.

"A gun?"

"Yes, a pistol. I saw it, under his jacket."

"What a sharp eye you have, my dear."

He thought of the young man and his little doll-like girl climbing the steps from the beach. Beware orphanage boys.

"No," he said, with a troubled frown, "I shouldn't have made that call."

Evelyn was counting stitches again—"...*zwei, drei*..." Now she interrupted herself and said, "But you did, my dear."

42

Slamming shut the door of the taxi, Phoebe turned, and paused to gaze up at the hospital's white-pillared facade. The place looked altogether too cheery and bright to be a house for the sick. It reminded her of a toy she had when she was a child, consisting of a set of painted wooden blocks that could be assembled and reassembled flat in its box into a seemingly infinite number of variants of a miniature palace. It was, she recalled, a Christmas present from Quirke, in the days when he was still masquerading as her favorite uncle. For this and other deceptions she had long ago forgiven him. One had to make do with life's building blocks, the unasked-for gift that couldn't be brought back to the shop and exchanged for something better.

She went up the steps and pushed through the tall swing doors. The nun behind the reception desk wore a pale-gray habit with celluloid cuffs and a stiff collar, and a comical little white hat topped with a pair of starched white butterfly wings.

"I am here to see Dr. Angela Lawless."

The nun, as if reacting to a challenge, shook her head vigorously and poured out a stream of Spanish. Phoebe, taken aback, made to speak again. Before she could do so, the telephone on the desk rang, and the nun answered it. Somewhere in the farther reaches of the hospital an electric bell began to blare—Phoebe recognized it as the same one she had heard earlier in the background on the telephone. The nun ignored it, only raised her voice until she was yelling into the phone. Meanwhile, Phoebe took out her diary and scribbled DR. ANGELA LAWLESS on a blank page at the back and held it up for the nun to see. The bell was still ringing. The nun put a hand over the receiver.

"*Ahí está ella,*" she said impatiently, pointing past Phoebe's shoulder.

Phoebe turned. On the far side of the reception area, at the entrance to a long, light-filled corridor, a youngish woman in a white coat, a doctor, obviously, stood talking to a younger nurse, her back turned to Phoebe. Slender, with narrow shoulders and dark hair cut short. Her ankles looked too frail to support even so slight a frame.

The nurse saw Phoebe staring, and said something to the woman facing her. The bell stopped ringing, leaving behind it a faint, tinny reverberation fading on the air. The nun had put down the phone and was addressing Phoebe again, again in Spanish. Phoebe paid her no heed.

Beyond the glass of the swing doors she saw a taxi pulling up outside and Strafford alighting from it. She had a dizzying sense of things rushing together into a vast, silent collision, like an event in stellar space.

The woman in the white coat glanced over her shoulder. It seemed for a moment that she might turn and hurry away down

the corridor in front of her and be swallowed up in its glaring,
icy radiance. Instead, she smiled, rueful, wry, remembered.

They went to a hotel farther up the hill, an ugly, white, many-
windowed cube surrounded by trees. On the way, they did not
speak. Phoebe thought of Lot leading his wife away from the cit-
ies of the plain—one backward glance and all would be undone.

Inside, the hotel was large and bright and brashly modern,
with a curiously antiseptic air—it might have been another,
newer version of the hospital down the road. They sat at the bar
on high stools beside a long, low picture window. The place was
chillingly spacious, with steel chairs and steel-legged tables. A
futuristic chandelier, made of countless splinters of frosted glass,
was suspended from the center of the high ceiling like a frozen avalanche. They were the only customers. Looking down
through the window they could see the crowns of the massed
trees below, their foliage a deep, blackish green in the strong sunlight, and, farther down the slope, the black roof of the hospital.

"Your papa recognized me, then," April Latimer said. "I knew
he did." She gave a small, hard laugh. "Of all the seaside towns,
in all the world, he had to come here."

Phoebe had so many things to say, so many questions to ask,
that she didn't know where to begin.

"He phoned me the night you met him for dinner at the restaurant," she said. "I didn't believe him, at first, that it was you."

"And then you did?"

"I don't know. I so much wanted it to be you that I thought
it couldn't possibly be."

April looked out over the treetops. She wore a white blouse,
the sleeves buttoned at the wrist, a narrow black skirt and black
shoes with flat heels. She had changed hardly at all. Her face especially was as Phoebe remembered it, starkly pale and narrow
with a sharp chin and large, vibrant, darkly shining eyes. There
was something new in her manner, though, a new brittleness.

Phoebe had always been a little afraid of her, in a thrilled sort of way. You never knew what April would do next.

A spring door behind the bar opened and the barman came out, drying his hands on a dishcloth. He was young, dark, lithe as a dancer. April and he exchanged a wry, complicit smile. April ordered gin.

Strafford came into view, walking up the hill. At the sight of him, Phoebe felt herself blush. Should she tell April who he was? She said nothing, though, only watched as the detective turned in at the hotel gates. She wished he had not followed her. His presence would only make everything more difficult.

The barman set April's glass in front of her. She said something to him in Spanish, and he gave a lazy shrug and went back through the doorway. The drink had a little parasol in it, made of pleated paper attached to a toothpick.

"Tell me what happened," Phoebe said. "Please."

April took a tube of lipstick from the pocket of her skirt and began applying it, narrowing her eyes to peer at herself in the mirror behind the bar. The lipstick was a violent shade of crimson, and turned her pale face into a primitive mask. She pressed a napkin between her lips, leaving a perfect imprint of them on the paper.

"What do you mean, what happened?" she said.

"Why did you run away and pretend to be dead?"

April laughed. "Did I 'run away'?"

"Well, didn't you? Everyone thought you were dead. Oscar—"

"Yes, well, I'm not dead, as you see." This was spoken with brusque finality. April put the lipstick away and plucked the parasol out of her glass and dropped it on the bar. She drank.

"Don't you want something?" she said to Phoebe. "Have some sangria—that's what all the tourists drink."

"No, thanks," Phoebe said. "I just had breakfast."

"Did you? God, I never eat breakfast."

The barman emerged again through the doorway. He eyed

the paper napkin where it lay on the bar, with the impression in it of April's lips. April saw him looking at it, and picked it up and tossed it to him, with another hard little laugh. It fluttered to the floor, and he bent to retrieve it. April turned away. The barman stared stonily at her profile for a moment and then went away again, kicking the door shut behind him with his heel.

"Why are you being so awful to him?" Phoebe asked.

"Gonçal? He doesn't mind—I sleep with him now and then." She was pensive for a moment, then said, "What a shock I got when I saw your old man at the hospital. Couldn't believe my eyes. Where did I meet him, by the way?"

"We were coming out of the Shelbourne one night, while he was coming in. He almost fell over us. I introduced you, and he said something stupid."

"Oh, yes? What?"

"I can't remember. One of his drunken gallantries."

April gave a little squeal of laughter.

"Wonderful!" she said. "Did he try to get off with me?"

"Well, you were with me, you know."

"Would that have stopped him? He had quite a reputation in those days, as I recall." She put a finger into her drink and stirred it, making the ice cubes joggle. "He's not bad-looking," she said thoughtfully, and sucked her finger. "For a man of his age, anyway."

She took another sip of her drink, and studied herself and Phoebe in the mirror facing them.

"Love your dress," she said. "Just the thing for Spain."

Phoebe smiled.

"Yes, I know. My stepmother says I must buy something bright."

"Bright? You?" April did one of her smiling grimaces, her mouth lifted high at one side. "Can't see it, myself." She dipped her head—like a finch, Phoebe thought, with that little sharp nose and those pale, pinched nostrils—and drank again from her glass. It was almost empty. "What's she like, that woman?"

"Who—?"

"Dr. Thing—what's she called?—your stepmother." She paused, and laughed. "Are there really stepmothers? I thought they were only in fairy tales."

"Evelyn is her name."

"She reminded me of one of those big carved heads on Mount Rushmore. Can't remember which one. Is she wicked? They're all supposed to be wicked, aren't they?"

"Only in fairy tales. She's very nice."

"They took me to dinner. Did they say? Ghastly—be thankful you missed out on that treat."

A sort of misery was welling up in Phoebe's breast.

"April, I don't know what to say to you," she said. She felt she might be about to cry. She mustn't—April would only laugh at her. "I didn't forget you. I thought about you all the time."

"Even though I was dead?"

"You weren't dead to me. Somehow, in some part of my mind, I knew you were alive." She felt the tears pressing up into her eyes. "Are you happy here," she asked, "here in Spain?"

April shrugged. "You know me, Pheebs. I don't like anywhere. The hospital is all right, I do some good."

"My father said you came to dinner with a—with a friend."

"Oh, Gerry. Yes. Jeronimo Cruz. My sugar daddy. He's the one who got me the job here."

"How did you know him?"

"He came to Ireland, years ago, to give a talk at the College of Surgeons. I collared him afterward, and we went to bed in his hotel. The Russell. He gave me a wonderful dinner there that night and pledged undying love. I kept in touch with him. Lucky I did. He's ancient, of course, but I like older men. If things had been otherwise I'd probably have made a go at your papa, at dinner the other night." She glanced sideways at Phoebe and grinned. "Yes, awful, amn't I. Once a nympho, always a nympho."

"Dr. Cruz, is he a good man?" Phoebe asked.

She expected April to laugh at so gauche a question, but she didn't.

"He's very high-minded," she said after a moment's consideration. "A little of it rubs off on me, I think—I hope. He makes me better than I am. What more can one ask?"

"Are you—I mean, do you—?"

"Are we living together? I suppose so." Her expression darkened for a moment. "He takes care of me. Heaven knows, I need it." She broke off, and craned her neck to try to see through the circular window in the door behind the bar. She called out something in Spanish, waited a moment, then picked up a handful of peanuts from a bowl on the bar and began to throw them one by one at the door. The barman appeared. The peanuts on the floor crunched under his shoes. He scowled at April, his already dark face darkening with anger. April took no notice, only waggled her glass on its base to indicate she needed a refill. Phoebe smiled at him tentatively, but he ignored her. He snatched the bottle from the shelf behind the bar and filled the glass halfway with gin. April spoke to him again, in Spanish, in a wheedling tone this time, batting her eyelashes at him in a vampish parody. He made no reply, and went away again.

"I shouldn't be drinking," April said, and laughed. "They'll smell it on my breath, and I'll be sacked, and then I'll have to find another sugar daddy to get me a new job."

Phoebe hadn't noticed Strafford coming in. She saw him now, sitting at a table in a far corner, with a cup of coffee, opening his book with the green binding. April would have done well in the time of Tiberius, she thought.

"Do you ever consider coming home?" she asked.

April stared at her.

"To Ireland? You must be joking. Anyway, I couldn't, even if I wanted to."

"Why?"

The barman came through the swing door again, and put a little folded paper packet on the bar and pushed it forward with a fingertip. April picked it up quickly and stowed it down the front of her blouse.

"*Gracias, cariño, te amo*," she said silkily, and kissed her fingers to the barman. He glanced at Phoebe and heaved an ironical sigh. When he was gone, April turned to Phoebe and winked. "My little *billet-doux*," she whispered.

"Tell me why you can't go home," Phoebe said.

April put on a vague look, and shrugged.

"Just can't." She drank from her glass and grimaced. "Jesus, it's neat gin," she said, and giggled. "I'll be completely pissed." She looked at Phoebe in the mirror. "I'm sorry I hung up on you, by the way," she said, not sounding sorry at all. "But you gave me a shock. A voice out of the past." She smiled impishly, and for a second Phoebe saw the younger version of her, the one she used to know, in the old days. Which weren't very old—what was it, four years since they had last seen each other? It seemed far longer than that.

"Tell me why you can't go back," Phoebe said again. "You owe me that much, at least."

April peered moodily again into her glass.

"You don't know my family, what they're like," she said. "Our house, our so-called home—God! Oscar called it Château Désespoir. I only found out what it meant when I started French in school. He was older, you see, and knew what was going on far better than I did. I mean, I knew what was going on—Jesus, my father was doing the two of us, me and Oscar, taking us in turns. Then, when Daddy died, Oscar and I carried on together, continuing the grand tradition."

"Did he rape you?" Phoebe asked.

April looked at her pityingly.

"Oscar? *Oscar?* Ha! The other way around, if anything. Not that I wanted him, you understand. It was—obsession. I tried to explain it to you once, but of course you couldn't understand what I was talking about. We all had it, the obsession, in that mad family. For all I know, Oscar and my mother may have been at it, too. It was like living in a rabbit warren. It all seemed perfectly ordinary to me, of course. Well, I'd never known anything different. The only thing that troubled me, really, was the secrecy—we were to tell no one, Daddy said, or Oscar and me would both end up in the reformatory."

Phoebe cast about the room. Strafford was deep in his book, or seemed to be.

April finished her drink and set the glass down on the bar.

"Poor Oscar," she said.

"Yes," Phoebe said. "Poor Oscar. You know I was there the day that he—"

April suddenly brightened, lifting her head and grinning.

"He did it in your father's car, didn't he—drove off Howth Head. An Alvis, too, wasn't it? God, how I laughed when I heard that." She laughed now, shaking her head. "He was never much of a driver, our Oscar."

"Oh, April," Phoebe murmured.

"What do you mean, 'Oh, April'? My brother is better off dead. His life was hell. Besides, Daddy had set him an example, hadn't he. And then it kept getting worse. When the patriarch blew his brains out, and that source of torment was cut off, Oscar was left with me to deal with."

"Do you feel—I mean—"

"Guilty? Why should I feel guilty? He did it to himself, I had nothing to do with it." She paused. "People like you, you have no idea. The world, this world—" She stopped, and shook her head slowly from side to side. Then she frowned. "Oh, Lord," she said, "I think I'm a bit drunk."

"Tell me why you can't go back. Please."

April gave a little belch. "Oops," she said, covering her mouth with her fingers. Then she frowned. "What did you say?"

"I asked you to tell me why it is you can't go home."

"All right," April said, leaning her elbows on the bar. "All right, then, Pheebs my love, I'll tell you."

43

There weren't many things Terry Tice was afraid of, but boredom was one of them. And unfortunately for him, he was easily bored. Returning from the beach, he was hardly in the door at the *lupanar* before he began to feel restless. The back of his neck was throbbing—his fair skin burned easily under the Spanish sun—and there was sand between his toes, which he couldn't understand, since he had kept his socks on the whole time he was at the beach.

The Girl started in on him straight away, rubbing against him and trying to get her hand inside his slacks, but he pushed her off.

"Leave it out," he growled. "What do you think I am, a screwing machine?"

Bloody insatiable, she was—didn't she get enough of it in her working day? But "a screwing machine"—he liked that. Sounded like sewing machine, which was why it was funny. Of course, it was wasted on her, since she didn't understand a word he said.

He lit a cigarette and went and sat moodily by the open window. The street below was all bustle and jabber, as usual. He already had a headache from the sun. The Girl said something to him in Spanish, asking him some question, and when he ignored her she flew into a rage and started shrieking at him. It was the first time he had seen her like this, and it was quite a sight. He sat back on his chair and folded his arms and grinned at her, saying not a word. That really got her going, and she flew at him and tried to hit him, which was a bad mistake.

Funny stuff, human bone. He had seen an X-ray of his own arm once, the time it got banged up when he was working for Jack Comer. Jack, known as Spot because of a mole he had on his left cheek, ran the East End betting rackets after the war. He was one tough Jew, was old Spot. That job that went wrong turned out to be the last one Terry did for the "43s," Spot's outfit—the day he was let out of the hospital, a message came down the line informing him his services would no longer be required by Mr. Comer. Unfair, that was, getting his arm smashed in the line of duty and then getting the sack. But you didn't argue with Spot, not unless you wanted to end up sitting on the floor in a moldy cellar somewhere with your belly split open and your guts in your hands.

His arm in the X-ray looked ghostly, the bone a gray shadow against the glossy black of the negative, or whatever to call it, and the fractures showing up as little fine cobwebby lines. The doctor gave him the X-ray plate to keep, but he lost it somewhere.

It was as easy as snapping a dry stick, just one good twist was all it took.

The Girl started to scream but he clapped a hand over her mouth and pushed her down on her back on the bed and got his knee into her chest. To tell the truth, he was almost as surprised as she was. He didn't like acting impulsively, but that was the way it was with impulse, the thing was done before you knew it—look what had happened with Percy down the docks that night. Anyway, hadn't she provoked him, shrieking the way she did and then coming at him with her fists?

Now she was holding on to her wrist and making mewling sounds behind his hand, like a cat, or a newborn baby, and her eyes were shut tight and big shiny tears were squeezing out between the lids.

"Take it easy, sweetheart," he said, baring his teeth and pushing his knee harder into her chest. "Take it easy, now."

Afterward he realized that he hadn't acted on impulse at all, that without knowing it he had goaded her until she lost her temper and gave him the excuse to do what he did. Amazing the way the mind worked by itself like that, sometimes. The mind had a mind of its own, you might say. Heh heh. He must remember that. Not that there was anyone he could say it to who would appreciate it.

Dede, the hairy guy who had given him the key and the little towel that first day, and who turned out to be the owner of the place, made a fuss, and threatened to get his *amigos* to come and break a couple of Terry's wrists, just to show him what it felt like. Dede didn't much care about the Girl, but he was under pressure already, with one chippie off sick with the clap and two others he had sent on their holidays before the tourist season got going in earnest.

Terry swore it had been an accident, that the Girl had tripped and fallen on her wrist. He knew she wouldn't contradict him. He had made sure, Spanish or no Spanish, that she understood what he'd do to her if she ratted on him—a snapped wrist would be the least of it. He could see Dede didn't believe him, about it being an accident, but he called for an ambulance, anyway.

The Girl wouldn't stop crying, all the way to the hospital she kept it up. Well, you could hardly blame her. Terry remembered,

from the Comer job that went wrong, what it was like to have
a broken bone. The driver was watching him in the mirror,
but said nothing. Terry in a state was not a person you'd want
to meddle with.

At the hospital a nurse took the Girl away to have her wrist
tended to, while Terry was given the third degree by a nosy
doctor with silver hair, name of Cruz. Terry put on the helpless
foreigner act, pretending he didn't know what had happened
exactly, since the Girl didn't speak English and he didn't speak
Spanish. It was an accident, he said. She had tripped and fallen.
He was only helping her because he felt sorry for her. Cruz was
deeply suspicious. He probably knew that the place Terry had
given the address of was a *lupanar*. But he couldn't prove Terry
had done anything, and in the end he went off, saying the Girl
would be kept in "for observation," and that Terry could phone
later and find out how she was.

It was as easy as that.

And it could have been easier, for it turned out he needn't have
broken the poor little bitch's wrist, after all. In a busy hospital,
no one notices you unless you're a doctor, or look as if you're in
need of one. He walked around the place, making sure not to
hurry, or to seem too relaxed. He went up in the lift, to the first
and second floors, and wandered along corridors that smelled
of antiseptic and cooked food. He even took a look into some
of the rooms—in one, a uniformed nurse was sitting beside an
old guy lying in bed, and he could have sworn she was giving
him a hand job under the blankets.

All the same, he knew this wasn't the way to find the target.
She could be anywhere—she could be on her day off. He would
have to go to reception and ask for her, by name. Which he did.

The nun or whatever she was behind the desk looked at him
as if he had landed from Mars. She couldn't understand what

he was saying. Was she stupid, or was she putting it on? It was only a name he was saying, after all.

"Law-less," he said again, speaking very slowly and struggling to keep his temper, "Doc-tor An-ge-la Law—"

And that was when he saw her. She was with two people outside, he could see them through the glass of the front door. One was a polony of about her own age, the other a lanky-looking fellow with fair hair. Terry had seen them both somewhere, earlier today, he couldn't remember where. Then the two turned away, and she was coming in. He turned quickly from the desk and moved away, leaving the nun staring after him. He strolled across to where there was a green board attached to the wall and pretended to read the notices pinned to it. The woman who had come in wasn't dressed like a doctor, but he knew she wasn't a patient, either, from the confident look she had about her. She stopped at the desk and signed her name into a ledger or something. She seemed a bit unsteady on her legs. Had she been drinking? She wasn't Spanish, with that pale skin. It had to be her. She didn't look like she did in the photograph, but he recognized her all the same, with that dark hair and narrow face and pointed chin.

She turned from the desk now and set off down a long white-painted corridor, at the end of which a big frosted-glass window glared with light from outside. She was a bit bow-legged, which was a thing he liked in a buer. He had adopted that word, "buer," and "polony," too. He was interested in words, and made a habit of collecting new ones. Percy had told him once he was "a bit of a connoisseur." Percy was being sarcastic, as usual, but he was more right than he knew. Terry *was* a connoisseur, in certain things, especially now that he had learned from Percy how to pronounce the word.

A buer and a polony were different, two different types. One was tough, with a smart mouth and game for anything. The other was more of a lady. Funny, that. How would you know which was which? He would, he'd know. This one, for instance, was a buer, while the other one, that he'd seen her with outside, in the black dress with the white collar, she was a polony.

He was wondering what to do. He had that fluttery feeling inside him that he always got when a target came into his sights. He set off after her. Passing by the reception desk, he spotted a clipboard on the counter that someone must have left there and forgotten. The nun was still on the phone, and took no notice of him. Smoothly he picked up the clipboard and walked along, frowning at it, doing his impersonation of a doctor. He saw the woman stop at the far end of the corridor and go in through a doorway.

What he took to be a real doctor, wearing a white coat, was approaching. Terry passed him by without a glance, concentrating on the clipboard and frowning, as if he were reading test results and the news was all bad. He came to the door where the woman had gone in, pushed it open and slipped inside.

It was a storeroom. There were shelves stacked from floor to ceiling, and on the shelves were boxes of pills and things, and bottles of stuff, and rolls of bandages and lint and sticking plaster.

The gun! For Christ's sake—he hadn't brought it!

She was half sitting on the edge of a metal table, turned away from him. He stood in silence with his back to the door. It seemed she hadn't heard him coming in. What was she doing? A slip of folded tissue paper was open on the table. The left sleeve of her blouse was rolled up, and a rubber tube was wrapped tightly around her arm above the elbow. As he watched, she lifted a syringe to the light, tapped the barrel of it with a fingernail, then slid the needle at an angle into a bulging vein in the underside of her arm.

He felt let down. Why? What did it matter to him if she was a junkie? It didn't matter, of course it didn't. And yet he was disappointed in her. He was like a hunter who had tracked down the animal he had been stalking only to discover it was already wounded.

She eased out the needle and closed her eyes and let her head fall back slowly, exposing her smooth white neck. He heard her sigh. Then, even though he hadn't moved or made a sound, she opened her eyes suddenly and turned her head and looked at him.

Why, oh why hadn't he brought the gun? The thing would have been over and done with in a second, and she probably wouldn't have felt a thing. Two to the chest and one to the head, *bang-bang bang*, that was the rule all professionals followed.

He was still holding the clipboard. It was made of some kind of stiff, thin metal, with sharp edges. He hefted it in his hand. It would do. He was good at improvising. He moved forward.

The woman said something in Spanish, and then, realizing he hadn't understood, she switched to English.

"Who sent you?"

The dope was taking effect, and her voice was slurred, but he could see by her eyes that she was still alert enough. And she was angry. Those eyes glittered. The pupils were the size of pinheads.

He smiled.

"It's all right, April," he said softly. "I have something for you, from the folks in Dublin."

She watched him. She was getting woozier, and her eyes were starting to go out of focus. All he had to do was wait a few seconds, until all the fight had gone out of her.

"The bastards," she muttered.

She moved so quickly he was caught off guard. He hesitated for no more than half a second, but it was enough time for her to reach out and lift a wide-mouthed beaker from a shelf in front of her and with a flick of the wrist—he thought for an instant of the Girl—fling the contents of it into his face. The liquid was colorless, and had a familiar, slightly tarry smell. He dodged aside, but he wasn't quick enough, and the stuff splashed on his jaw and the side of his neck.

At first, he felt only the wetness, and a coolness that rapidly turned warm. He staggered forward, with the clipboard lifted like a blade. He drew back his arm, ready to slice at her. She stepped behind the table and put her hands against the edge of it and pushed it at him across the rubber-tiled floor.

A drop of the stuff she had flung at him had landed on the soft flesh just below his left eye. That was where the pain started. Then his jaw and the side of his neck seemed to catch fire. He gave a scream that surprised even himself.

His eye. Had the stuff got into his eye? For as long as he could remember he had been terrified of going blind. He often dreamed about it, and always woke in a sweat, shivering.

She was crouched behind the table, her hands still braced on the edge of it, watching him like a wild animal. Why wasn't the dope doing its work?

He dropped the clipboard and put his hands to his face and felt the terrible heat against his palms. The acid was eating into his skin. He aimed a wild punch at her but she reared back, out of his reach.

Christ, the pain.

He swore at her, and turned and ran to the door and wrenched it open.

Water.

He stumbled along the corridor. He could smell his own flesh scorching. What was the acid? Not sulfuric, not as bad as that. Phenol, he thought. Yes, that was the stink he had recognized.

He found a lavatory. He pushed open the swing door, and it banged against the wall and came back at him with such force it nearly knocked him down. He leaned over a handbasin and turned on the cold tap. At first the water made the pain worse, then the coolness set in. Phenol. Could have been worse. He had seen what real acid could do. One of Reggie Kray's girls had got a bottleful of hydrochloric straight in the mug. He came across her a couple of years later. She looked like Charles Laughton in *The Hunchback of Notre Dame*, only worse.

The gun. He'd get the gun, and find her. Oh, yes, he'd find her.

44

He thought the Girl was going to faint when she saw him. She got up from the bed where she had been lying on her side, nursing her bandaged wrist. Her face was gray from the pain, and there were beads of sweat on her forehead and on her upper lip. She began to say something to him but he pushed her out of the way and went to the mirror hanging by the window. He looked worse than he had in the hospital. The skin on his jaw and the side of his neck was livid, and there were patches of powdery white stuff that he hadn't managed to wash off.

He ran water in the sink and soaked one of his shirts and pressed the wetted cloth to his face. He sat down on the side of the bed. He was breathing hard, and now and then a breath would catch in his throat and come out as a sort of whimper. The Girl was going on and on at him, crying, and tearing at her hair with the fingers of her good hand. She was like something you'd see in the pictures. He would have given her a wallop if he felt more himself. But he was saving his energy for the Latimer bitch.

The question was, where to look for her. Would she still be at the hospital? She would have to go home sometime. This wasn't a big town. He would wait until it was dark, then he'd wrap a scarf or something around his face and go on the prowl. She might live miles outside the city, though somehow he didn't think so. She wasn't the rose-covered-cottage-in-the-country type.

Would she go to the cops? Not right away, with a head full of hop and a trail of needle marks up and down her arms. Maybe she wouldn't go at all. Junkies tended to steer clear of the filth.

He thought again about the pair he had seen her with outside the hospital. They were her friends, or certainly the one in the black dress was, that was plain to see. Maybe she'd go to them. But who were they? They had the look of tourists. They'd be bound to be staying in a fancy hotel. And there weren't many of those.

The shirt had warmed itself on his burning skin. He went to the sink and soaked it again under the tap. The Girl was sitting on the chair by the window, nursing her bandaged wrist in her lap like a baby. He grabbed her, sinking his fingers into her bony shoulder, and hauled her to her feet. She shrank away from him in fright, the whites of her eyes flashing, and began to babble what sounded like a prayer.

"Shut up!" he shouted. He pressed a handful of banknotes into her brown little claw and mimed drinking from a glass. "Whiskey," he said. "You know? Whiskey? Drink? Spirito?"

She nodded quickly and ran out of the room. He didn't care whether she came back or not. Though he was badly in need of a drink. He only took spirits when he had a pain, or couldn't get to sleep, or when old ghosts rose up and tried to frighten him.

He sat down again on the bed and swung his legs up onto

the covers and stuck a couple of pillows against the headboard and leaned back against them and closed his eyes.

A pulse was beating in his jaw. He was in a bad place, but he could bear it. He had got worse hurts at Carricklea, and he had survived them.

He bit on the pain as if he were biting on a bullet.

The Girl did come back, bringing him a bottle wrapped in a paper bag. He couldn't make out the label. It wasn't whiskey, but some kind of sweet, sticky stuff. It didn't matter, he drank it, anyway, straight from the bottle. He was beginning to feel better already. He would be all right.

The alcohol trickled along his veins, doing its work. He took another few slugs from the bottle, then corked it and put it away, on the far side of the little table that stood beside the bed. He was going to need a clear head.

Worse than the pain, in a way, was the sense he had of having been insulted. Yes, insulted. It wasn't just her, the doped-up bitch, slinging the stuff out of the beaker into his face. They were all in on it, the junkie, and the skinny one in the black dress, and the dozy-looking longshanks with the floppy hair, and the others, for he knew there must be others that he hadn't encountered yet. They had all spat on him, one big collective spit, that burned into his sense of himself as the acid had burned into his skin.

The Girl brought an enameled basin and a clean cloth and began to bathe his burned skin. They sat together side by side on the bed with the basin between them. It was funny, really, he thought, the two of them here, in pain, him with his face and her with her wrist. She had put ice cubes in the water and the coldness felt good, almost like an anesthetic. His face was still sore and stiff, but either the pain was easing or he was learning to cope with it.

Burns and scalds he had always feared. One night in a place

in Greek Street he had found himself in the middle of a bar-
ney, and took a bullet through the fleshy part of his arm just
below his left elbow. He hadn't even known he was shot until
it was all over and the bodies were being hauled out into the
lane at the back and shoved into a brewer's van to be taken away
and dumped. Next day he couldn't move his arm, and worried
that the slug might have severed a nerve or something. One of
Ronnie's doctors, an alky with a permanent drop on the end
of his nose, patched him up and told him to keep his arm in a
sling and take it easy for a week or two. Three nights running
he couldn't sleep for the pain, but he didn't mind. A hole in
your arm would heal with no one the wiser, but a burn to the
face left you marked for life.

The Girl was coming at him again with the soaked rag, but
he pushed her hand away and got up off the bed. His mood
had shifted. He was angry. The back of his shirt was damp. He
looked at himself again in the mirror at the window, turning
sideways to get a better look at his jaw. He touched the puffed
and angry skin here and there with his fingertips. Maybe it
would heal, maybe it wouldn't leave a scar. Anyway, he could
get a skin graft—they could do amazing things, nowadays, those
plastic surgeons.

He sat down on the cane chair by the open window. The
street below was swarming, as always. Didn't these fucking spics
ever get tired of rushing around the place and yelling at each
other?

Behind him the Girl was saying something, asking him a
question, by the sound of it, but he ignored her.

He lit a cigarette. The hot smoke rasped in his throat. He
thought of having another drink from the bottle, but didn't.
Stay sober. Stay in charge.

Black dress, white collar, pale northern face. Where had he
seen her, where?

He took out the gun from where he had hidden it under the

mattress on his side. It was a German model, .32 caliber, not great, but it packed a punch and was accurate enough. Not a patch on the little beauty he had let slip into the Irish Sea, of course.

He was strapping the holster under his left arm when the Girl put a hand on his shoulder, saying something to him in a sing-song whisper. She wasn't trying to get him in the scratcher again, was she? A couple of hours ago he had deliberately broken her wrist, and now she had the hots for him again? He turned his head sideways and looked at her. Leaning over him, she gave him a sly, swollen smile, and took the cigarette from his fingers and put it to her glistening, pouting mouth and drew in a slow drag of smoke and let it trickle out again at the corners of her lips. He shook his head. She was insatiable.

"That thing between your legs will wear out from overuse, sweetheart," he said to her, and made to push her away again. Then he stopped, and frowned.

The steps up from the beach, the sunlit seafront, the high, white facade of the hotel, and a polony in a black dress with a white collar waiting there for a taxi.

Yes.

45

Quirke was lying on the bed with his shoes off, trying to read Calderón—in an English translation, of course—and not enjoying it much. Why would a Spanish dramatist set a play in Poland? *Life Is a Dream*, that's for sure. The telephone on the nightstand rang, and he snatched up the receiver before the first peal had finished—Evelyn was asleep, lying on her side with her back turned to him, the silk of her dress drawn tight across her shoulder blades. He was afraid she would wake—her sleep, for him, was a magical state to be preserved and guarded against all interruption—but he needn't have worried. It took a lot more than a tinkle on the telephone to wake this woman.

It was Phoebe's voice.

"She's here," she said. "Come down and meet us in the bar."

He replaced the phone and sat motionless, listening to his

wife's soft, slow snores. Slipping on his shoes, he saw her sleeping face reflected in the mirror on the back of the open bathroom door. He turned and leaned down to her, half hoping she would wake just enough for him to kiss her. The dress she wore was his favorite, pale cream crepe de chine splashed over with big scarlet blossoms of peony roses. He studied the fat little bead of flesh in the center of her upper lip, the smooth plane of her forehead, the parchment-pale eyelids filigreed with tiny violet veins. The last thing he saw, when he had stepped into the hall and was easing the door shut behind him, was the gauze curtain languidly billowing up like the sail of a blazoned galleon as it turned aslant of the wind and set forth.

The door closed behind him with a click.

Never to be lost, the memory of that moment already receding from him, with the big-bellied curtain and the sun in the window and, beyond, the indigo-blue sea stretching off to a blurred horizon.

They were seated in a huddle, the three of them, at a table in a far corner of the bar. Passing by the model three-master in its glass case, he ran his finger along the top edge of the wooden frame, as if for luck. It, too, probably imagined its voyage was just about to begin.

Phoebe looked at him blankly as he approached, seeming not to know him. Strafford, too, glancing up, took a moment to adjust to his presence. What was the matter with them? They looked as if they had witnessed a car crash.

Music was playing somewhere, softly, blandly.

"Well, Dr. Lawless," Quirke said, attempting a jaunty tone, "we meet again, in altered circumstances."

April Latimer sat as he had seen her sit that first time, in the bar under the arches, with her thin shoulders drawn in around her and her knees pressed together and her fists lifted in front of her, the knuckles touching. But she was not the same person. It was as if an animal, half-wild and long lost, had come creeping back in search of sustenance and shelter, furious at itself and the world for being thus demeaned.

She muttered something that he didn't catch, and looked away. Her face was drawn and her skin was ashen. He noticed the faint, rapid tremor in her hands. He saw the sleeves of her blouse buttoned tightly at the wrists. He looked at her eyes, the pupils like tiny dark stars. He understood.

"Someone attacked her, at the hospital," Phoebe said in a rush. "She threw acid in his face."

Quirke sat down slowly. A voice in his head, that seemed not his own, demanded of him sharply, *What have you done?* But why?

"Who was it?"

He had addressed the question to April Latimer, but it was Phoebe who answered.

"That fellow we saw earlier out there"—she gestured toward the window—"coming up from the beach." *Orphanage boy.* "He was going to kill her—wasn't he, April?"

April turned to her dully, seeming to peer at her as through a veil of clotted cobwebs. The drug, whatever it was, was wearing off, Quirke could see. Her thin shoulders drooped.

"Someone must have sent him," she said. "Someone must have told him to—"

At that moment, two things happened simultaneously. Strafford stood up suddenly, looking across the lobby toward the entrance and reaching a hand inside his jacket. A voice spoke behind them.

"Oh, look," Evelyn said gaily, "it's happy families!"

She was coming toward them from the lift, in her peony frock.

"Down!" Strafford shouted, and everyone stared at him.

His right arm was outstretched, and he had something in his hand. There was a sense of being onstage, of an unseen audience holding its breath.

The sound of the shot was impossibly loud.

Halfway across the lobby a slight, doll-like young man in a striped shirt and fawn trousers that were too short for him had stopped suddenly and now was lowering himself slowly to his knees. He, too, had a gun in his hand.

For a moment, Phoebe thought it was indeed all a performance, some silly, lifelike show the hotel had put on to entertain the guests.

"Stop!" Quirke said loudly, not knowing who it was he was shouting at. He was still seated, his injured hand lifted like a club and the other clutching the arm of his chair, the knuckles white.

The mannequin kneeling on the floor was trying to speak. His expression was one of amazement and fury. His left jaw and the left side of his throat bore a livid rash. His cheek on the other side had been torn open, revealing a bloodied mess of shattered teeth and splintered bone. The bullet had entered there and traveled upward, tearing through the soft palate and lodging at the base of the brain. His right eye was bulging in its socket, and now it slowly slithered out, attached to a string of shiny, purplish flesh.

Evelyn took a step toward him.

"Poor child," she said, in a strangely soft, subdued voice, "my poor child!"

She put out her hand to him. His one eye regarded her with what seemed like bemusement. It was as if he knew her, or someone like her. He lifted the gun and fired, then toppled forward on his face.

Evelyn turned back to Quirke inquiringly, as if he had called out to her, which he hadn't. Then she looked down at the bloodstain spreading on the front of her dress, a flower-head unfurling among the other scarlet blossoms printed in the silk. Her eyelids fluttered and, lifting her arms out from her sides in a graceful, drooping gesture, she collapsed.

Shouts, people running and an old man in a bright-yellow

cravat at a far table pressing his hands to both his cheeks and saying, "Oh! Oh!"

Quirke knelt on one knee. Evelyn lay on her side with her cheek cradled on her arm. It was how he had seen her, in bed, upstairs, when he turned from the door to look at her and the moving curtain. Her eyes were closed, but now she opened them—opened them, and seemed to smile.

"So you see, my love," she whispered, "she was right, that nun of yours. Laughing will end crying."

Quirke began to speak but she lifted a hand weakly to silence him. She had managed, for the last time, to have the last word.

DUBLIN

46

A spring storm had broken over the city. The wind-driven
rain was coming down in undulant gray sheets and Leinster
Lawn was awash. Ned Gallagher stopped on a turn of the stairs
by a window and stood a moment to rest. Lately he had been
experiencing bouts of breathlessness, and sometimes he woke
in the night with a constriction in his chest. He was working
too hard. The stresses on him were too great.

He looked out gloomily at the rain. So much for April show-
ers. He had stepped in a puddle on the way down from the
Taoiseach's office, and his left foot was soaked.

The Chief Whip's office was on the top floor. Best view in
the House. It was an old joke.

Ned Gallagher resumed his climb. Why had he been summoned here this morning? What business could Dick Fitz-

Maurice have with him? He was a civil servant—civil servants weren't answerable to the Chief Whip. He felt a deeper stirring of unease. He had heard nothing from Spain. God grant it hadn't gone wrong down there. No sooner had he offered up the prayer than he knew, he just knew, that it wasn't going to be answered.

The Chief Whip's secretary showed him into what was popularly known as the Torture Chamber. Dick FitzMaurice rose from behind his desk and greeted him in friendly enough fashion— "Good morning, Ned, thanks so much for coming. I suppose you got drenched"—which was encouraging. Dick Fitz wasn't known for warmth.

The two men shook hands, and that was when Gallagher noticed the Minister. He was standing in shadow by the tall window at the far end of the room, his back turned, his hands in the pockets of his trousers. At the sight of him, Gallagher's overworked heart skipped a beat.

"Sit down, sit down," Dick Fitz said to him. There was a silver cigarette box on the desk, and Fitz turned it toward him now, the lid open. "Smoke?"

"No, thanks," Gallagher said, clearing his throat. He sat down. The sock inside his shoe was wet and warm. Horrible sensation. He could feel his heart wobbling.

Bill Latimer turned from the window and crossed the room. He took a cigarette from the box on the desk, and lit it with a slim Colibri lighter. He hadn't greeted Ned Gallagher, hadn't even looked at him. Bad omen. He grasped the back of the chair that stood beside the one where Gallagher was seated, and moved it a good three feet away to the left and sat down on it. *Cordon sanitaire*, Gallagher thought.

Dick Fitz resumed his place behind the desk and riffled through a sheaf of what appeared to be telegrams.

"I thought it best to see the two of you together," he said, keeping his eyes on the olive-green slips of paper before him.

He was a lithe, trim fellow in his early forties. Looked as if butter wouldn't melt in his mouth, until you found yourself fixed in the pencil beam of his pale-blue stare. He wore a three-piece tweed suit, a white shirt with a thin blue stripe and a blue-and-white polka-dotted bow tie. The tie wasn't a ready-made one, but the real thing, that he knotted himself. It was his trademark. His nickname was Dicky Bow. He had been educated by the Jesuits at Clongowes, and then by the Prods at Trinity College. An all-around man.

He looked up now and smiled, first at Ned Gallagher, then at the Minister. It wasn't really a smile, only the shape of one. Both men gazed back at him with a mixture of foreboding, calculation and contempt. Dick FitzMaurice was that rarest of things, an honest politician.

"We've been contacted by the embassy in Madrid," he said. The telegrams crackled in his hands. "These were coming in throughout the night."

"Don't tell me," Bill Latimer said. "Franco has been assumed bodily into Heaven."

Dick FitzMaurice greeted this with a wintry smile. He had bad teeth, crooked and discolored, and broken, some of them. It was said he had a terror of the dentist.

"There has been an—an incident, in the north, in San Sebastián. Nice place, I've been there—went on my honeymoon, actually. The seafood is very good." He frowned. "It's all a bit confused, still. But it's certainly bad, very bad. A woman was killed there yesterday, shot dead in the lobby of a hotel, the"—he peered at one of the telegrams—"the Hotel Londres. Dr. Evelyn Quirke." He looked at Ned Gallagher. "You know who she is?"

"Quirke's wife, the State Pathologist?"

There was a pause.

"That's right," Dick Fitz said. "You knew they were down there, did you?"

How mildly the question was put, how innocent it sounded. Gallagher shifted in his chair.

"No," he said, "I just—I knew Quirke was married to a doctor."

"A psychiatrist, yes."

The room was silent. Bill Latimer had still not acknowledged Gallagher's presence. I've become a nonperson, Gallagher thought, and almost laughed. He was curious to know by what means the Minister would try to wriggle out of this one. Well, he could wriggle all he liked, he would only draw the noose tighter around his own thick neck. They would go down together, the two of them, Gallagher would make sure of that.

Dick Fitz sighed, and rose from his chair and paced slowly along the length of the room and stopped by the window, in the spot where Bill Latimer had stood earlier. He still had the telegrams in his hand.

"As I say, it's very confused. I've spent the last hour trying to understand what happened. I spoke to the Ambassador in Madrid. Dr. Blake—Quirke's wife, that is—was shot by a so-far-unidentified assailant. No one knows who he is—no papers on him, nothing."

"Is he refusing to talk?" Bill Latimer asked, his voice toneless and flat.

"He's dead," Dick Fitz said, without turning from the window. "He was shot by one of our people, fellow called Stafford, a detective."

"What was an Irish detective doing down there?" Ned Gallagher asked, playing the innocent.

"Chief Superintendent Hackett, down in Pearse Street, sent him there, along with Quirke's daughter."

The little bitch! Bill Latimer thought.

Dick Fitz turned, but stayed by the window.

"Quirke was convinced he had met someone, someone he recognized, and asked his daughter to come down and tell him if he was right. She went to Hackett, and Hackett sent his Stafford fellow to—I don't know. To look out for her, I suppose."

A gust of raindrops rattled against the windowpanes, and a ball of smoke rolled out of the chimney above the fireplace, where a small coal fire was burning. Gallagher caught an acrid whiff of the smoke, and thought of Hell.

"Who is the person Quirke thought he recognized?" Bill Latimer asked, in the same dead tone as before.

Dick Fitz took a deep breath.

"Your niece, Minister," he said. "April Latimer."

Tea was ordered. Ned Gallagher, with a graveyard laugh, wondered aloud if there might not be something stronger on offer, given the circumstances—"I've heard tell you keep a bottle of Crested Ten in a drawer in your fine big desk there."

Dick Fitz, once again seated, looked at him stonily. No booze, then. Gallagher coughed into his fist and looked off to the window, where the rain still streamed. Must be an east wind, he thought. He felt strange. It was as if he weren't really there, or was there but entirely detached. Didn't they say that sometimes a patient undergoing surgery will feel himself drifting up to the ceiling and staying afloat up there, surveying the proceedings on the operating table? That was how he felt. He was suspended on high, the surgeon was working away on him, but the operation was going badly wrong.

Dick Fitz leaned back in his chair and joined his fingers at their tips.

"The Ambassador tells me he spoke at length with the detective, Stafford—or Strafford, is it? He, in turn, had spoken to the young woman—your niece, Minister, though she's going under another name, I forget for the moment what it is. She has been working down there, as a doctor, for some years. She has a strange, not to say a shocking, tale to tell."

"Aye, she's a great teller of tales," Bill Latimer said, and leaned forward and took another cigarette from the box on the desk and brought out his lighter again. Dick Fitz was eyeing him coldly.

There was a light tap at the door, and the secretary appeared bearing a tray with tea things on it. Dick Fitz gestured at her where to set down the tray. She spoke not a word, and soon was gone.

"You don't seem surprised to hear that your niece is alive," Dick Fitz said, addressing Latimer.

Latimer gave him back stare for stare, and blew a stream of smoke contemptuously across the desk in his direction. Ned Gallagher could feel the pent-up anger of the man; even though he was sitting a yard away from him, the heat of it reached him like a blast of scorched air.

"Nothing that girl does could surprise me," he said.

Dick Fitz was rummaging among the telegrams again. He was playing for time, Ned Gallagher saw. Or no, he was playing with them, like a cat with a couple of mice.

"The story she tells," Dick Fitz said, still pretending to be engrossed in his papers, "is of a family in turmoil, and of the past crimes of—of certain of her relatives."

Bill Latimer made a sound, a sort of grunt that might have been a laugh.

"Crimes, is it?" he said harshly. "One man's crime is another man's duty."

Dick Fitz braced his hands against the edge of his desk.

"There's duty, and there's sedition, Minister," he said. "Your niece told Strafford how you ran arms and ammunition into the country, and supplied them to the IRA in Belfast—"

"Sedition?" Latimer almost shouted. "The Six Counties is a failed state, or would be, if it deserved to be called a state at all. I acted as a patriot—"

Dick Fitz pushed himself to his feet and leaned forward across the desk.

"Don't talk to me of patriotism," he said to Latimer, his voice tight with sudden rage. "I am as much a patriot as you are, Minister, but I abide by the law. You committed a felony by arming a band of gangsters—"

"Gangsters, he says!" Latimer said with a burst of laughter, turning at last to Gallagher. "Gangsters!"

"—and when your nephew, Oscar Latimer, discovered what you were up to, and told his sister, his sister came to you and

confronted you—and what did you do? You drove her out of the
country, under God knows what sort of threats, and pretended
to the world that she was dead, murdered by her own brother."

Latimer drew back his head and looked at him with a broad,
brazen smile.

"Every family has its troubles," he said. "And every family
solves them in its own way. It's no business of yours, or of anyone else's, how I chose to fix the things that were broken."

Dick Fitz, his anger under control, sat down slowly and leaned
back in his chair. He turned to Ned Gallagher.

"It was you who arranged a false passport for her, I suppose?"
he inquired, in almost a conversational tone.

Gallagher made no reply, only sat looking miserable, with his
hands in his lap. Keep quiet for now, he told himself. Afterward
he would find some way of putting the knife into Bill Latimer's
broad back. He was damned if he would take the blame for that
man's sins. Only, please, God, he prayed, please, don't let this
bastard know that it was me who hired the fellow to go down
and shut that young one's mouth for good.

"Are we done here?" Bill Latimer said, making to rise.

"Not quite," Dick Fitz replied.

Latimer lowered himself back on to the seat, making a grinding motion with his jaws.

"It's nothing to do with me if some madman shot Quirke's
wife," he muttered.

"The Ambassador tells me," Fitz said, "that the detective is
convinced Mrs. Quirke wasn't the intended target."

"Then who was?" Latimer snapped.

Dick Fitz took up the bundle of telegrams and tapped them
on the desk on their edges, squaring them off. His manner had
changed, had become brisk and businesslike.

"I have spoken to the Taoiseach," he said. "We have agreed that,
while these tragic events in Spain are being investigated, certain
measures will be put in place. You"—he looked at Latimer—"you
will tender your resignation forthwith, giving whatever reason

you choose. And you, Mr. Gallagher, will take leave of absence, for an indefinite period. When are you due to retire?" Gallagher, seeming frozen where he sat, said nothing. "We might speed up the process. Your pension will suffer, of course, but I fear that can't be helped. And now, gentlemen, I'll bid you good day."

He stood up. Bill Latimer remained seated, the cigarette in his fingers sending up a swift, thin stream of smoke.

"I'll destroy you, Dicky Bow," he said softly. "I'll have your fucking head on a platter—"

"Dr. Latimer," Dick Fitz said calmly, "the head that rolls here won't be mine. I told you, I've spoken to the Taoiseach. There will be no cover-up. Times have changed. If you're found to be implicated in what happened in Spain, you'll be extradited—"

"By Christ—!" Latimer cried, struggling to his feet.

"—or else," Dick Fitz went on inexorably, "you'll be tried here, for the attempted murder of your niece, and the killing of Dr. Evelyn Quirke. That's all I have to say." He pressed a button on his desk. "My secretary will show you out."

Latimer stood motionless for some moments, fixed on him savagely, then turned and strode out of the room. Ned Gallagher still sat, still frozen into immobility, blinking, his fists in his lap. He looked old suddenly.

"If I find out you're involved as deeply in this affair as I think you are," Dick Fitz said to him, "you'll be spending your retirement behind bars. Now get out of my sight."

But still Ned Gallagher couldn't move. He felt as if he might never move again, but stay paralyzed here forever, lost inside himself.

The rain beat against the window. In Spain, the sun was shining.

★ ★ ★ ★ ★